AN EXTRAVAGANT DUPLICITY
BEATRICE HYDE-CLARE MYSTERIES
BOOK XI

❦

LYNN MESSINA

potatoworks press • greenwich village

Copyright © 2023 by Lynn Messina

Cover design by Ann-Marie Walsh

ISBN: (ebook): 978-1-942218-62-3

ISBN (Paperback): 978-1-942218-65-4

ISBN (Hardback) : 978-1-942218-66-1

This is a work of fiction. Names, characters, places and incidents either are the product of the author's imagination or are used fictitiously. Any resemblance to actual persons, living or dead, events or locales is entirely coincidental.

All Rights Reserved

Title Production by TheBookwhisperer.ink

Published 2023 by Potatoworks Press

Without limiting the rights under copyright above, no part of this publication may be reproduced, stored in or introduced into a retrieval system or transmitted in any form or my any means (electronic, mechanical, photocopying, recording or otherwise) without prior written permission of the copyright owner and publisher of this book.

The scanning, uploading and distribution of this book via the Internet or via any other means without the permission of the publisher is illegal and punishable by law. Please purchase only authorized electronic editions and do not participate in or encourage electronic piracy of copyrightable materials. Your support of the author's rights is appreciated.

To Ann-Marie Walsh, whose kindness and creativity astound me

Chapter One

If compelled to give the reasons she refused to allow her son to take lessons with Gentleman Jackson, Vera Hyde-Clare would have listed expense first. Engaging in the art of pugilism required not only tutelage, which came at a premium, but also equipment and rigging. By the time Russell had acquired all the necessary accoutrement, the financial investment would be double the estimate he had provided.

She knew this to be fact because she had seen it happen time and again with her friends. A child developed an interest in a sport or leisure activity, and then a few months or years later the household would be overwhelmed by debt.

Poor Mrs. Potter—she could barely afford new hair ribbons since her son had taken up yachting. Wilfred's determination to win the regatta in Barton had necessitated an ever-increasing fleet of boats, and the family lived under the constant strain of looming penury. (Could their anxiety also have a little something to do with the series of bad investments Mr. Potter made in a minerals company? Well, yes, that was almost certainly a factor. But everyone knew a sailing habit doubled the precarity of any circumstance.)

After cost, however, Vera would have cited brutality.

Boxing was such a savage diversion. All those clenched fists smashing into all those chins; all those cheeks bruised like apples at the bottom of a barrel. All that blood!

It chilled her to the core of her being, and she found it incomprehensible that an occupation as uncouth as bare-knuckle brawling could be perceived as an elegant pastime of gentlemen.

John Jackson had much to answer for, imbuing the sport with scientific principles! As if the mathematical analysis of how to land a blow magically divested the action of its barbarity.

And yet, if the loathsome pursuit was indulged in by a personage no less exalted and refined as the Duke of Kesgrave, was it not incumbent upon her to temper her judgment? Was she not obligated to concede it might have a redeeming quality or two?

Unequivocally, yes.

Nobody would dare imply that the duke's taste was anything but impeccable.

That being the case, he *had* recently aligned himself with Vera's own drab, spinsterish niece, so it was possible his infallibility was not quite as inviolate as one would—

With an abrupt shake of her head, Beatrice, Duchess of Kesgrave, halted the thought in the middle of the sentence. She had resolved to stop assuming she knew every idea and notion that passed through her relative's mind, and the only way to do that was to actually stop assuming she knew every idea and notion that passed through her relative's mind.

It was a challenge.

Having spent twenty years in the other woman's care, Bea could not conceive of her as anything other than a villainess

—a comedic one, to be sure, with elements of absurdity, but a villainess nonetheless. Aunt Vera, possessing a breathtaking lack of generosity, always formed the meanest opinion about a subject and met every situation with a miserly understanding. Vaguely aware of these limitations, she often sought to soften her position with clarifying statements that inevitably rambled with clumsy imprecision, further obfuscating her stance.

Although these attempts at coherence frequently caused Bea to smile with perverse enjoyment, they did not outweigh the cruelty to which the woman had subjected her for much of her life. Consequently, she had a difficult time seeing her relative as a fully formed human being capable of complexity and growth.

Aunt Vera struck her as more closely resembling a fish—able to perform a small assortment of basic tasks over and over. Not even the revelation that her harsh treatment of the orphan entrusted to her care was based on a gross misunderstanding of the girl's parents could significantly alter her behavior.

She was simply too much of a turbot or a mackerel to overcome the pettiness that lived in her heart.

Or so Bea believed.

And then, two weeks ago, Vera offered to accompany the Dowager Duchess of Kesgrave to Cambridgeshire to attend the funeral of the septuagenarian's son. The peeress roundly refused to accept her grandson's escort and an argument was brewing, possibly a heated one—definitely a protracted one—and into this fray stepped the inordinately timid Mrs. Hyde-Clare with a helpful suggestion.

It was an unfathomable turn for a variety of reasons, not the least of which was that Bea's aunt was not renowned for solving problems. She was more famous for wringing her hands over the slightest awkwardness and lamenting the lack of decorum. For her to offer gallantly to take the two-day journey was an astonishing act of generosity, for it would expose her to an intolerable amount of discomfort.

Traveling by itself was always an unpleasant enterprise, what with the confined space of the carriage and the lamentable condition of the roads and the harrowing threat of highwaymen, but to undertake it in the presence of an elderly noblewoman was a form of torture for Aunt Vera. She found everything about the British peerage overwhelming, from its noble bearing to its family crests. (It was appalling to her, all that excess—to be so magnificent as to warrant *three* lions!)

Given how breathless finely veined marble made her, she was likely to suffocate before they left London.

Never in a million years could Bea have imagined her relative making such an audacious proposal, and she found it remarkably difficult to reconcile the generous act with the woman she knew. Even as Aunt Vera opened her mouth to suggest it, Bea had braced herself for yet another harsh critique of her hoydenish conduct. (In this case, running after a suspected murderer in the middle of a bustling street with her skirts raised to reveal her ankles.) No matter what she did, her relative always had a complaint.

Except this time.

This time she had a solution.

Confounded, Bea was forced to consider the possibility that she might not in fact have privileged access to her relative's mind.

Perhaps she did not know what Aunt Vera was thinking at all.

Well, no, that was going too far in the opposite direction.

After two decades of exposure, she had *some* idea and could reasonably conclude that her offer to the dowager was an anomaly. The fact that the two women happened to rub together well made the event's singularity more pronounced, and Bea was convinced nothing like it would ever happen again.

Even so, she nevertheless found herself determined to be fair and resolved to withhold judgment. Going forward, she would give her aunt the benefit of the doubt.

Alas, it was more easily said than done, and Bea found herself often falling into the old habit, ascribing thoughts to her relative based on the tilt of the other woman's chin and the rigidity of her shoulders.

Like now, for instance.

The harsh line of Aunt Vera's lips grew thinner and thinner the longer her son talked—a clear indication that she disapproved of his words. Rarely could she hold her tongue for more than a few minutes, and it had already been a full ten.

They were gathered in the drawing room at 19 Portman Square, convened there at the request of Russell, who had issued an invitation to Bea and the duke asking them to participate in a family conversation.

That was the way he described it in his note: a *conversation*.

'Twas a curious thing to receive, a formally worded missive from her cousin, and Bea promptly rearranged her schedule to comply with the request. Kesgrave, who had had a more interesting afternoon of riding in the park with Nuneaton planned, was likewise too intrigued to decline.

After attending thoughtfully to his guests, including his parents, who he made sure had tea prepared specifically to their liking, Russell had launched into an extensive description of his experience at Gentleman Jackson's. Most surprising to him was the genial company he had found at the salon. When petitioning for the right to take lessons, he had not considered the camaraderie of like-minded fellows.

"All I wanted when I began my training was to perfect my uppercut," he said.

At this statement, Aunt Vera compressed her mouth so tightly her lips disappeared, and Bea felt a disconcerting itchiness between her shoulder blades as she struggled to hold fast to her resolution.

Without question, Vera Hyde-Clare's patience was at an end. She had indulged her son with painstaking tolerance—accepting the invitation affably, receiving the cup of tea thankfully, listening to his speech silently—and all she had gotten in exchange for this extraordinary act of child-rearing was a dissertation on the benefits of violence. Whatever pact she had made with her husband to allow the training, it certainly did not include submitting to the provocation of juvenile taunts.

Did Russell really think she would endure such an incitement without summarily rescinding her approval and demanding he withdraw at once from—

No, Bea thought, shaking her head again.

Aunt Vera's pinched look could mean any number of things, such as dissatisfaction with the room's temperature or irritation with the state of the curtains. Both were decidedly imperfect, with the latter possessing a rather large U-shaped stain along the edge about halfway up and the former subject to the unusually chilly weather. Given that such conditions exposed her to charges of lax housekeeping by the august Duke of Kesgrave, she could be composing a sternly worded lecture to the housekeeper, Mrs. Emerson.

It was possible, Bea thought fairly.

Yes, but not likely.

With his speech, Russell was waving a red flag at a bull, and it struck Bea as a particularly ill-advised decision. The last thing he should do was draw more attention to his new hobby. The much better way to serve his goal was by

AN EXTRAVAGANT DUPLICITY

pretending not to take lessons at all. Every time he left the house for 13 Bond Street, he should act as though he were visiting the tobacconist or calling on a friend.

Seemingly oblivious to the damage he was doing his cause, Russell described a strike he had dealt Ripley—that was, Viscount Ripley, second cousin to the Marquess of Eastleigh —that knocked his lordship's nose so hard, blood seeped from it.

"For a moment he claimed to see double," Russell added giddily. "He said there were two of everything—two sparring partners, two Jacksons, two clocks, *four* of his own fists."

If he thought the potential to befriend young peers through the sport of boxing would endear the occupation to his mother, then he was even more buffleheaded than Bea had supposed. As Vera Hyde-Clare could not bear the presumption of her son sharing a tailor with men of noble rank, she was hardly more likely to welcome the prospect of his assaulting them physically.

Planting a facer on a viscount!

Had Russell abandoned every notion of modesty?

Did he not recall his place at all?

Unable to stand it one second more, Aunt Vera leaped to her feet, her hands clenched tightly at her side, her eyes flashing with anger, as she wailed that she would not permit it.

She would never permit it!

How dare he sully them all by even having the temerity even to suggest it!

"You ungrateful child!" she cried with unrestrained agitation. "I knew this would happen. You've had a small taste of the power and now you want more. That is what violence does: It spreads and destroys until everything has been devoured. I held firm against your boxing for years, and then I go away for one measly week and come back to find my son

7

so drunk on the glory of bare-knuckle brawling, he wants to participate in a public fight. I will not have it! I am sure your father feels the same way, and he will say so as soon as he is given the opportunity. And the duke! What is he to think of us? We have always striven to be an unassuming family, to stay beneath the notice of our betters, and then Beatrice began poking her nose into other people's affairs, as if it is any business of ours whom Lady Skeffington decides to attack in the library—in the privacy of her own home, no less. Is no place safe anymore from the glare of interest?"

It was an incredible speech.

Even for a woman who had made a career of nonsensical blathering, it was an extraordinary outburst, and no one in the room was immune from its effects. Kesgrave's lips quirked as he sought to hide his amusement in a cup of tea, and Uncle Horace's face turned bright red at the inexplicable assumption his wife had made. Flora, who had been curiously out of sorts for the past week or so, stared at her mother blankly, while Russell goggled in astonishment.

Bea smothered her own smile while she waited for someone to address Aunt Vera's concern. From the grimace on her uncle's face, she assumed he had something to say, and Russell would surely be impatient to correct his mother's egregious misconception.

Neither spoke.

Aunt Vera continued to breathe heavily, further unsettled by their silence, which seemed to confirm her worst fears.

Then Flora said calmly, "The law."

Swiveling her head to glare at her daughter, Vera squawked, "What?"

"Given that murder is illegal, even for peeresses with whom you went to school, the law gave Bea the right to poke her nose into Lady Skeffington's affairs," Flora replied waspishly. "You are the one who just said violence spreads if not checked. Well, Bea held her ladyship's violence in check. I would think you would laud her for that, not continue to berate her all these months later."

Aunt Vera gasped and waved her arm behind her back as if to locate the chair nearby before she collapsed to the floor in disbelief. Gently, she lowered herself to the seat and pressed her hand against her chest. "I cannot believe you would speak to me like that, you ungrateful child."

Her surprise was understandable, for her daughter usually treated her with either amused patience or fond affection. Sometimes Flora rolled her eyes lavishly behind her mother's back, but she always kept her tone respectful.

Whatever bedeviled her now, Bea thought, left her cousin with little tolerance for Aunt Vera's antics.

Equally disconcerted by his sister's display, Russell pursued his lips and insisted sullenly, "*I* am the ungrateful child. This is *my* meeting, and nobody will change the subject until I have said my piece. I could have been sneaky about it, but I decided to be open and aboveboard and you will respect my maturity!"

Exhaling heavily, Aunt Vera assured him he had said quite enough. "And I have given my answer. You will not enter a public match."

"I don't want to!" Russell insisted.

"Then a private one," his mother replied dismissively. "You will engage in no more fights."

Russell sputtered angrily, his color high as well, and Kesgrave pressed closer to Bea to inform her that now was a good time to intercede. "I appreciate your forbearance in holding your tongue, but in a moment the discussion will descend into a squabble between your cousins."

It would, yes, inevitably.

Almost all conversations between the siblings ended in a spiteful exchange of insults. Their father had been very sparing with his approval during their childhood, and they were both almost desperate for his approbation. In recent months, Flora had earned it by displaying more intelligence than anyone had believed her capable of, scattering Latin phrases among her conversation. Russell had only recently acquired it by keeping a cool head in the immediate aftermath of a steam engine explosion. Emboldened by his father's esteem, he had announced he was taking lessons with Gentleman Jackson, then dared anyone in the household to stop him, even the housekeeper.

As his mother was in Cambridgeshire at the time, nobody did.

When Aunt Vera discovered what had transpired in her absence, she had shown unprecedented tact, withholding her disapproval so as not to undermine her husband's authority.

But she had been struggling for more than a week to restrain her anxiety and now it appeared to have corrupted her ability to reason.

Russell partaking in a title fight!

Aunt Vera's gross misunderstanding of the situation was more outlandish than anything Bea could ascribe to her.

It was for that reason she had no intention of interrupting. She could not conceive what her relative would do next.

"If you wish to avoid a quarrel, then I suggest you intervene," Bea replied as Russell threw himself back into the chair with a gloomy expression, as if his dream of winning a championship bout had indeed been thwarted. "I am too deeply engrossed in the unfolding drama to say a word."

Kesgrave demurred, citing his lack of standing. "I am not family."

"Coward," she observed softly.

He accepted the charge without comment.

Flora, displaying further impatience, told her mother she was making a ridiculous fuss over nothing. "Although I have seen few signs of intelligence in my brother, I am sure he is clever enough to avoid humiliation by displaying his meager skills in public."

Russell, straightening his posture in the chair, said his right hook was a prime rounder and that he would acquit himself quite well if he wanted to enter a mill on Highgate Common. Aunt Vera whimpered in distress, Flora cackled scornfully, and Uncle Horace remained silent.

Bea looked at the duke pointedly, as if to indicate that he could speak now if he so chose.

He did not.

Russell glowered ferociously and muttered that he had not intended to spar anywhere except at the salon, but if Flora continued to goad him, he might just change his mind.

"Ah, yes, there is his much-vaunted maturity," Flora murmured airily.

But in fact he did display a great deal of it by not responding to her taunt in kind. Instead, he smoothed his features and said his presentation had gone wildly off course. Seeking to correct that, he explained that he had not mentioned landing a facer on Ripley's nose to prove his bona fides as a boxer. "I was citing it as evidence of his temperament. He is an easygoing chap."

At the reminder that her son now punched the relatives of marquesses, Aunt Vera winced, but it was not as deep as the flinch evinced by the word *chap*.

Truly, it was horrifying that her own flesh and blood could speak so nonchalantly about the nobility. Where was his overweening awe that made him ramble awkwardly in the presence of a better?

Unaware of his mother's discomfort, Russell continued. "Ripley is like that with everyone, you see, tolerant and good-natured. No matter how bruising the blow, he never loses his temper, which is how I know his family's understanding of the situation is off target. And that is the reason I have gathered you here today. As I said, I want to be aboveboard about the matter. There have been secrets in this family in the past and I do not want to perpetuate the cycle, most importantly because you, Bea, have been at the center of it."

Startled to find herself singled out, Bea wondered if Russell had discovered that the lowly law clerk with whom she had recently been infatuated was in fact a figment of her imagination.

It did not seem possible, for Russell displayed little interest in things that did not directly pertain to him and he would have no reason to launch his own investigation. Flora would not have told him either, for she delighted in knowing things her brother did not.

Most assuredly, Russell did not suspect the truth about Mr. Davies.

To what, then, was he referring?

Her investigative bent in general?

But that was widely known.

Satisfying her curiosity, he added that he thought it was reprehensible that his mother and father withheld vitally important information about her own parents from her. "I know how damaging that has been to your life."

Aunt Vera recoiled as if struck, but Uncle Horace advised him not to comment on things he could not properly understand. "We made the best decisions we could based on the information we had at the time. I am not certain how this unfortunate history relates to your lessons with Gentleman Jackson, but I trust you will rectify that soon or risk losing them."

In recognition of his parent's authority, Russell acknowledged the complexity of the situation and even apologized for speaking out of turn. Vera, grateful that her son was still able to display some good sense, thanked him, then immediately cringed again when he reiterated his central thesis that secrets caused harm.

Identifying himself as unwilling to participate in clandestine behavior, he said, "That is why I am seeking my cousin's assistance in the presence of all of you. So that you may know what is going on."

"Yes, but what *is* going on?" Flora asked snappishly. "You have said nothing comprehensible and only succeeded in giving our mother vapors. If that was the purpose of this meeting, then next time you may hold it privately, for I have no need or desire to witness it."

Russell blinked at his sister in surprise, while Bea, who knew something was being asked of her even if she could not say what that was, marveled at Flora's malice. Although the girl frequently ridiculed her brother, her remarks were rarely so cutting. Whatever had put her in a churlish mood had made her mean as well.

"But it is obvious, is it not?" he replied, examining each of them in turn, a faint hint of disappointment clouding his eyes as he noted their lack of comprehension.

It was impossible not to bristle at his response, for the idea of being so lackwitted as to fail to meet Russell's expectations was a daunting one.

Naturally, Bea had her suspicions, for there were few things with which one would reasonably seek her assistance, and help with solving a murder certainly topped the list. But if there was a dead body lurking somewhere in the background, Russell had done a poor job of identifying it. The only person he had mentioned was a viscount named Ripley, whom her cousin had discussed in the present tense, indicating he was alive.

Had someone else been killed at Gentleman Jackson's?

Surely not.

The salon was too well attended for an event of that

nature not to be an on-dit, and there had been no mention of it in the *London Daily Gazette*. Of a certainty, Twaddle-Thum would have found some way to use a corpse in the famous boxing rooms to further deride Bea.

How is it possible, he might have wondered in one of his loathsome screeds, that her Outrageousness—because, yes, after several attempts at saddling her with an insulting sobriquet fell flat, he had finally settled on one that satisfied him—did not take lessons with Gentleman Jackson to complement her many other masculine traits?

Aunt Vera, her voice shrill with confusion, announced that nothing was obvious. "I do wish you would explain why we have been summoned here if not to be made aware of our forthcoming humiliation," she said, before nipping at her bottom lip in distress and apologizing to the duke for presuming to assign him to any group, let alone one so patently beneath him. "A man of your rank and breeding is immune to humiliation, for your participation immediately elevates the questionable behavior to acceptable conduct. It is why you did not pause to consider the consequences of marrying Beatrice, for which I am grateful."

But the source of her gratitude was not readily apparent, at least not to Vera, and she added that she was grateful for his confidence. "*Not* that you saved Bea from spinsterhood. She was not a spinster yet and had many interested prospects. Indeed, a plan was in the works for her to marry a ... to marry a ... a ..."

Reluctant to say *law clerk* in the duke's presence just in case he had yet to realize just how dire the situation had been before he had kindly stepped in, she allowed the thought to trail off.

"Regarding Kesgrave's social sway, Mama," Flora said with cynical amusement, "does that mean Russell could fight publicly if the duke did it first?"

Aunt Vera turned bright red, and Uncle Horace ordered her to stop teasing her mother. Then he told his son to bring the meeting to a close because he was already late for an appointment. "I was supposed to meet Wilkinson at my club fifteen minutes ago."

"As I just finished explaining, there is no way Ripley could have done it," Russell said. "He is too genial to have even thought of anything like it."

Although Aunt Vera snapped that nobody knew what *it* was, the other occupants of the room in fact had a good idea of the viscount's situation and Flora irritably asked who was dead.

"His grandfather," Russell replied. "That is, the viscount's maternal grandfather, a cit called Roger Dugmore, who resided in St. James's Square. It is a very large house and Ripley is staying there with a parcel of cousins and one of his aunts. You see, the old man, who was in fact quite old, had a fall while climbing out of bed five days ago. It was dreadful. A deep cut along his forehead. And, well, he died—in the fall—but Ripley had had a vicious row with him about money only the day before *and* he was seen creeping out of the old man's room very early on the morning in question. And now everyone in his family thinks he is a depraved killer and he cannot bear the way they look at him, all scared and suspicious as if he might murder them next. So, knowing of my connection to Bea, he asked if I could ask *her* to do him the kindness of paying a call to the house and proving to his family that he did nothing wrong."

Finishing his explanation, he tilted his head forward to look beseechingly at his cousin. "I know the situation is a little unconventional and it is not the way you typically conduct an investigation, but you must understand how difficult it is for him. To have his own family suspect him of murder when he wouldn't hurt a fly!"

It was true, Bea thought, for it was unusual for her expertise to be sought. More frequently, she had to impose her presence on unwilling subjects and ask impertinent questions they did not want to answer. Although she had demonstrated an impressive proficiency at identifying murderers, she was nevertheless called upon repeatedly to prove her skill. The prospect of her interest being welcomed rather than resented appealed to her and she thought it might be a fitting last—

Ah, but no, she would not think of that either, she told herself sternly.

No assuming she knew what Aunt Vera was thinking.

No contemplating life after the cherub.

All that was permitted was staying focused on the event unfolding before her, which in this case was Russell's sparring partner's possible guilt.

Or, rather, his presumed innocence.

Deciding to accept the invitation, she straightened her shoulders and opened her mouth to gather more information just as Dawson entered to announce a visitor.

"Mr. Holcroft to see Miss Hyde-Clare," he said.

Chapter Two

As many desperate schemes had been conceived and executed with the purpose of creating this exact circumstance—that was, Sebastian Holcroft calling on 19 Portman Square to see Flora—Bea was taken aback by the angry scowl that swept across her cousin's features. Bea had been dragged to Almack's less than forty-eight hours after escaping a deadly assault, the evidence of her attacker's finger still faintly visible on her skin, so that Flora could sparkle charmingly in hopes of piquing her beau's interest. Likewise, Mr. Caruthers, Holcroft's disgraced cousin whom Flora accidently brought to a murder scene. The poor man just wanted to nurse his shame privately in his rooms, but Flora could not allow it. Determined to impress Holcroft with her charity, she forced the former solicitor to accompany them to Tuck's Court, where they stumbled upon the bludgeoned corpse of Kesgrave's uncle.

And now, at long last, the object of her affection and ardent pursuit stood in her entry hall and she glowered.

Flora, raising her chin slightly, told the butler to inform the visitor that she was not at home to guests.

"Very good," Dawson said as he slipped out of the room.

It was a pointed response, Bea thought, the way it made clear that her cousin was in residence but unavailable.

The development was baffling.

All of them, even Kesgrave, had endured weeks of Flora wringing her hands over Holcroft's defection. After a heady initial courtship, the gentleman had proved elusive, taking a pet over a minor flirtation and then leaving town to attend to family business. Perhaps the trip's timing was unfortunate, but it could not have been avoided. Having narrowly escaped a violent death at the behest of his father's oldest and dearest friend, he had felt compelled to comfort his sire.

It was a reasonable compulsion, and Flora claimed to understand it even as she lamented his absence. All evidence indicated that Holcroft was grappling with a deeply painful familial issue, and yet she continued to place herself at the center of the crisis, convinced that his grief and distraction were somehow about her. All her actions had been calculated to lure him back to London as if he were enjoying a sojourn in the country, not providing solace.

And now he was back—finally!—and she refused to see him.

Bewildered, Bea glanced at Kesgrave, whose expression revealed neither confusion nor curiosity.

He does not want to get involved, she thought.

Smart man.

Also reluctant to allow herself to be drawn deeper into the affair, Bea tried to seek out Russell's gaze to indicate she wished to discuss the Ripley matter further, but he was staring at his sister with wide-eyed wonder.

His parents were as well.

Aunt Vera's jaw even dropped a full inch in her surprise.

Seemingly oblivious to the stunned confusion of her family, Flora sat calmly in her seat, her hands clasped loosely

AN EXTRAVAGANT DUPLICITY

in her lap, her eyes blinking with bland indifference. Incapable of holding his tongue for long, Russell asked her if she was dicked in the nob.

"Or are you just hard of hearing?" he added with a facsimile of genuine concern. "Dawson said Holcroft was here: H-O-L-C-R-O-F-T. You have been sighing incessantly over him for weeks, which has been deadly dull for the rest of us."

His mother, contributing to the conversation only a horrified gasp at the vulgar description of her daughter's mental state, leaned forward to hear the answer.

As a result, it fell to Uncle Horace to chastise Russell for his language.

Noticeably, he took no issue with the sentiment.

Indeed, he appeared to endorse it by adding that everything his daughter had said in the past month indicated an affection for Mr. Holcroft as well as an eagerness for his return to London. "That you would deny him now is perverse."

Flora, her brow furrowed darkly, replied that Holcroft had paid a call on her a week ago, which was how she knew they had nothing more to discuss. "He is not the man I thought he was. That is all," she said sternly, as a lone tear hovered tremulously over her eyelashes and slipped down her cheek. She wiped it away smoothly as she continued to stare stonily at her father, as if daring him to draw attention to her misery.

Uncle Horace, declining to delve deeper into what was patently a thorny subject, murmured something about trusting his daughter to know best just as Russell screeched, "Aha! There, you see, she has been intolerable because of Holcroft. I told you, Mama, did I not, that she had some bee in her bonnet? All week she has been barking at us at the slightest provocation. You noted the loose stitching in her glove, and she snapped that she was neither blind nor

19

unaware of the defects of her wardrobe. I said then that something was bothering her, and you insisted it was just the weather. But it was Holcroft all along!"

Recalling the incident, Vera nodded firmly and said, "Wretched man, turning my own daughter against me. I cannot pretend to be shocked, what with the quality of his connections. There is a certain level of decorum that can only be bred, not bought."

Whereas previously Flora had been utterly indifferent to her mother's inexplicable dislike of her suitor—inexplicable because he was from an established family and in possession of a large fortune—she now found her condemnation unbearable and tears spilled out of her eyes.

Glaring at her brother, she said indignantly, "I have not been intolerable. I have been very, very tolerable. You are the intolerable one, for you do not understand anything at all. Only minutes before noting the loose stitching on my glove, Mama had called my complexion pale, and it is decidedly cruel to say someone's glove stitching is loose after pointing out their pallor. Everybody knows that except you."

Exposed now to the sort of scene he had spent much of his married life striving to avoid, Uncle Horace rose to his feet and said that Wilkinson would sell his horse to someone else if he did not appear soon to discuss his offer. Aunt Vera, who had not realized her husband was in the market for a new mount, asked how much he intended to bid before noting that Erasmus was in good shape, barely six years old and well-muscled.

"He is an excellent specimen," she added.

Russell, determined to benefit from what he hoped was a general loosening of the family purse strings, observed that his own horse was eighteen years old and prone to stumbles. "Pearson dashed past me in the park the other day, and you know what a terrible seat he has."

In fact, his mother did not. She possessed no information about her son's friend's riding skills and resented the implication that she should be expected to keep abreast of such trifles. Uncle Horace said Pearson had recently bought Dearborn's filly, a fine example of horseflesh, and Flora pointed out that Persephone was only fourteen years old, not eighteen. Russell huffed angrily and said he should know the age of his own horse.

Arguing with her brother restored some of Flora's composure, and she agreed to this statement with vicious civility. "Yes, you *should* know, and yet you do not."

As the squabble between the siblings intensified, Aunt Vera pressed her husband on the need for such an unplanned extravagance. Bea looked at the duke, whose weary expression indicated he had had enough of her relations for one day, and suggested they depart while the rest of the company was distracted. As Russell had already given her the viscount's address, she did not require any more information from him.

Kesgrave consented at once to this proposal, but just as they were rising to their feet, the drawing room door flew open and Holcroft strode in. He was followed by a harried Dawson, whose face was bright red from either embarrassment or exertion.

"As I explained, Miss Hyde-Clare is not at home to visitors," the butler huffed heatedly. "If you will kindly give me your card, I will make certain she gets it."

Flora, whose entire body had recoiled in horror as Holcroft crossed the threshold, recovered her equanimity with impressive speed. Feigning surprise, only the slight breathlessness in her voice hinting at any apprehension or discomfort she might be feeling, she said, "Oh, do I have a caller? I did not realize because I was too engrossed in a matter of life and death to pay attention to trivial social concerns. You see, I am consulting with my family on the suspicious death of a patriarch, and based on my experience, I have decided to launch a full investigation. That is because I am capable of making my own decisions, Mr. Holcroft. Although I might strike some people as too beautiful to be able to ratiocinate logically, I am a competent human being who is able to accurately assess the danger to which she exposes herself. Now you may leave your card with Dawson and I will consider it along with the other dozen I have received today. Because, yes, Mr. Holcroft, I am *very* popular."

This speech astounded the members of her family, who each took exception to varying assertions. Her father repeated the word *capable* as if it were suddenly a foreign concept, while Russell chortled over her description of herself as *beautiful*. Her mother pinched her lips even tighter, something Bea had not thought possible, and asked what Flora meant by exposing herself to danger.

"If it is riding your horse astride, then I must most heartily object, for I cannot condone your making such a scandalous display of yourself," Aunt Vera continued. "And if it is something utterly ruinous such as smoking cheroots with Miss Fenwick, then I will send you to your room with nothing but bread and water for a month."

It was typical of her family, Bea thought, to focus only on the words spoken and give no consideration to the context in which they were offered. If they had a little more interest in the world around them, then they might have wondered at Flora's insistence on being allowed to make her own decisions. It implied that she had recently been denied the privilege, presumably by Holcroft, as he was the target of her ire. A cautious gentleman, he most likely assumed he was ensuring her safety, which was a logical supposition, given the reckless way Flora had charged into the Davies affair, determined to solve the murder of a man who did not actually exist. Her efforts had brought Holcroft and her to the brink of death.

Despite the fracas caused by Flora's outburst, Holcroft's expression remained untroubled as he greeted the occupants in the room with genial warmth. He inquired about Mr. Hyde-Clare's health, complimented Mrs. Hyde-Clare on the charming decor of her drawing room and congratulated Russell on his cravat, which bore a loose resemblance to the Barrel Knot. Then he apologized for bursting in unannounced and explained he would never have indulged in such boorish behavior if it were not absolutely necessary.

"Sensitive information regarding the patriarch in Miss Hyde-Clare's investigation has come to my attention and I knew it was vital that I impart it at once," he explained, deftly manipulating the snippet of information he had been given to his advantage. "I hope you will allow us a brief tête-à-tête to discuss it, and then I will be on my way."

He motioned to a cozy seating area in the far corner, a seemingly benign gesture that nevertheless caused Aunt Vera to shudder. The trio of chairs was for display purposes only because their legs were too rickety to support a user's weight for long. Replacing them was on her list of improvements she sought to make if only her husband would consent to the expense, something that would never happen as long as he prioritized his horse over their home.

She need not have worried, however, because Flora refused to comply with Holcroft's suggestion, insisting that she did not have a moment to spare. "I was just this minute running out to interview my first suspect. I…I am…ah… taking Bea's carriage," she said, foundering momentarily as her mother inhaled sharply. "Yes, that is right. I am taking the duchess's carriage because she and the duke have agreed to assist me with my investigation."

Russell gawked at the impudence. "*Your* investigation! Why, I like that very much!"

Bea, incapable of smothering the grin that rose to her lips at Flora's improvisation, said softly to the duke, "There, you see, your grace, you no longer have cause to fear being supplanted by Flora as my associate, for we have both been relegated to her assistant."

He laughed lightly at this observation as Aunt Vera reminded her daughter that they had been on their way to the milliner when Russell waylaid them with the family meeting.

"You were to order a new bonnet," she said.

Flora's lashes fluttered wildly at this information, indicating that she had indeed forgotten, and although a look of regret flashed across her face, she stood firm against the temptation of a lovely poke confection with ribbons and feathers. "I do not need a new hat."

Of all the remarkable statements spoken in the drawing room that afternoon, this simple denial was the most astonishing.

Flora Hyde-Clare did not need a new hat?

One might sooner say the King of England did not require a throne!

Her mother pressed her hand against her chest, as if to calm the palpitations that arose suddenly, and said that she had thought after the milliner they could stop by the modiste. "According to Mrs. Ralston, Madame Bélanger has just received a new shipment of silks from France."

Flora did not waver. Although owning a ravishing red creation by the coveted London seamstress was her most cherished desire, she knew better than to succumb to her mother's trick—and that was exactly what it was, Bea thought.

With her parsimonious little heart, Aunt Vera would never stand the expense of a Bélanger gown.

The deception was in the use of the phrase *stop by*, Bea decided, picturing the family's carriage pausing briefly in front of the modiste's gaily dressed window before continuing to Portman Square. Her relative had quite pointedly not said they would enter the shop or make a purchase.

Flora, incapable of going so far as to say she did not need a new dress, suggested they make the visit another time—tomorrow, perhaps, if her investigation had concluded by then.

Russell, irritated by her repeated claim of ownership, said, "It ain't your investigation. It is Bea's. I don't know why you think Ripley would entrust his reputation to you. You have never done anything noteworthy."

In fact, his sister had uncovered a rapacious scheme at the heart of the country's Chancery Court that resulted in the ignominious resignation of one of the most powerful men in England.

But her family knew none of that.

During the period in question, in which Sir Dudley's veniality was revealed, Flora was supposedly confined to her bed with a crippling bout of food poisoning brought on by the consumption of rotten eggs.

"Lord Ripley's situation is not yours to bestow like an elegant bouquet of flowers," Flora countered before nimbly adjusting her argument to include her rebuffed suitor's recent statements. "Mr. Holcroft knows the gentleman as well and is just as concerned about his future. That is why he is here. He is to escort us to him right now. I trust you will excuse our hasty departure, but a man's life hangs in the balance."

Although this comment regarding her visitor, whom she had refused to see only five minutes before, constituted such a violent change in attitude as to almost cause whiplash in its listeners, Holcroft displayed no confusion. He announced at once that Ripley waited upon their pleasure and that they should depart soon so as not to keep the viscount waiting.

After all, the man's life hung in the balance.

Russell frowned in confusion as his father hailed the situation resolved and dashed from the room before anyone could protest. Aunt Vera watched him leave, a helpless look on her face as she stared at the doorway through which he had passed for several seconds before turning to gaze at her daughter with the same befuddled expression. Something about the event struck her meaningfully—perhaps, Bea thought, the juxtaposition of her husband's desire for expensive horseflesh and Holcroft's deep pockets—and her stance on Flora's beau underwent a drastic alteration.

Her expression lightening, she heartily endorsed the plan, asserting that there was nothing more precious than a man's life. "And a viscount's as well!" she added with breathless excitement before rushing to clarify that she did not mean to imply that a noble life was in some way more valuable than an ignoble one.

Firmly, it was not.

But that modification revealed what she feared was an untenable prejudice *against* the aristocracy, whom she did consider to be superior to men of common birth. Then, recalling her own husband and son, she amended the statement to mean men of low birth. "As there are so many honorable and good men of common birth. Mr. Hyde-Clare, for one, and I am sure you, Mr. Holcroft, possess many fine qualities despite your disgraced relations."

Blushing hotly at her indiscretion—making veiled reference to the disbarred cousin in mixed company!—Aunt Vera repeated the phrase *many fine qualities* two more times before falling into silence.

Holcroft, seeming to recognize an ally, agreed with every

word Mrs. Hyde-Clare stammered, and even lauded her insightfulness.

It was a response of which only a thoroughly besotted suitor was capable, Bea thought in amusement.

"Thank you, Mama, yes," Flora said before her parent could reply. Then she bid her goodbye and, refusing to acknowledge Russell, swept from the room with an air of purpose. Holcroft promptly followed.

Kesgrave grinned at Bea and noted that they had been demoted even further, to mere chaperones. She agreed as they crossed to the hall, adding, "I can easily imagine the glee with which Mr. Twaddle-Thum will report it. He will say something like: Her Outrageousness suffered a genuine outrage when she discovered the only thing she had to add to the investigation was her carriage."

The duke, allowing it was likely, suggested the infamous prattler might accompany the observation with a description of the conveyance, noting how well sprung it was.

"*Inappropriately* well sprung," Bea amended, "for one should never attend to a murder victim in comfort. If we had any decency we would arrive in a hack."

"A donkey cart, I should think," Kesgrave offered.

Delighting in the distinction, she nodded appreciatively and said to avoid criticism altogether, she should give up all forms of transportation save walking.

Kesgrave shook his head and asserted that Twaddle would mock her for her ostentatious austerity. "The only way to thwart him is to deprive him of fodder."

"Retire to my office of rout cake enjoyment and leave the investigating to Flora, you mean?" she asked, stepping outside into the cool air, which was damp with rain. Although the unseasonably chilly weather gave the plan a certain cozy appeal, she would never discharge her duty so cavalierly. Her cousin was, to be sure, far more capable than anyone gave her credit for, but the viscount had expressly sought her assistance. She could not simply abandon his lordship in his time of need.

There was, to be sure, an element of self-interest in her public-spiritedness, for it would in all likelihood be her last chance to conduct an investigation. As soon as Kesgrave learned of her condition, he would—

No, we are not doing that now, she reminded herself.

But even as she pushed the thought from her mind, she knew the situation was untenable. The vague suspicion that had struck her in the wake of the Huzza affair had been confirmed by a series of uncomfortable early-morning episodes and a monthly that failed to arrive on its prescribed day.

Or on any of the days that followed.

A week later she was certain of her situation but had yet to inform the duke.

He deserved to know—for personal reasons, yes, because she thought the prospect of his pending fatherhood would genuinely delight him, but it was also a matter of state. So much was at stake—five hundred years of unbroken lineage, a dukedom, an estate of unnerving vastness—and she felt the weight of history bearing down on her womb.

As that thought made her queasy, albeit in an entirely different way, she redoubled her efforts to think of something else.

Holcroft and Flora—yes, that situation required her attention.

And it did indeed, she observed, for her cousin looked as though she was about to punch her former beau on the nose.

Alas, a chaperone's duty was never done.

Approaching the couple, she heard Flora coldly refuse Holcroft's offer of assistance. "I do not require your escort, as the duke and duchess will accompany me to St. James's

Square. I am certain you will honor my decision, as you have displayed much respect for my autonomy. It is not as though you withheld secret information from me for four weeks, five days and seven hours and allowed me to descend into a dark well of sadness, confusion and regret because then you would be a monster."

Stung by the accusation of monstrousness, Holcroft tightened his shoulders and raised his chin. Scowling fiercely, he seemed on the verge of arguing against the unfair characterization but when he spoke, he made no reference to it. Instead, he explained that he had told her the truth: He did know the family. "Howard Lewis, Viscount Ripley, went to school with my youngest brother, Chester. I have not seen him in a decade, but the connection between our families is well established. I can make the introduction."

Unimpressed with the offer, Flora replied in the same strident tone that the Duchess of Kesgrave needed no introduction. "Furthermore, our presence has been requested by his lordship. He is expecting us!"

As cogent as this argument was, Holcroft could not permit it to stand, for he owed it to his own rigid code of honor to do everything possible to assist the viscount. "I cannot stand by and allow an innocent man be accused of a crime he did not commit."

"And yet you *can* stand by and treat me like the veriest fool," Flora replied with excessive sweetness. "Your code is fascinating, sir. As uninterested as I am in hearing more, I do not have the time to indulge you. A man's life hangs in the balance!"

Although this statement grew no less hyperbolic the more it was repeated, Bea reiterated it in an attempt to move the pair forward. "No time to waste with bickering in the courtyard. Bicker in the carriage."

Holcroft had the grace to blush but nevertheless nodded

stiffly and thanked the duchess for her understanding. Flora, huffing angrily, marched across the gravel to where the groom waited.

"Why are you encouraging this madness?" Kesgrave asked.

"Why are you not?" she replied. "Aren't you curious what he did to cause Flora to respond with such fury?"

Firmly, he said no.

"Liar," she murmured, her heart oddly light as they walked toward the carriage. Thanks to Russell's intervention, she was embarking on one of her favorite activities with her most favorite person for one final time, and nothing, not even a pair of quarreling lovers, could spoil her buoyancy.

Oh, but that could—her awareness that this outing would be her last—and she thrust the thought aside.

Flora and Holcroft, she reminded herself.

And in truth it was not only a distraction, for Bea was genuinely fond of her cousin and wanted her to be happy. She would never presume to interfere in Flora's relationship unless the girl asked specifically for her opinion, but she did desire to understand what had transpired between the two.

Based on what Flora had revealed, the rupture seemed to be almost entirely Holcroft's fault. Without providing any explanation, he had summarily removed himself from her life. The many excuses he had offered—taking a pet over a minor slight, visiting his family—had merely been pretexts to hide the truth.

Considering the increasingly extreme lengths to which her cousin had gone to regain his attention, Bea thought anger was a rational response. It had to be humiliating to realize she had dragged poor, disgraced Mr. Caruthers to the scene of a murder for no reason at all. With each passing day, the girl had grown more convinced that something had gone greatly awry with the blossoming romance that had seemed so promising only a few weeks before, and everyone around her chastised her for being unnecessarily dramatic.

Even Bea had done it.

The needless extravagance had seemed so in keeping with her estimation of her cousin: If Flora could not have the giddy breathlessness of returned affection, then she would have the blighted despondency of thwarted love.

And yet Flora had been right all along.

That realization was almost enough to turn Bea against Holcroft because it revealed to her not only her own prejudices, a development no sensible woman appreciated, but also the depth of his cruelty. But it was the implausibility of this notion—of Holcroft being deliberately cruel—that held her back. Although she did not know him very well, as she had interacted with him only a handful of times, she believed wholly in his decency. Coming upon Flora as she stood on the pavement outside of Lyon's Inn, the mystery she had wrested from Bea firmly in her grasp, he refused to abandon her to the machinations of fate. Instead, he offered his protection and helped her pursue her ends.

It was this act of open-mindedness that endeared him to her. He could have overpowered Flora or threatened to reveal her presence to her parents. He could have controlled her behavior in any number of ways.

And then, when her fake murder investigation somehow transformed into a real murder investigation exposing the venality at the heart of the Chancery Court, he attributed its success to her. He did not claim credit for any of it, insisting on Flora's bravery and ingenuity.

It could have gone the other way, Bea knew, for the notion of a competent woman was so alien to most men that they were simply incapable of discerning their contributions. If a noble deed had been performed and there were only male persons in the room, then one of them must have done it. No other explanation was possible.

Holcroft was not a frivolous man.

If he had decided that distancing himself from Flora was the only way to keep her safe, then he had done so after a great deal of thought and consideration. It was not a choice he would make lightly, and although Bea understood why her cousin was annoyed by the lack of respect for her autonomy, she was more fascinated by the mystery it presented: What threat had loomed so large that Mr. Holcroft resolved to end their association rather than expose Flora to it?

As the carriage rolled down Dover Street, she turned the question over in her head.

Chapter Three

※

Viscount Ripley was all shirt points.

There was more to him, obviously, such as lively brown eyes and a languid demeanor, but when one looked at him one could see only his starched collar skimming the lobes of his ears. It framed his chin, giving the bottom half of his face an incomplete quality, like a painting yet to be fully conceived.

Holcroft, who recalled a shy boy who loved licorice and catching frogs in the pond, was astonished by his appearance, for he had never seen him looking quite so modish.

At least, that was what his lordship told him as he led them down a long hallway lined with shell-shaped sconces inlaid with porcelain. "The last time you saw me, Holcroft, I was a child, running wild in the country with dirt caked on my cheeks. Now I am an *homme du monde*," he explained, drawing out each syllable with lavish floridness. "It is startling, I am sure, for you could not have expected me to rise so quickly to the heights of society. I have been here barely a month and already I am having tea with the most celebrated peeress in the kingdom."

Ripley paused on the threshold of the drawing room and looked at Bea with a mixture of hope and pleading, an indication that he did not quite possess the confidence he projected. "You *will* allow me to serve you tea, won't you, your grace? I do not think partaking in a light refreshment makes the seriousness of the situation any less solemn."

Although he stated it firmly, the comment was more of a question and Bea agreed with the assessment.

Visibly relieved, he gestured to the settee and invited her to take a seat.

Watching him navigate his shirt points—the way he moved his head with gingerly care—she could not decide whom he was imitating. It was not Brummell, for the style was too ostentatious, nor Edward "the Golden Ball" Hughes because his adherents sported the signature black cravat.

Nuneaton, perhaps?

That struck her as precisely the sort of mistake a cawker would make: distilling the complexity of the viscount's sartorial presentation down to an overly stiff collar and an exaggerated drawl.

And Lord Ripley *was* young.

At two and twenty, he was the same age as Russell, but his efforts to appear worldly only made him seem younger. He was like a child trying on his father's tailcoat.

Holcroft, who had secured his position on the outing with a pledge to be of use, stepped forward to make the formal introduction. His first bid, attempted in the entry hall upon their arrival, had been thwarted by Ripley's enthusiasm. Elated by the opportunity to impress an old friend, the young man had launched into a lengthy oration detailing the many sweeping changes to his person before his visitor could say more than a few words. The energetic narration had accompanied them all the way to the drawing room.

Ripley rebuffed his efforts once again, insisting that his

honored guests required no introduction, especially the illustrious Duchess of Kesgrave. Then he added that he had had the pleasure of meeting the duke earlier in the week. "It was in Oxford Street, in front of Pratt's, on a Tuesday."

Kesgrave, unaware of the acquaintance, apologized for not recalling it. The viscount excused him at once, asserting that it was too much to expect a man of the duke's consequence to remember every dandy who strolled by him on the busy thoroughfare.

Although this reply sounded like a display of gracious humility, upon further questioning it was revealed to be the actual truth. Their encounter had been a fleeting exchange comprised of Ripley stepping to his left to allow the duke to pass. It was brief, yes, but the viscount appeared thrilled by his literal brush with greatness.

The fatuous grin he wore, however, dimmed as he noticed for the first time Flora's presence in his home, and he owned himself incapable of placing her, as she was not famous.

Holcroft stiffened at the oafish remark, but his distemper was not in evidence as he made Miss Hyde-Clare known to their host.

Her name, however, did little to explain her presence, and Ripley's expression remained puzzled as he invited her to sit down as well. "As honored as I am for the opportunity to receive the duchess's cousin, I worry that being seen to entertain a large party while the house is in mourning sets the wrong tone. I would be loath to earn a reputation for frivolity."

The observation, so patently opposed to the reality of his shirt points, defused the situation beautifully. Flora, whose cheeks had turned bright red at the charge of intrusion, nodded her head in an exaggerated show of understanding and murmured that it would be wretched to be perceived as silly.

Holcroft's belligerence likewise decreased, and he leaned back into the cushion as a footman entered with the tray. He placed it on the table beside the settee, and securing his employer's approval, left the room.

"It is a difficult balance to strike," Ripley continued as if Flora had not spoken, "for a swell of the first stare such as I must straddle the line between fashionable and frivolous—a harrowing feat all on its own. Few of us are able to cultivate an outlandish peculiarity with the same effortless grace as the duchess."

Although the description did not strike Bea as quite the fulsome praise its speaker believed it to be, it was nevertheless an improvement on *ghoulish,* which was the adjective more commonly ascribed to her. Amused by her own low standards—and aware of the duke's twitching lips—she thanked the young viscount for the compliment.

"Of course," Ripley replied gravely. "I find your trajectory to be hugely instructive. Not since Brummel has someone so staggeringly inconsequential risen to the height of popularity."

Flora, whose previous treatment of her cousin indicated a similar opinion of her former stature, exclaimed in protest. "The duchess was never inconsequential."

Ripley waved his left hand in dismissive acknowledgment of her critique. "Insignificant, then. Either way, I am in awe. Do allow me to pour you tea before we turn to the reason you are here. As you can imagine, I am undone by the circumstance and my nerves are stretched to the point of breaking. Several times in the past week I've had to employ the Austrian method of meditation, which was taught to me by Archduchess Louisa Clementina, second cousin twice removed from Francis II, the Holy Roman Emperor."

Having *read A Comprehensive History of Meditation as Studied by the Author: A Compendium in Three Volumes,* Frederick Mark's excellent account of the history of the meditative practice, Bea could only conclude this Austrian strain was a recent invention, devised, presumably, to give inane viscounts further opportunities to impress their guests with the importance of their connections.

In that purpose it failed, for Flora, perhaps still bristling from Ripley's flippant dismissal of her cousin's consequence or even her own, noted that she preferred the Anglo-Saxon style of meditation. "I cannot support anything that is associated, however loosely, with Napoleon's wife because I am English, you see."

The viscount colored faintly at the implied lack of national loyalty, his eyes narrowing. Rather than issue a curt reply, however, he chose to ignore the slight altogether, which was the far more cutting response. Turning to Bea, he owned himself pathetically grateful for her willingness to prove his innocence. "It has been a terrible five days, lumbering under the weight of suspicion while struggling to contain my grief. Truly awful, your grace. I can barely bring myself to climb out of bed in the morning, let alone allow my valet to dress me in the *fabuleux* manner the ton has come to expect. I had even decided not to go to the salon yesterday because bearing under the weight of all that suspicion in addition to the wearying pall of sadness is exhausting. But then I thought, No, Rip, you must soldier on—it is what Grandfather would want. So I put on my best waistcoat despite the weariness in my heart and went, and that is when I discovered that Mr. Hyde-Clare is your cousin. It felt like more than a stroke of good luck," he added as he served the tea. "It felt preordained."

Although her purpose in coming to St. James's Square was not to relieve the young man of his undue burden but to discover if the burden was justified, Bea offered no correction. Instead, she asked him to tell them about his grandfather's death. "My cousin says he was found on the floor of his bedchamber with a cut in his forehead, presumably caused by falling against the night table."

"Grandfather banged his head in a fall, yes, but it was not against something as mundane as a night table," he rushed to explain. "It was a pier table by Thomas Chippendale made in 1775 to my great-grandfather's specifications. It is unique and beautiful and far too significant a piece to be hidden away in a bedchamber. It deserves pride of place in the drawing room, but Grandfather refused to consider it, insisting it remain buried in his bedchamber, where only he could admire its stupendous craftsmanship."

Bea, accepting the cup of tea, nodded as if this information was vital to her investigation, which, to be fair, it might yet be, for she never knew which seemingly insignificant tidbit would prove pivotal. "And your family think you had something to do with his fall because you had an argument the day before he died?"

Frowning severely, his lordship told her she did not have to be delicate about it. "My family think I murdered him as surely as if I had driven a dagger into his heart. As I said, it has been a terrible few days. Imagine what it is like trying to eat your *hareng fumé et salé* while half a dozen people glare at you with grave mistrust. Suspicion of murder is completely ruinous to a young man's digestion. That I can tell you!"

Flora, who found kippers to be difficult to digest regardless of their preparation, murmured consolingly. Ripley bestowed a grateful look upon her.

"What was the argument about?" Bea asked.

"*Argument* does not begin to describe the incident," he replied with a dramatic shiver. "Grandfather yelled at me for twenty minutes without pause, and his face grew so red from the exertion, the truth is, I did worry about his health. I thought he might have a fit of apoplexy and fall dead right there in his study. But he *was* sitting down and his heart was strong. His gout bothered him and from time to time he would have a nasty cough but all in all he was in good health for a man of his years."

"How old was he?" Bea asked.

"Eighty-four this past March," Ripley replied. "I wanted to be here for his birthday celebration, but I had not yet managed to wiggle out from beneath my mother's thumb yet. She is very protective of me, you see, because my father died in a duel when he was only a few years older than me. As she likes to say, I am all she has, although that is not strictly true because she has her roses and the ladies she plays whist with and also the vicar, who is very kind to her. Plus there is my older sister, who is constantly breeding, so she already has a parcel of grandchildren to occupy her. Even so, she is excessively attached to me, which is the very devil, and I can waste no time in establishing myself in London because I do not know how long I have before she finds some way to haul me back to the village. I thought Grandfather would understand the urgency of my situation, which requires me to act boldly to earn the respect of my peers. Everyone knows gambling is the best way to make a name for yourself in London, and that is why my losses, which might seem large, are actually quite small."

Holcroft muttered, "Good lord," which earned him an irate glare from the aspiring Pink, and Kesgrave, whose opinion could not have been much better, sought to confirm his large losses were the source of the quarrel.

"*Seemingly* large," Ripley corrected petulantly. "But modest when one considers the value of notoriety. One cannot *buy* the beau monde's attention. It has to be earned with acts of audacity, as I said. Although Grandfather was upset about my minor-when-considered-in-the-larger-context losses, he took particular exception to the ladybirds. That was the source of the quarrel."

Failing to anticipate the turn from debts to spotted red insects, Bea said, "What ladybirds?"

The viscount placed his saucer on the table with a clatter as he said, "Exactly! What ladybirds! You do not know about the ladybirds because that confounding Mr. Twaddle-Thum failed to report on them, which is vexingly unjust. He devoted *two* columns to Lord Fernsby."

Despite the force of his response, it provided no illumination and Bea was compelled to ask who Lord Fernsby was.

"An ignorant puppy who wagered his entire fortune on ants," Holcroft replied in disgust.

"It was a *race*," Ripley said, making what he thought was a meaningful distinction.

Holcroft, his tone oddly weary, replied that ants cannot race.

The viscount's brow furrowed angrily and for a moment he seemed on the verge of arguing in favor of the sentience of ants. But he restrained himself and complained again about Twaddle's unjust treatment. "I staked two hundred pounds on which of three ladybirds would arrive at the top of a tree trunk first, and the wretch did not acknowledge it at all."

Although Bea was stunned by the profligacy of the wager, her cousin took issue with its lack of creativity. "Perhaps his uninterest was due to the derivative nature of the venture. Next time you should bet on something original, such as which leaf crosses a pond first."

Annoyed by the criticism, Ripley pulled his lips together in an impatient moue and yet he could not quite smother his interest in the idea. A thoughtful look entered his eyes, and Bea assumed he was calculating which type of leaf crossing what body of water would result in the most thrilling contest.

He was, she thought again, impossibly young.

AN EXTRAVAGANT DUPLICITY

"And that is why Mr. Dugmore yelled at you for twenty minutes?" she asked. "Because you lost an astronomical sum on a ladybird race?"

"He simply had no idea what it is like for a young man to try to establish himself in London these days," Ripley grumbled. "He came to town in the middle of the last century. He powdered his wig, for God's sake! I had no choice but to be bold and daring, and it was exceedingly horrid of him to take me to task for doing what was necessary. He would never have known if one of his cronies had not tattled on me."

"But you *wanted* Twaddle to write about it," Flora pointed out. "Would he have not discovered the truth regardless?"

He aimed another querulous look at her and said there was a tremendous difference between his grandfather reading about his triumph in the dailies and his getting a report sotto voce from an interfering crony with nothing better to do than spread lies. "Notoriety is worth any amount of familial disapproval. But to remain obscure *and* be subjected to threats of disinheritance? The worst of both worlds!"

Bea put down her teacup and leaned forward at this mention of an actual motive. "During your heated argument the day your grandfather died, he threatened to disinherit you?"

Ripley exhaled heavily and said, "See, now you are looking at me just like they do. Yes, during that argument Grandfather threatened disinheritance. But you say it like it was noteworthy. It was not! He had been making that threat since almost the day I arrived in London. At one point, he showed me his will, pointed to the section that pertained to me and said all he had to do was strike out those lines and I would be gone. But he was just making a fuss. Like my mother, he worried that I would follow in my father's footsteps and wind up destitute in a field with a bullet through my head, which is ridiculous because I would never agree to pistols at dawn.

Rise before eight for the pleasure of providing a hostile opponent with target practice? No, absolutely not!"

Although threatening disinheritance was a tried-and-true method for keeping a young hothead in line, the warnings appeared to have had no effect on the viscount and Bea wondered if his grandfather had made a move to follow through on his threat.

If he had contacted his solicitor, then it might have behooved the viscount to eliminate his grandfather before the changes could be enacted.

Disinheritance was always an excellent inducement to murder.

Firmly, Bea reminded herself there was no reason to believe Mr. Dugmore's accident was anything but the mundane fall it appeared to be. Just because the viscount's family thought the circumstance was suspicious did not mean it was.

In all likelihood, all she would wind up proving was that an eighty-four-year-old man with gout was unsteady on his feet.

Even so, it would be remiss of her to not at least try to find evidence of wrongdoing, and recalling what Russell had said about his lordship's movements, she asked why he was in his grandfather's room so early on the morning of his death if he preferred to sleep late.

"Circumstance demanded it!" he exclaimed with an air of agitation. "I knew Grandfather kept his correspondence in his bedchamber, and given the losses I suffered that night, it became vital that I find out who was running to him with malicious tales about me before he could malign my good name even further."

Given the apparent constraints on his financial situation, Bea found his attitude toward his debts shockingly cavalier and asked him how much he owed in total and how he planned to satisfy it.

Coloring slightly at the query, Ripley insisted that a gentleman never discussed money. "It is decidedly *mauvais goût* to mention actual sums. Indeed, I hold to that principle so strongly I have not done the math myself. But I am sure it is fine. Whatever I cannot pay with this quarter's allowance will be settled with next quarter's. There is no reason for anyone to kick up dust."

But obviously there was, for his funds could not be without limit, and it seemed highly probable that he would not only blow through next quarter's funds in short order but also the next several quarters'. Even if Dugmore was not a stodgy old man with eighteenth-century notions of propriety, he would be alarmed by his grandson's spending.

The greenhorn equated profligacy with popularity.

Although she was only a few years older than the viscount, she regarded him as a callow youth and could only imagine how incredibly young and foolish he must have appeared to a man of his grandfather's years.

A veritable babe in arms.

With these thoughts in mind, she suggested they take a look at the bedchamber.

Ripley leaped excitedly to his feet and cried, "Hurrah! You have decided to take up my cause. I am so very grateful, your grace. Now you must not be shy. Please ask me for anything you need. The entire house is at your disposal, including all the servants. I believe in the Mayhew case, you conducted your interviews in the servants' hall? I do not think anything so rustic is required here, but if being belowstairs is necessary to your process, then by all means, make use of the servants' hall. And have no worry about outstaying your welcome. You must remain as long as it takes to prove Grandfather suffered an unfortunate fall. If you have to stay for a week, then you will stay for a week."

"It will not take as long as a week," Bea said.

Awed by the confidence in her voice, the viscount shook his head. "You are everything Mr. Twaddle-Thum described and more."

Given the virulent gossip's penchant for wild exaggeration, Bea was far from flattered by the remark, but rather than register her disfavor she smiled blandly and rose to her feet. As Ripley led them through the house, he conducted an impromptu tour of the establishment's most impressive features. The chandelier in the entrance hall was made of rock crystal in the *lustre à tige découverte* style, the painting at the top of the stairs was by Jan Steen, and the handrail was patterned on Inigo Jones's design for the Banqueting House in Whitehall.

"And of course the pier table, which might be the finest example of Chippendale's baroque style still in existence," he added as they arrived to the second floor. "As I said, Grandfather was greatly attached to it, and he lambasted me when I arranged for the footmen to bring it down to the drawing room and put a conventional night table in its place. He had a habit of responding with immoderate anger to even trifling situations, which was why I was not worried he would cut me off. The truth was, my grandfather was a grumpy old man with gout raging about anything that caught his attention: a stain on the settee, a scratch in the table. All he wanted was peace and harmony, he would yell as he was despoiling everyone else's peace and harmony. Inevitably, something new would capture his attention and he would forget all about the stain or scratch—although the staff did scurry to fix the imperfection. Grandfather's love of harmony applied to all aspects of his environment."

Dismayed by his reasoning, Flora sought to confirm that

he genuinely believed a debt of several hundred pounds was equal to a scratch in a table.

Ripley stopped halfway down the hallway and regarded her with curiosity. "Oh, but what scratch? Which table?" he asked, wrapping his fingers around a door handle. Then he took a deep breath and let it out in short, sharp bursts.

Inhaling again, he explained that he was performing an Austrian meditation technique. "I am apprehensive about entering Grandfather's room, which I have not been in since the footmen took the body away. Nobody has been inside because my aunt ordered the room shut. My cousin Matthew thought he could move in without anyone else noticing, and naturally I objected because it is the loveliest set of rooms in the house. Aunt Celia was infuriated by our arguing over it while her father lay in the cellar and said neither one of us would get the bedchamber. And then she shut the door to everyone, including the servants."

Properly fortified by the Austrian method, Ripley opened the door and they entered the room, which was dark, with heavy curtains obscuring the eastern light. Only faint slivers of daylight slipped in along the edges. He apologized for the gloom and hastened to open the drapes, revealing a large, comfortable space with expert plasterwork and intricate wood carvings. A fireplace with a marble mantel and detached fluted columns decorated the long wall, and a mahogany bed, commodious and canopied, rested in the center of the floor. Before it, its width running the length of the bed, was a primrose rug decorated with thistles and marred by a brown stain. The blemish meandered like a blot of ink and spread outward as it followed the slope of the floor toward the bed. It grew fainter as it drew closer to the table, almost fading entirely before reappearing as a round blotch.

Rushing over from the windows, almost as if to block their view, Ripley said, "Mary did it! The stain, I mean. She was the one who found Grandfather when she brought his tea in the morning. She brings his tea every morning at eight-thirty. She was so startled, she dropped the tray and the pot spilled everywhere as you can see. She was cleaning it up when Aunt Celia ordered everyone from the room."

The explanation made sense to Bea, who recalled how dark the room had been when they had entered. Carrying the tray, the maid would not have had a hand free to open the heavy curtains. Rather, she would have walked directly to the pier table to put down the tray before admitting the light. That would explain why the stain was so close to the bed. She had gotten within two feet of the body before realizing it was there.

To get a better sense of the scene, she asked Ripley where Mr. Dugmore had been found, and the viscount all but clapped in response. Hailing the question as an example of the investigative spirit that animated Mr. Twaddle-Thum's accounts, he dropped onto the rug to show them, forgetting the dignity of his shirt points in his enthusiasm to imitate a corpse. He lay at an angle away from the pier table, his back mostly following the line of the bed frame and his legs slightly under it.

"He was like this," Ripley said, his cheek pressed against a lavender flowerhead.

"With his eyes looking toward the door?" Flora said.

As if surprised to find she was still there, Ripley regarded her with vague confusion for a moment before answering in the affirmative.

Flora nodded thoughtfully and asked where precisely on Mr. Dugmore's forehead the bruise had been.

"It was a gash, not a welt or bump," Ripley replied irritably as he rose to his feet, annoyed by either her belittlement of the injury that had felled his grandfather or her efforts to wrest the mystery from the elegant grasp of the

Duchess of Kesgrave. "And it was here, a little toward the left side, approaching the temple."

Bea contemplated the bed and tried to imagine Dugmore's movements based on the position of the wound. Waking, he would have swung his legs to the edge of the bed, placed his feet on the floor and stood. Falling from that position should have propelled him forward, onto the open swathe of rug. Depending on what had caused the tumble, he would have landed with a hard crack or a soft thud.

Either way, his left temple was unlikely to bear the brunt of it.

But it was dark with the curtains closed and the fire but an ember after the long night. In that case, opening the drapes would have been his first priority—except Dugmore's eyesight was poor if the spectacles resting on the table were an indication.

Now she pictured him standing as he reached for the eyeglasses, a simple enough maneuver but one that could nevertheless have grave consequences. If he misjudged the distance, he might have tipped forward too far or he could have suffered a fainting spell. Balance was in general harder to sustain for older people, or his legs might have given out beneath him.

Any manner of things might have facilitated the fall, and she could see how he would knock forward and then collapse backward, so that he landed in a supine position.

Flora, arriving at the same conclusion through her own extended process, smiled in pleasure when Holcroft corroborated her theory before remembering she had no interest in his approbation. Then she scowled at him and turned her attention to the pier table, announcing that it was indeed an exquisite example of Chippendale's Baroque period. Her admiration overcame some of his lordship's resentment, and he trotted over to make sure she noticed the delicate acanthus carvings along the border.

Amused, Bea contemplated the sinuous splotch and marveled at Aunt Celia's doggedness. She understood her anger, for it was highly disrespectful to bicker over a man's room when his cadaver had not yet cooled, but it seemed a little excessive to refuse the servants access as well, especially when there was a large spill to clean up.

And some blood, she thought, detecting a thumb-size smudge on the rug near where Ripley had lain his head. She lowered to the floor to examine it more closely and wondered again why the aunt would not want this evidence of her father's suffering removed at once.

Holding her thoughts on the notion of proof, Bea pondered the other reason someone might close off a room: to hide incriminating evidence. If an object had flown off in the heat of the struggle—a button, an earring, a hairpin—then the killer might not have noticed it was gone until later. Then she would be desperate to retrieve it.

But how to search her father's room without raising the suspicions of the servants, who would be constantly in and out, scrubbing the rug and preparing the space for its new occupant? And all that cleaning and preparing—it would create significant peril for a killer who had left behind a readily identifying item such as a locket with an inscription.

It was five days later, however, and still the prohibition remained.

Did that mean Aunt Celia had yet to find the missing article?

Thoughtfully, Bea tilted her head and noted there were several inches between the frame and the floor, plenty of room for a small object to skitter through.

It could not be that simple.

No, of course not.

Under the bed was the first place the killer would search.

Well, second, she allowed, after the bed itself.

There was nothing to find, and yet she was already there, on the rug in the deceased's room, eye level with his mahogany bed. She might as well take a look.

It might be the most futile theory of her brief career as an investigator but certainly not her most implausible.

Cautiously, she lowered to her stomach and slipped her head under the frame.

Ripley let out a piercing squeal, startling Bea, who lifted her head without recalling her position and banged it against the frame. She yelped in pain as Flora asked the viscount with wry derision if screeching was also an Austrian technique. Holcroft told him to control himself, and Kesgrave helped Bea to her feet, his expression a mix of concern for her welfare and amusement at her predicament.

Well he should laugh, Bea thought without any censure. It was utterly absurd, crawling beneath beds based on the flimsiest of theories. The least she could do was wait until after interrogating a suspect before deciding she was the killer.

Or she could first decide whether a murder had actually taken place.

As yet nothing about the incident seemed nefarious.

Tragic, yes, because it could have easily been avoided if Dugmore had waited for the maid to open the curtains, but not nefarious.

Dismayed by the injury his elation inflicted, Ripley rushed to Bea's side to apologize. "I was so excited to see you crawling under the bed, I forgot myself. It is just that you are willing to go to any lengths to prove my innocence and I am so grateful. We will both be shown to great advantage, I think, in the article Mr. Twaddle-Thum will inevitably write about my ordeal."

The reminder of her vulnerability, of the likelihood that

her actions in this room would not only find their way into the pages of the *London Daily Gazette* but also be exaggerated, so that in the published account she would be fully underneath the bed with only the soles of her shoes peeking out, made her feel doubly silly.

Slithering on the floor!

Was she truly so desperate for a murder to investigate?

She was, yes, very much so.

Bea harbored no illusions. An intelligent woman, she had perceived at once what it meant to carry the next generation of the illustrious Matlock family, what was at stake, and she knew the eccentricities of a newly married woman would not be tolerated in an expectant mother. Kesgrave could not allow her to dash around town like a Bow Street Runner, interviewing dangerous crime lords and chasing homicidal law clerks.

It would be madness.

To ease her disappointment, she reminded herself that her practice of identifying killers would have ended soon enough regardless of her condition. London simply could not continue to serve up an endless supply of dead bodies. It was already hugely improbable that she had somehow stumbled from one victim to the next, seemingly without pause, and her luck could not hold.

Without fate dropping corpses at her feet, she would have been forced to resort to other means to find victims and what would those be? Loitering in front of the magistrate's office? Posting a sign in Berkeley Square announcing her services? Asking Mr. Twaddle-Thum to send referrals?

There were no viable options—and nor should there be.

She was the Duchess of Kesgrave, for God's sake, not a character in a Minerva Press novel.

Determined to be reasonable about the termination of her career, Bea was nevertheless terrified of what it would

AN EXTRAVAGANT DUPLICITY

mean for her marriage. Kesgrave had only known this Bea—investigative Bea, courageously-staring-down-murderers Bea—and she could not convince herself that he would like the other Bea.

Not even *she* liked the other Bea: meek Bea, mute Bea, drab Bea.

Rationally, she knew it was absurd to believe she would revert to a lesser version of herself the instant she stopped her peculiar occupation. Rather, the reversion would happen slowly, over years, a gradual wearing away until she was back to where she started: silently cowering next to a fern hoping nobody noticed her.

It seemed inevitable to her that the duke, demanding conventionality in this one respect, would begin to expect it in others. Whatever exhilarating digressions had been tolerated in the first heady months of marriage, he was still an exalted member of the British aristocracy superintending a centuries-old institution redolent of dignity and decorum.

Tradition exerted its own force, like gravity, and eventually it drew everything back to the surface. Not even a feather could resist its pull.

There had been a wild originality to their relationship from the beginning—Kesgrave perching on the branch outside her window in the Lake District, Bea kissing the mustache off his lip in the carriage—and she did not know what would remain after it was gone.

It was with these cheerful thoughts in mind that Bea had contemplated the dark space beneath Dugmore's bed and she could not blame herself for trying so hard to find something sinister in the aunt's behavior. The patriarch's murder would be her last opportunity to savor the keen satisfaction of solving a mystery.

But she could not make something exist simply by wanting it to be real, she thought with amusement as

Kesgrave brushed his hand along the back of her head to reassure himself there was no bump.

"It is nothing," she said before walking over to look at the pier table herself.

Flora moved suddenly to the right, in front of Holcroft, effectively blocking his view, and Bea neatly stepped around both of them to examine the piece. Its light-colored wood contrasting brightly with the rich mahogany of the bed and other furniture, including an impressively large bookcase along the far wall, the table featured a rectangular top with carved panels in an acanthus design supported by cabriole legs tapering to claw-and-ball feet. Admiring the quality, Bea could understand why Dugmore would insist on keeping it in his bedchamber for his exclusive enjoyment. Pressed against the edge of his bed, near the headboard, it was an elegant place to rest one's books, spectacles and candleholder.

Flora, examining the decorative floral design along the edge, nodded in that world-weary way of hers and said, "Ah, yes, just as I expected. You can see it here, where his head hit. There are traces of blood. You are right to call it a gash, Ripley, for I can see from this evidence that the wound bled quite profusely."

Ripley whimpered at the prospect of blood marring the Chippendale and lightly shoved Bea out of the way in his eagerness to make his own inspection of the wood. Holcroft peered at the stains from the far end of the table, a less prestigious vantage but adequate to the task.

As the three convened over the night table, Kesgrave commented on the advancement in Flora's investigative method. "Usually, she stands over your shoulder and affirms your conclusions. Shall we gracefully accept our demotion by standing over hers?"

He was teasing, Bea knew, and she smiled to signal her amusement, but it cut a little too close to the bone. With her actual relegation imminent, she did not want to stand in admiration of her cousin's conclusions. She wanted to draw a dozen of her own.

It was she, after all, who had made the occupation of female investigator de rigueur if not respectable. Flora would still be worshipping Incomparables like Miss Petworth if Bea had not all but tripped over Mr. Otley in the library at Lakeview Hall, and it was only fair that she get to examine the pier table.

It was *her* murder!

But even as she had the petulant thought, she knew it was absurd. Mr. Dugmore had not been murdered. He was an old man who knocked his head as he stumbled out of bed, and Ripley was a callow attention-seeking youth who had hatched a scheme when he discovered he was sparring with the Duchess of Kesgrave's cousin. He had even said it himself as he crowed with delight at her presence in his home, eagerly anticipating Twaddle's interest.

The fatuousness of the whole scene struck her as a fitting end to her brilliant career as an investigator, and rather than chafe at things she could not change, she consented to the duke's suggestion.

Chapter Four

Flora made a thorough inspection of what she deemed the "fall range," pressing her nose against the pier table's surface and examining every inch of its gilded frame. She perused the items on the table, scrutinized the fibers of the rug and ran her fingers over carvings in the headboard. Methodically, she sifted through the bedclothes, drawing back the sheets and blankets in turn, and Bea, noting her careful treatment of the linens, wondered if her cousin was looking for clues or admiring their quality.

They were, to be sure, finer than anything 19 Portman Square had ever seen.

Regardless, Flora's exhaustive search revealed nothing beyond her own personal fondness for silk counterpanes, and concluding her review, she absolved Viscount Ripley of all wrongdoing.

"The culprit—and I use that term lightly—is the pier table," she announced with an aura of self-importance. Confident in her determination, she offered to discuss her findings with his family in hopes of putting their minds at ease.

His lordship, however, neither sought nor desired her exoneration. "I do not know who you are."

Stiffening at the insult, she explained that she was Miss Hyde-Clare, cousin to the Duchess of Kesgrave and cousin-in-law to the sixth duke. "We were introduced upon our arrival, but that was over an hour ago so perhaps you forgot."

"Yes, yes, I know who you are," he replied with a dismissive wave of his hand. "But I don't know *who you are*. Has Mr. Twaddle-Thum chronicled your adventures? Did Lord Bentham try to kill you in your sitting room? Have you inspired a fashion craze that has left most London jewelers out of stock of diamond-studded magnifying glasses? In short, Miss Hyde-Clare, how much respect do you command among the *ton* and how will your vindication advance my career?"

Although the questions were demeaning, Ripley imbued them with sincere curiosity, as if he truly did not know the answers. Possibly, he might have overlooked something vital about the presumptuous girl before him, who might only appear to be talking out of turn. If she would just present her bona fides so that he may examine them.

Unable to reply affirmatively to any of these queries, Flora shrunk back just as Holcroft stepped forward, his expression uncharacteristically pugnacious.

"Miss Hyde-Clare does not need to justify herself to you," he said coldly. "She is a young lady of remarkable accomplishments, among which is ensuring that if you *were* guilty of murdering your grandfather you would get a fair trial for your crime."

Flinching slightly at Holcroft's belligerence, Ripley nevertheless remained obdurate. He could not accept exculpation from anyone whom Mr. Twaddle-Thum had yet to recognize. "If I wanted the opinion of any old Jack or Harry Smith, I would have called the Runners."

"You understand nothing, you ignorant puppy," Holcroft exclaimed scathingly. "Mr. Twaddle-Thum holds Miss Hyde-Clare in such high esteem he has refrained from mentioning her name in his column as an emblem of his respect."

Confounded by this statement, Flora opened her eyes as wide as they would go and squawked, "He has?"

Bea, too, was struck by the comment, for it indicated an unimagined intimacy between the staid gentleman and the disreputable gossip.

Did Holcroft know who he was?

It seemed very much as though he did.

The revelation held no interest for Ripley, who advised Miss Hyde-Clare to be a little less impressive, for there was no point in being notable if Mr. Twaddle-Thum refused to note it. "I know it sounds harsh," he added with an apologetic look at Holcroft, "but it is just a matter of practicality. How can I expect my cousins to accept her judgment if I do not?"

Holcroft sneered at this nonsensical reply, and Bea, who knew well what it was like to be overlooked and ignored, said she supported any conclusions her cousin drew.

Ripley, who had not summoned an emissary of the Duchess of Kesgrave but Her Outrageousness herself, opened his mouth to argue against this injustice. But he barely squeaked out a syllable before thinking better of it and forcing a smile. "That is charming," he said without conviction. Nevertheless, he extended his arm to Flora. "Come, then, Miss Hyde-Clare. Let us go put my family's mind at ease."

Although Flora looked disgruntled enough to snub the offer, she consented without comment and allowed herself to be led from the room by the viscount. Far from appeased, Holcroft stomped after them.

Following with Kesgrave at a sedate pace, Bea said, "Our

Mr. Holcroft is a dark horse, fraternizing with Twaddles. What do you make of that?"

The duke agreed the connection was unexpected, as well as the revelation that Twaddle appeared to have standards. "That is, if he refused to lend his consequences to the ladybird race because he recognized the coxcomb's desperate ploy for attention. As he ordinarily delights in mocking the caprice of the aristocracy, I have to assume there is some discretion involved."

"Let's hope he continues to disoblige him by giving our visit the same treatment despite the many fascinating details his spies will inevitably uncover, such as my bumping my head on the bed frame," Bea said, her cheeks growing warm at the memory. "It might be petty of me, but I find the idea of that silly stripling being denied his greatest ambition satisfying."

"He has already been thwarted by your insistence that he accept Flora in your stead," he replied with a faint smile. "I thought he was going to stamp his foot like a child and say no."

"The viscount has too much respect for his dignity to indulge in a fit of pique," she said as they arrived to the drawing room, where they were introduced to Matthew Gaitskill. Several inches taller than his cousin, he had the same warm brown eyes and prominent chin. His hair was cut à la Brutus, his clothes were austere, and his manner was brusque. He could not understand why Flora was burdening him with information he had shown no interest in acquiring.

"The only suspicion I harbor against Ripley is that he is more of a fool than I'd thought possible," he said impatiently.

"But you did observe his lordship leaving your grandfather's room at six-thirty on the morning of his death," Flora reminded him. "Did that not strike you as odd?"

"It was the damnedest thing, seeing Rip up before noon," he conceded. "He takes such pains with his toilette, he usually does not leave his room until well after breakfast has been cleared. Then he forces the servants to lay the table for him again. Very inconsiderate stuff."

"Oh, I say, that is not fair!" Ripley protested. "Mrs. Keene swears it is no bother at all."

"Yes, because housekeepers are famous for complaining to their employers about additional work," Matthew said scornfully, before turning to Kesgrave and apologizing for the outburst. "I am just struggling to understand why you are here—why any of you are here."

"Lord Ripley wants to put his relatives' minds at ease in regards to your grandfather's death and called on us to use our expertise to confirm that Mr. Dugmore did in fact die from a knock against the table," Flora explained.

But this explanation shed no further light on the subject, for the cause of his grandfather's death had never been in doubt. "I fail to see why my cousin wasted your time with this nonsense other than he is a general sapskull who wastes *all* our time," Matthew said.

Ripley's cheeks darkened with embarrassment as he glared at his cousin with fervent dislike. "That is a bald-faced lie! He does think I killed our grandfather. He accused me directly."

"I said it was your fault, you dolt," Matthew replied in exasperation, "not that you killed him. Good God, I do not believe you have the pluck to kill anything larger than a ladybird, which I am certain you massacred by the hundreds in service of your daft stunt."

His eyes hot with fury, Ripley swore that he did not harm a single ladybird in the pursuit of his thrilling race, which was too brilliant an event for his cousin's leaden mind to comprehend. "My ardent respect for the creature's athleticism would never condone abuse. And I do have pluck! Only a man of extraordinary courage would dare to attempt a paisley waistcoat with striped pantaloons!"

Matthew looked at the duke with amused disdain and said, "Really, your grace? You are lending your consequence to this drivel? You have nothing better to do with your time than entertain fairy stories from my cork-brained cousin?"

Insulted on his guest's behalf, Ripley replied that Kesgrave had time for drivel, nonsense *and* folderol. "For that is what it means to be a duke—to have infinite amounts of time for trivialities—and for you, a man who spends *hours* dangling a length of string in the water, to question his activities is the height of hypocrisy."

Gravely, Kesgrave thanked the viscount for his passionate defense, then asked Matthew to explain his earlier comment. "In what way do you consider your grandfather's death to be Ripley's fault if you do not think he pushed him against the table?"

"His asinine exploits," Matthew said succinctly, before adding, "They put such a strain on our grandfather's heart that he could barely rise in the morning. Of course he toppled over as he tried to stand!"

Ripley shook his head violently. "That is a lie. He is lying! He is just like Grandfather, old-fashioned and stodgy, and believes this should be a private matter, discussed only among family and dealt with only among family. They do not want the attention her grace will draw to his nasty suspicions. He wants to condemn me privately and send me back to the country to rusticate with the cows."

"My God, it is like talking to a brick wall!" Matthew snapped. "Get it through your thick skull, Rip: I do not suspect you of anything. I do not believe you have the wherewithal to murder our grandfather even to save your inheritance."

"Ha!" Ripley said, as if catching his cousin in a lie. "So you admit I have a motive!"

Matthew furrowed his brow at the accusation, seemingly at a loss to understand the point the viscount thought he had made. "I agree unequivocally that you had cause to wish our grandfather dead. He believed a man should suffer the consequences of his actions and you refused to heed all his warnings. But that is precisely my argument: Even *with* the huge inducement of disinheritance, I do not believe you capable."

And still the viscount was not swayed. "Then why did you tell everyone you saw me coming out of his room only a few hours before Grandfather turned up dead? You had to have suspected *something* or least wondered about me. Why did you think I was in his bedchamber if not to do him harm?"

"I assumed it was some childish prank or game," he replied impatiently. "Or that you had wagered with one of your equally juvenile friends to see who could steal the most intimate object from a slumbering victim. I figured you had taken his nightcap."

"That is only what he will admit to *now*!" Ripley cried, greatly distressed by his cousin's attempt to revise history. "Let us ask someone else. There must be someone else who is at home. Aunt Celia? Jesse?"

Only one other relative was in residence: Clifford Parr, son of Dugmore's middle daughter, Grace, and brother to Jesse, two years younger, who was also staying at the house in St. James's Square for the season.

Having insisted on the interview, Ripley was far from pleased it was taking place. "Clifford is the worst one of us, an obsequious toadeater who did everything Grandfather asked. And I am convinced he spied on me in exchange for money."

As these words were muttered under his breath, only those nearest to him could hear them, including Bea and the duke. Unaware of his cousin's censure, Clifford greeted the company, thanking them for their interest. Although he possessed the rich brown hair color of the Dugmores, his face was narrower and he had a dimple in his chin. He spoke diffidently, his voice hesitant, as he admitted that he had not suspected Ripley of killing their grandfather. "That is, I agreed with Matthew when he said your antics would take ten years off anyone's life. But I did not believe it literally because I didn't think Grandfather had ten more years left. Five, definitely. Seven, maybe. But a full decade? With his gout and sclerotic outlook?" He shook his head. "It seemed like hoping for too much."

This second exoneration no more pleased Ripley than the first, and he swore again that his cousins were only making a show for the duchess's benefit. "I swear, the moment you leave, your grace, they will again point their fingers and call me a murderer."

As neither man had done this previously, per his lordship's own account, Bea was disinclined to believe it. She turned to Kesgrave, who nodded slightly, and then announced that they would be leaving.

Greatly distressed, Ripley contended that they could not leave without interviewing the servants. "At least talk to Mary! She is the maid who discovered his body. You have been here for scarcely an hour. You spent the *entire day* at the Mayhews!"

Thoroughly out of patience with the viscount, whose nonsense he had been forced to endure for almost *two* hours, Holcroft declined the offer, which spurred Flora to accept it. Owning himself grateful for her uninvited presence, Ripley instructed a footman to summon Mary, and although Bea wanted to belay the order, she could not bring herself to undercut her cousin's authority in front of Holcroft. Therefore, she sent an apologetic look to the duke and waited for the maid to appear, which she did quickly enough.

Mary was a young woman, with light eyes and wide nostrils, and although she displayed no hesitance in describing the scene as she found it, she faltered when it came to discussing the deplorable state of the room. "I had so little time to do anything before Mrs. Gaitskill evicted me from the room and shut the door. I had barely begun to scrub the rug, let alone remove the sheets and blankets to ensure they got a good cleaning."

"Do not trouble yourself about it," Matthew said kindly.

The maid darted him a grateful look but still appeared deeply mortified. "It was my mess, though, wasn't it? Most of it, at least. And everything happened so fast, I can barely recall it properly. I just remember opening the door and noticing that it was darker than usual. Ordinarily, some daylight comes in through the curtains, but they were closed up right and tight. I continued with my routine, putting the tray on the table before opening the curtains and lighting the fire, and then when I got within a few feet of the bed, I saw him lying there and was so shocked I dropped the tray. That's when my memory grows dim. I don't remember what I did next."

"You screamed," Clifford said grimly. "You screamed as if your lungs were on fire, which created a ruckus in the entire house. Even I heard it downstairs in the breakfast room. John ran into the room first and then he called for help. By the time I arrived he was trying to find a pulse. I opened the curtains and all three of us gasped when we saw the cut in his forehead. The game was clearly over, but I said we should summon his physician regardless. Dr. Pritchard took a while to arrive, which was horrible, because I had hoped to keep the truth from Aunt Celia until he could assure her himself that there was nothing anyone could have done to save him. She values his expertise and trusts him implicitly. But that was impossible, and she was quite distraught and it was almost noon before the whole matter was sorted and Grandfather was settled in the cellar to await the undertaker."

Mary nodded, as if to affirm the description, and she said softly, moisture gathering in the corners of her eyes, that she remembered the gash. That was clear in her mind, for it was wide and deep and red against his snowy scalp. "It was awful. The poor master. He did not deserve to go like that after all his suffering."

As the maid struggled to hold in her tears, Matthew rebuked his cousin for making the poor girl cry. "My mother says there is no harm in your youthful enthusiasms, but I think there is a casual cruelty."

Outraged by the charge, Ripley denied it passionately and sought Mary's support to bolster his claim, putting the servant in the awkward position of having to refute one of her employers. Matthew cited this as further evidence of his cousin's wantonness, and while the two men argued, Kesgrave quietly thanked Mary for attending to them. Then he announced their departure and led the party from the house with indecent haste.

As soon as they settled in the carriage, Holcroft apologized to Bea and Kesgrave for wasting their time. "I should have thought better than to give my imprimatur to this outing. From my brother Chester's reports, I knew Lord Ripley could be silly and irreverent, but I assumed maturity had cured him of the worst of it."

Flora, tugging at the edge of her glove, begged him to stop taking responsibility for other people's actions. "This is my investigation and as such *I* will apologize to the Duke and Duchess of Kesgrave for wasting their time. You see how I am capable of making my own decisions?"

Holcroft pressed his lips together rather than rise to the taunt, and Flora, seemingly annoyed by his display of control, turned to stare out the window. She held that position for the rest of the journey to Portman Square, her silence deeply sullen, and refused Kesgrave's offer of escort.

"It is only a few steps. I am capable of doing at least that little on my own!" she snapped, then immediately clapped one hand over her mouth, dismayed at having spoken so harshly to the duke. She rushed to apologize but Kesgrave would not hear a word of it, insisting he had not meant to undercut her independence.

Imperiously, she said, "It is not *you* who undercut it."

Holcroft flinched but said nothing as he watched the girl climb the front steps and slip into her house. Even after she disappeared, he kept his gaze focused on the empty doorstep and only looked away when the carriage jerked into motion.

Bea, who knew well the desolation of a hopeless passion, felt as much sympathy for Holcroft as she did for her cousin. It was not in her nature to intrude on someone else's personal feelings—except, of course, when the identity of a killer was at stake—and even if she were so inclined, she did not know the gentleman across from her well enough to conduct an intimate conversation.

Asking him about London's most notorious gossip, however, was another matter.

Resolutely, she said, "Tell me about Mr. Twaddle-Thum."

Holcroft, demonstrating that his ability to think had not been wholly undermined by heartbreak, said at the exact same time, "I cannot tell you anything about Mr. Twaddle-Thum."

But Bea would not be fobbed off with a stern reply and a firmly set jaw, not about a matter of such outsize importance. It should not have shocked her to learn that the gossip had widened his sphere of interest to include her family. It was the inevitable next step, for his column required more fodder than a single woman could provide and if there were not

AN EXTRAVAGANT DUPLICITY

enough stories about the Duchess of Kesgrave, then her grace's relatives would have to suffice.

And yet she was surprised.

Twaddle's interest in her was so intent, so focused, it sometimes felt to Bea as though nobody else existed and every time he turned his gimlet eye on another subject, she was a little taken aback.

It was a relief, to be sure, not to read yet another swooning account of her own antics. Seeing them described in print, the way Twaddle's giddy cynicism molded her actions into something strange and unfamiliar, was always unsettling. Her fondness for rout cakes, for instance, which she knew to be benign because a large majority of her acquaintance enjoyed them as well, sounded in his retelling like a wild indulgence.

His description of the sugar on top—a gentle sprinkling that he recast as a generous shower—felt particularly damning.

She had been naïve, she realized now, not to wonder about her family's vulnerability. Of course they would be subjected to Twaddle's scrutiny as well. As little as Aunt Vera had to recommend her, she was certainly more interesting than a rout cake, and Flora had conducted her own investigation. What kind of scurrilous rumormonger would he be if he failed to uncover Flora Hyde-Clare's connection to the largest political scandal to strike the judiciary in a decade?

Well, medium-size scandal, Bea amended, recalling how little attention Sir Dudley Grimston's resignation had actually garnered. She had expected it to create a significant fuss, for the bland reason given to justify it—irregularities in the way he performed his job—struck her as almost an inducement to dogged reporters to require the Chancery to define its terms.

Irregularities how?

Holcroft's comment to Ripley in defense of Flora offered

one possible explanation for Mr. Twaddle-Thum's peculiar silence on the subject. Although it stretched credulity to believe he had refrained from writing about it out of respect for her cousin, Bea knew some aspect of that claim had to be true. Holcroft was simply too circumspect to make statements that were not accurate.

By the same token, he was not the sort of gentleman to befriend the most rapacious gossip in London. That meant something far more interesting than she had imagined was going on.

Oh, yes, definitely, but what?

The answer depended on what Holcroft was willing to share, and she rested her elbows on her knees as she leaned forward. "You mean you *won't* tell me about Mr. Twaddle-Thum. You are choosing to withhold vital information about my family."

Holcroft's expression did not change, and his posture remained rigid as he replied with cool authority. "I am sorry you feel that way, but I must hold to what I believe is the right thing to do. That said, I do hope you know that I would never do anything to endanger Miss Hyde-Clare. Her well-being is of the utmost importance to me, and if necessary, I would eagerly sacrifice my own happiness to ensure hers."

Although issued in clipped tones, the words conveyed a passion Bea had never associated with the sober-minded Mr. Holcroft. Possessing none of the wild romanticism of a Donne sonnet or the "my bounty is as boundless as the sea" speech from *Romeo and Juliet,* they nevertheless left her in no doubt as to the depth of his feelings for her cousin.

Embarrassed by this unexpected baring of the man's soul, Bea tilted her eyes slightly away from his form, toward the window to the left, where drops of rain splattered against the pane. As disconcerted as she was by the odd intimacy, she still wanted to know what had passed between him and Flora, and it required all her self-control not to ask.

Such an interrogation would be too intrusive, even for her.

Kesgrave, however, possessed none of her scruples and observed that Holcroft's eagerness to make a sacrifice appeared to be the source of the disagreement between him and Flora. He spoke smoothly, simply, with a lack of self-consciousness that Bea found disarming. She would not have thought it possible—a man of his rank and breeding broaching a personal matter with so much comfort and ease.

"Flora appears to resent your high-handedness," the duke said. "You made a decision regarding her safety without bothering to consult her, and based on the increasingly flimsy excuses you have given in recent weeks to avoid her company, I have to assume this decision was to sever the connection to protect her from some threat known only to you."

Stunned by these deductions, Bea stared at Kesgrave.

She had not questioned Holcroft's behavior. Blithely, she had assumed his absence was the inevitable consequence of learning the man who was like a second father to him had arranged his murder. The discovery seemed like the sort of thing that would divide one's focus and demand repeated sojourns to the country to comfort one's family.

Flora had known. Unable to articulate her unease, she had realized on a visceral level that something was wrong. All of her various plots and schemes had been devised to circumvent a barrier she had not even been able to see.

And yet Kesgrave had seen it.

Seemingly oblivious to Flora's endless preoccupation with her missing beau, he had not only paid attention but also pieced together a narrative.

An accurate one, she thought, judging by Holcroft's expression.

"I will not presume to speculate how Twaddle entered the picture," the duke continued. "Given your earlier remark it is reasonable to conclude that at some point he became aware of Flora's part in Grimston's downfall. That he did not write a dispatch gleefully drawing the connection to the duchess indicates that you somehow persuaded him not to write it, which in turn implies a decency of which I would not have thought him capable. If you could assure Bea that neither Flora nor any other member of her family will be exposed to danger via Twaddle, then I am sure she will be satisfied and cease pestering you."

Kesgrave, looking at her meaningfully, waited patiently for her to affirm his statement. Obviously, she would agree. Pressing Holcroft further would be churlish, and she had no wish to offend her cousin's suitor.

Despite their recent falling-out, Bea remained convinced the pair would ultimately make a match of it.

But it stung, she thought. To sit less than a foot away from a man who had stood less than a foot away from the relentless gossip was excruciating. She wanted to leap across the carriage, grab him by the lapels and compel him to reveal everything he knew. Holcroft was the closest she had come to actually being able to do something about Mr. Twaddle-Thum, for she was entirely without recourse in the situation. One simply could not confront one's cheerful tormentor, for any attempt made to halt his ridicule would immediately result in more ridicule. If she offered him two hundred pounds in exchange for his silence on Tuesday, then a withering ode to her generosity would appear on Wednesday.

"That is true, yes," Bea said with more affability than she felt. "I just want to know that Flora is safe from him."

"She is," Holcroft replied promptly. "I have his word he will not write a single word about her barring an outrageous event such as a challenge to Miss Petworth to duel or a swim in the Serpentine."

Although he spoke confidently, Bea found little comfort in his reassurances, for her cousin was likely to do either. "Or both," she immediately added, "were the challenge to take place in Hyde Park."

Holcroft chuckled lightly and amusement lightened his features, giving his handsome face an appealing brightness. "That is precisely what *I* said," Holcroft replied as the carriage turned left onto Mount Street. "And you must know that while I did meet him, I did not *meet* him, if you will allow the distinction. He is a master of disguise, and I have no idea of his true identity. For all I know, he is one of the boys in my own stables."

But Bea pounced on even this minor piece of information. "So he is young or at least young enough in appearance to pass as a stable boy?"

Holcroft laughed again and said he supposed so. "But do not hold me to it. If you do discover he is a wizened old man as set in his ways as Mr. Dugmore, I hope you will not accuse me of deliberately misleading you."

Although she readily agreed to his caveat, she did not believe an octogenarian could successfully pass for someone much younger. It was not only a matter of appearance—the wrinkles and the liver spots and the yellowed teeth—but also a function of stiff joints and aching bones. The way an old man moved in the world was vastly different.

That meant Mr. Twaddle-Thum's age most likely fell somewhere between twenty-five and fifty-five.

'Twas an unhelpful conclusion, for a thirty-year range did little to narrow the field of suspects. Tens of thousands of men in London met that general description, and although Bea told herself it was futile to speculate about his identity, she could not seem to make herself stop.

The asymmetry of their relationship struck her as patently unfair. He knew everything about her, and she knew nothing in return.

And it would, she realized, only grow worse when news of her condition reached his ears, which would presumably be only minutes after it arrived at the duke's. The rapacious prattle's accounts of her relatively mild exploits were already paeans to breathless exaggeration, and she could easily imagine the heights of hysteria to which he would rise when the line of succession was at stake.

Her baffling eccentricity would become a treacherous peculiarity.

Distracted by this new horror, she was surprised to realize they had arrived at Holcroft's residence. Holcroft, thanking the duke for his concern regarding his scapegrace cousin, Mr. Carruthers, promised to pass along his well wishes. Then he bid Beatrice adieu, climbed out of the carriage and closed the door gently behind him. Watching him walk up the steps to his home, she wondered what he would do next to earn Flora's forgiveness. He could not have imagined such an absurd outing when he had called on Portman Square that afternoon.

Even so, it had done him no harm and perhaps some good, as it allowed him to spend more time with Flora. Now he could be in no doubt as to the tenor of her objection, which would allow him to formulate a response that addressed it directly.

Turning to the duke to commend him on his forthrightness, she was surprised to find him regarding her with an air of expectation.

It was startling and unsettling and for one moment she thought he knew.

Her heart dropped like a lead pipe in her chest, landing in her stomach.

Her mind felt leaden as well.

All that time to think about the cherub and yet she had no glib reply at the ready.

A queasiness roiled her stomach as she stared at him blankly.

It did not matter, for the duke required no comment.

His eyes glinting with eagerness, he said, "Now that we've dispensed with our charming investigative associates, shall we return to St. James's Square to find out who killed Roger Dugmore?"

Dumbfounded, Bea stared at him.

Chapter Five

Amused by the utter blankness of her response, Kesgrave laughed.

A blond curl fell into his lovely eyes, fathoms deep and stunningly blue, as he chuckled with heartfelt sincerity, and Bea, baffled by his behavior, realized with an alarming thickheadedness that he was teasing her. Given to preposterous conclusions based on flimsy pretexts, she often expressed that exact sentiment, demanding they return to the scene of the crime or conduct an interview with a suspect.

Anticipating that response from her now, he had said it himself.

Unmistakably, it was a joke.

It could be nothing else, for he had made few comments during their two-hour visit to the Dugmore residence and displayed little interest in the proceedings. At no point did he lean over to peer at an item more closely or ask a follow-up question to an answer he deemed insufficient. He certainly did not bump his head on the bed frame while searching for a locket.

If anything, he had appeared bored.

Confident in her understanding, she smiled in return, not at all put out by the treatment, for she frequently skewered his conceits and received no resentment in return.

Replying in kind, she said that while she considered Ripley to be a leading contender on the strength of his motive, the suspect she really wanted to interview was the ladybird who had won the race up the tree. "She might have spotted something."

Although the pun was worthy of a wince at the very least —in truth, it deserved a groan or a wholesale reevaluation of her wit—the duke leaned forward and took possession of her lips. Gently, lightly, he brushed his hands along her shoulders, applying so slight a pressure as if afraid he might break her. The response in Bea was immediate, and she felt desire slither through her body, slinking through her limbs as her own arms rose up to wrap around his neck and pull him closer.

"This is a first for me," he announced softly.

Pressing kisses along his jawline up to his ear, she said, "Unless Jenkins magically replaced the carriage while we were driving in it, I am reasonably certain the conveyance is very familiar with this particular activity."

"Well, yes," he conceded, "but no. I meant the investigation. For the first time ever, I noticed something my clever wife missed and I am eager to celebrate."

Although the remark pricked her ego, she was enjoying his touch too much to take offense. Instead, she laughed throatily and said, "And this is how you choose to celebrate, by seducing me in a carriage?"

"This is how I choose to celebrate everything," he replied, threading his fingers through her hair. "Finish calculating the rents? Seduce my wife in a carriage. Wind my pocket watch? Seduce my wife in a carriage. Climb the stairs to the house? Seduce my wife in a carriage. Although to be clear, it does not have to be a carriage. Despite my reputation to the contrary, I am not a stickler. Any surface will do."

It was astonishing what these words did to Bea, how they melted her bones and dissolved her flesh and transformed her into something else: a quivering mass, a bundle of need. She reared up, throwing her weight forward, and with a slight laugh of surprise, the duke tumbled backward until he was half-lying on the bench. Ferociously, she reclaimed his lips, and as she groaned low in her throat, she heard it—his actual statement—and realized it was not a prick of the ego at all.

It was a stab.

Pulling back suddenly, her breath heavy and thick, she said, "What do you mean I missed something?"

"The nightcap," he said with a light chuckle.

Bea did not say, "What nightcap?"

It was on the tip of her tongue, for she was thoroughly baffled by the comment, but she could not bring herself to ask. It was a matter of pride.

Having overlooked the clue once, she could not overlook it again.

Consequently, she struggled to recall all mentions of the garment.

Matthew had said something about it, had he not?

She struggled to recall his words.

In the quiet, with her eyes closed, she heard them: *I assumed it was some childish prank or game. Or that you had wagered with one of your equally juvenile friends to see who could steal the most intimate object from a slumbering victim. I figured you had taken his nightcap.*

But he had not been sporting any such item when he bashed his head against the table. That was apparent from the maid's description of the gash as a bright red spot against his bald pate.

Presumably, then, it had fallen off before he had tried to rise and lost his footing.

If that was the case, then it should have been in the bed, but thanks to Flora's thorough inspection, they knew there was nothing there except the linens themselves.

The maid could have cleared it.

That was definitely possible.

Mary, seeing it lying on the sheet, might have compulsively picked it up, folded it and returned it to its proper compartment.

And yet she had been troubled by the state of the room because Mrs. Gaitskill had not allowed her to adequately clean up the spill. She had barely begun to scrub at the stain before the room had been closed to bring an end to the unseemly bickering between cousins.

So what did it mean?

That the killer stole the sleeping cap?

Very well, then, but why?

Kesgrave, who was watching her closely, noted the exact moment she reached the same conclusion as he and welcomed her to his investigation. "I suppose this makes you my assistant. If you continue to display such quick thinking, I am sure you will be promoted to senior assistant in no time. And you must not worry about Flora. I promise she will never supplant you no matter how many secret compartments she finds."

He was pleased with himself.

Oh, yes, he was delighted to have gotten one up on her, and Bea, seeing the mischief glimmer in his eyes, could not muster an iota of resentment. She had spent far too many years on the fringes of society not to be tickled by the prospect of the imperious Duke of Kesgrave trying to even some imaginary score with the drab Miss Hyde-Clare.

Tempted to kiss him again, she held herself back. They

were turning onto King Street and would be in St. James's Square in a few minutes. "I did miss it, and it is reassuring to me to know I may rely on you to spot the things I fail to notice. Thank you."

He dipped his head, nobly accepting his due. Then he added, "It is understandable that you would overlook it given your level of distraction."

Nonplussed again by his seeming omniscience, Bea forced herself to show no response. Although it sounded as though he was making reference to the cherub, the topic was something far more mundane: Holcroft's sudden reappearance, Flora's fury.

Kesgrave continued. "It was kind of you to hold back and allow your cousin to direct the investigation. She showed herself to be quite able in the Chancery affair, and with Holcroft undercutting her confidence, it seemed important for her to demonstrate that competence."

Agog, Bea shook her head and said, "Your level of insightfulness today is unsettling."

And she meant it, for it seemed as though there was a reasonably good chance he would intuit her condition simply from the way she drew her breath or held her shoulders.

"I am this insightful every day," he drawled with the sort of languid haughtiness she had found intolerable in the Lake District. "I just rarely get an opportunity to demonstrate it before you arrive at the conclusion yourself. I should send Flora roses to thank her for creating a fuss engrossing enough to pull your attention away."

"You are not insightful at all if you think Flora would not thwack you repeatedly over the head with the roses for relegating the devastating blow of Holcroft's betrayal to merely a 'fuss,' " she said as the carriage came to a stop in front of the residence and she looked out the window at the elegant home, with its gracious columns and pediment. She could hardly believe she was back after ... how many minutes away? ... and found she was genuinely pained at the prospect of giving an absurd coxcomb exactly what he wanted.

But there was nothing to be done.

Murder was murder—even if she failed to discern it at first—and it fell to her to follow the evidence wherever it led.

"And now I must question your understanding if you believe a Hyde-Clare would ever dare to lift a stem against my ducal person," he replied with amusement. "Present company excepted, of course."

Bea refuted the charge by pointing out she had never assailed him with anything floral or otherwise. "I only *imagined* throwing fish patties with olive paste and veal cutlets at you during dinner at Lakeview Hall," she reminded him as they climbed out of the carriage, mounted the steps to the house and knocked. The butler answered promptly, and if he was at all surprised to see them again so soon, his expression revealed none of it as he welcomed them inside. Stoically, he led them to the drawing room and announced their presence.

Lord Ripley squealed.

Just like when he spotted Bea slipping under his grandfather's bed, the viscount could not contain his joy and shrieked loudly. Then he immediately clapped his jaw shut and took several sharp, short breaths.

"Ah, yes, Austrian method," Bea murmured to the duke.

With a high-pitched laugh, the viscount hurried across the elegant room to welcome them. "You have returned! By all things wonderful, you have returned to allow me to make amends for my cousins' boorish reception earlier. I am most grateful. But of course you have, for the Duchess of Kesgrave is nothing if not kind and generous. Why else would you devote so much time to identifying other people's killers? You are munificence itself, and I am humbled by your presence. Humbled to pieces, your grace. I am but gravel you may stride upon on your way to grander things. Do come in!"

Waving his arms in various directions, Ripley urged them to sit down, then ordered the butler to fetch rout cakes. "We need rout cakes and more tea at once, Bevins. And tell my valet I will not require him for another hour because the Duchess of Kesgrave and I have much to discuss. Now do be quick about it, Bevins. You do not want Mr. Twaddle-Thum to report that you kept Her Outrageousness waiting for her beloved rout cakes, do you?"

Despite the threat of this dire outcome, the butler remained impassive and as he left to return to the kitchens, Ripley reminded him to make sure there was a generous sprinkling of sugar on each one. "And by 'generous,' I mean 'liberal,' not the faint smidgeon my grandfather sanctioned," he added as he sat down in an armchair opposite the settee, mindful as ever of his shirt points.

"I was going to have them delivered to Kesgrave House as an apology for my family's appalling behavior. Matthew and Clifford have lived among the *haute ton* much longer than I and yet they understand nothing of how it functions. The Duchess of Kesgrave investigating a murder in our home would have increased the status of every member of our family, even my sister, Maud, who has not visited London in almost seven years. All they had to do to bring about that felicitous event was display a little bit of suspicion toward me —not a huge amount, just a hint. And what do they do instead? Hold to some arbitrary notion of modesty. It is mortifying, your grace, to claim kinship to men who have no sense of spectacle. Even if they did not suspect me, they might have done the decent thing and *told* you they did. Nevertheless, our scheme worked, for they were so embarrassed by the episode, both claim now to believe I am innocent. So do let us revel in that victory—and in your return visit. A second one in a single day! I am certain that must be worth something. You did not call on the Mayhews twice in one day, did you?" he asked as he adjusted his position yet again, loosening his shoulders to make it appear as though he were lounging comfortably against the cushion.

Obviously, he was not.

Attempting to ape Nuneaton's effortless indolence, he seemed at pains to find the right height for his chin or the correct angle for his elbow.

Unable to remember the exact number of times she visited the Mayhew establishment during her investigation, Bea would never have gratified him by supplying it even if she could.

Getting to the heart of the matter, she said, "Having reviewed the evidence, the duke and I agree that an investigation is in order to figure out what precisely happened to your grandfather."

The effect of these words on the viscount was comical, for he seemed at once utterly bemused and extremely pleased. A brilliant smile swept across his face at the prospect of her spending more time in his home. Twaddle was guaranteed to take notice of him now!

And yet the notion that there was something to discover about his grandfather's death was all wrong, for he had invited her there to prove what did *not* happen and now she was proposing to discover what *did*.

"I am sorry, your grace, but I do not understand," Ripley said with measured hesitance. "Are you saying you think my grandfather was murdered after all? But Matthew swears he believes I had nothing to do with it now, and that is thanks to your intervention. My name has been cleared and I no longer have to bear the inordinate weight of my family's suspicion. Your interest is appreciated, of course, but no longer required."

The new diffidence in his tone was neither surprising nor alarming, for it must be very unsettling indeed to discover that the homicide investigation you had initiated as a high-spirited lark to gain attention was now a gravely serious enterprise.

An actual murder was no fun at all!

"That is what we are saying, yes," Bea confirmed. "As such, we will need to inspect Mr. Dugmore's bedchamber again and interview members of the household to establish where they were during the time of the murder and possible motive."

The viscount, striving for indignation, asked if *he* was a suspect, but he could not quite muster the fury to imbue the question with outrage. Instead, the query sounded anxious and scared, and he shook his head, unable to comprehend how his innocence could be in doubt when it was he who had brought them there.

"Why would I call attention to my grandfather's accident if I was the one who had done it—and gotten away with it! I know I am generally thought to be an exquisite with more taste than sense, but not even I am so imprudent as to send *myself* to the gallows. I suppose I could be a diabolical genius who, having executed the perfect murder, sought to match wits with the greatest lady Runner of our age," he said, his voice turning contemplative as the possibilities occurred to him. "Or I could be an overly confident popinjay who thinks he is a diabolical genius but is in fact just an addle-cove who left unequivocable proof of his guilt."

Bea said yes.

Both explanations were under contention because nothing could be dismissed in a murder investigation, and yet she knew a third option was most likely: He was exactly as he appeared—a resourceful young puppy who seized an opportunity to exploit his grandfather's death for social gain.

AN EXTRAVAGANT DUPLICITY

But that conclusion could not be assumed; it had to be proved.

At her abrupt agreement, Ripley flinched visibly and gripped the arms of the chair. "You know, I have always wanted to be considered mad, bad and dangerous to know like Lord Byron, but now that I am suspected of murder, I must say it is deuced uncomfortable."

The observation was, Bea thought, the first sign of intelligence she had seen in him.

"How do we begin? With the interviews or the inspection?" Ripley asked, shifting awkwardly in his seat, as if unable to find a suitable position for the gravity of the situation. First he rested his chin on his hands, then he gripped his fingers and laid them on his knees. He held his arms stiffly for several seconds before shaking them out and letting them fall to his side. "I suppose rout cakes are too frivolous now. I wonder if we should have just the tea. Or maybe we should have coffee. That is a serious drink for men who read the newspaper and furrow their brow in concern over the deplorable state of world affairs. My uncle in Shrewsbury had a cup every morning as he perused the *Times*'s coverage of the war."

As if summoned by these words, the housekeeper entered the room with the tray, and Ripley visibly recoiled at the cheerful assortment of pastries. Although he wanted to send them away, he restrained himself and thanked Mrs. Keene for her prompt delivery.

When she left, he apologized for the frivolity on display. "It is just that I never imagined this conversation. I ... uh... I shall pour, shall I?"

Bea, whose appreciation of rout cakes had never interfered with an investigation or vice versa, said, "Please do."

The task—having something constructive to do with his hands—seemed to calm him down and when he met her gaze over the rim of his teacup, his eyes were not as apprehensive as before. He was able to focus on her without blinking wildly or looking away.

"The interrogation it is, then," he said with an uneasy laugh. "I do most humbly submit. Please feel free to ask me anything."

Bea, selecting a rout cake, asked when he had entered his grandfather's bedchamber. "What was the time?

"Six o'clock," he replied promptly.

"Six o'clock on the dot?" she said.

"Oh, I see," he murmured with a knowledgeable intonation in his voice. "You want to know the *time,* not the time. Of course you do, for your method depends on precision and detail. That is slightly harder for me to answer because I do not make a habit of watching the clock. I find timekeeping to be tedious. But if I had to give an exact minute, then I would hazard it was 6:08 because I woke at six on the dot, as you say. I know that because the clanging of that infernal thing"—he pointed to an ormolu clock hanging on the opposite wall—"woke me. I then stumbled to the privy, still sightly muddled from the night before. I had not intended to drink, but I encountered Berrycloth at the Red Lantern, you see, and he wanted to play a few hands of vingt-un with me. I tried to refuse but he *insisted.*"

He paused here, as if to allow her a moment to properly grasp the significance of a famous whipster demanding his presence, and she marveled at his naiveté. Clearly, the gentleman had recognized the country bumpkin as the easy touch he was.

Regardless, the viscount was determined to be flattered and spent several minutes fawning over the other man's ingratiating manners, intricate cravat and baffling skill with cards. Finally, he announced that he returned home a little after five. "And because my losses were a little steeper than I had expected, it occurred to me that the same interfering busybody who had run to Grandfather with stories about me before would run to him again. So I decided right then and there that I would find out the name of the man who tattled, only I must have fallen asleep in the drawing room because I woke up a little while later with my head on the arm of the settee. I rose unsteadily to my feet, clambered to the privy and crept to his room—all of which I would say took eight minutes, making it 6:08 when I *entered* Grandfather's room. It was around six-thirty when I left because Matthew was on his way out to the heath and when he saw me coming out of Grandfather's room, he said, 'Awake at six-thirty, are you? I guess you are the early bird today. I hope the worm is worth it.' To be honest, I was surprised to find out it was still so early. It felt as though I had been looking for the note for hours. I suppose that was my frustration in not finding it where I expected. And the brandy as well. I was still a trifle disguised from the evening's indulgence."

Bea found it remarkably easy to picture the viscount stumbling around in his grandfather's bedchamber in the dark, slightly foxed.

Oh, but not in the dark, she thought, recalling what Mary had said about the drapes.

"You opened the curtains so you could see better," she said.

Ripley raised his chin in offense and asked her what kind of muddlefish did she think he was. "Opening the curtains on a sleeping man! I would never be so reckless! I merely spread them apart a little so I could have some light to search by. But I closed them before I left so nobody would suspect a thing. How could I know that Matthew would be right outside the door?"

In his enthusiasm to shut the drapes, he drew them tighter than usual.

Filing that information away, Bea asked where the viscount had expected to find the letter.

"With the others," he said succinctly, then, anticipating the inevitable next question, confessed he had been reading his grandfather's correspondence regularly since arriving to London. "But only the ones from my mother! I mean, Grandfather did not communicate regularly with anyone, not even his solicitor, with whom he prefers to conduct business in person when in Tamworth, so there was no true danger of my reading something I ought not. But even if there was, it was vital that I know what was said between them. Mother was vehemently opposed to my coming to London, and I had to make sure she would not convince him to send me home. The dear old thing is so oppressive. She never lets me do anything I want to do. It is because of my father. He was reckless, a neck-or-nothing rakehell who lacked the sense of a dormouse. *He* got killed himself in a duel over a lightskirt—another man's lightskirt, if you can believe it!—so *I* was buried in the country for decades."

The introduction of his mother raised a salient issue, and Bea took the opportunity to ascertain his lordship's financial situation. The title, obviously, came from his father's side of the family. What else did the viscountcy provide?

"Very little, I'm afraid," Ripley said with a sharp frown. "My father was a reprobate in every sense of the word and had bankrupted the estates soon after attaining possession of them, although to be fair three out of four of the houses were already mortgaged to the hilt. The previous viscount was just as much of a wastrel. But the crushing family debt is what made it possible for Grandfather to arrange the marriage. He paid off the mortgage on the family seat, organized the sale of the other houses and provided my father with a tidy allowance in exchange for marrying my mother. My mother likes to tease that she was sold for a title."

Bea could not imagine the former Miss Dugmore found the joke very funny. "So the threat of disinheritance was genuinely perilous for you. If your grandfather cut you out of the will, you would have no source of income?"

He shook his head violently, insisting his mother would never allow him to fall into penury. "She has a generous portion of her own and would always provide for me."

"The same mother who has kept you buried in the country for twenty-two years and resisted your efforts to come to London?" she added blandly. "She would gladly support a way of life that exposes her son to the same dangers that ruined her husband and her husband's father?"

"Well, no," Ripley said, the teacup clattering on the saucer as he returned it to the table, his nerves frayed by the question. "Any income provided to me by my mother would come with conditions, and I see where you are trying to go but you are wrong. Grandfather would never have followed through on his threat. I had no reason to wish him ill."

"Your cousin Matthew believes differently," she pointed out. "And you had just suffered another loss, one steep enough to make you worry about your grandfather finding out from his crony."

Although the viscount's complexion grew ashen, he managed to keep his voice smooth as he replied, "If my wits had not been addled by alcohol, I would not have worried so much about Grandfather finding out about my losses because the sum of a hundred pounds is really not that great. I reacted too strongly, that is all. But I am aware now of how it looks and can only wonder at my cousins' lack of imagination in not suspecting me of something truly foul. At this juncture, I am half convinced I murdered him."

Bea washed the rout cake down with a sip of tea and asked about the will, confirming that it had been read and ascertaining the name of the executor. "And you were left the expected portion?"

A little more, in fact, but he was hardly pleased with the development because the bequeathment came with onerous restrictions. "It was all left in a trust until I am thirty, paid quarterly, which I did not anticipate. I thought control would be transferred to me when I reached my majority. As expected, all the property went to Matthew, with the exception of Paltry House, which was given to Melody, along with a modest allowance for its upkeep. Clifford and Jesse received generous settlements as well, without, I might add, the same conditions as mine. They gain control of their monies immediately. I thought that was decidedly unfair, but when I threatened to contest the will, Mr. Rothbart, the executor, laughed and called me a puppy."

An apt description, Bea thought, before asking which cousin was Melody.

"Aunt Celia's daughter and Matthew's younger sister," he replied. "There is another daughter, Dora, who is between them in age, but she is married and lives in Surrey."

"And you have a sister as well? Maud, I believe," she said, recalling an earlier comment he had made. "She also lives in the country?"

"Correct," he said. "There are seven cousins in total. Dora, Matthew and Melody are the children of my aunt Celia, who is the eldest of the three daughters. Like my own father, theirs died while they were very young. An accident in the stables that is too gruesome to repeat. Then there are Clifford and Jesse, whose mother is Grace, the next eldest. Her husband, my uncle Seymour, died heroically in battle, shot up by some Frenchies as he saved his men from certain death. He was a regular Trojan! And of course there is Maud and myself. Our mother is Ruth, the baby of the family."

Although it was impossible to hear the words *too gruesome*

to repeat and not immediately desire details, Bea refrained from asking a dozen questions and curtailed her interest to information relevant to the current situation. "And of the three granddaughters, only Melody received a bequest?"

Ripley insisted it was not true, for his sister had been given a matching set of diamonds from their grandfather and other cherished baubles. "I am certain Dora did as well. Grandfather would never been so unfeeling as to leave them out."

But Bea noted the discrepancy in material value between property and trinkets. The dispensations were far from equal.

"First of all, they are not *trinkets*," his lordship countered haughtily. "They are beloved items of great sentimental worth. Secondly, their situations are not similar. Dora and Maud have comfortable homes with their husbands and children. Melody has nothing—no home, no husband, no children. She refuses to wed, despite Grandfather's efforts to marry her off. He found an excellent prospect for her, but she won't even consider him. And her mother is no use, what with all her charity and good works. Aunt Celia thinks that is a fine future for a woman, helping destitute orphans, the grimy little things! Grandfather had to provide for Melody or she would end up dependent on Matthew, which would be a miserable existence for anyone."

Given Ripley's earlier complaints about the patriarch's old-fashioned attitudes, Bea found his willingness to support his granddaughter's independence startling.

It was, his lordship agreed, an unexpected act of generosity. "I think he felt obligated because he was the reason Aunt Celia never remarried. Her husband left nothing but debts behind, so after he died, Grandfather invited her and my cousins to live here, in London. He needed a hostess, you see, and Aunt Celia was very well suited to the role. But he could just as easily have paid for them to stay in Tamworth. As a result of the arrangement, Melody was allowed an excessive amount of independence and accompanied her mother on her good works, which has given her some rather strange ideas. She says she does not want to marry but instead devote herself to charity. Grandfather did not like it but accepted it out of respect for the sacrifices Aunt Celia made on his behalf."

"Mrs. Gaitskill does not object to her daughter abstaining from marriage and children?" Bea asked, taken aback by her tolerance as well.

"I think she expects Melody to change her mind. She is only twenty-one and might still have her head turned by a handsome suitor," Ripley said. "Aunt Celia already has three grandchildren from Dora, and Matthew is sure to marry soon. He is thirty-three, which is the ideal age to wed. And I suspect she would rather reside with Melody in her cozy house in Peckham than with Matthew and his wife. Again, I can only conceive of the arrangement as torture for anyone who is not Matthew, although perhaps Aunt Celia feels differently. A mother's love can, I understand from the parables, work miracles."

Having found fault with his one cousin, the viscount felt obliged to complain about them all, and Bea enjoyed a second rout cake, then a third, while he grumbled about Melody's piousness, Clifford's obsequiousness and Jesse's obtuseness. When she felt satisfied with her snack, she interrupted his tirade and announced that they were ready to inspect Mr. Dugmore's rooms again.

Chapter Six

The bedchamber looked the same.

Horrified by her failure to accurately assess the scene during her first visit, Bea had expected the room to appear slightly altered, as if all the details she had missed in her distraction would stand out in sharp relief. And yet as she drew closer to the imposing bed, nothing struck her as different. The fluted columns of the fireplace were just as beautiful; the canopy's ornate silks were just as sumptuous. The whole room, with its swaths of mahogany furniture and expert carvings, was comfortable and welcoming, and it was easy to see why the cousins would feud over its possession.

Stopping short of the tea stain on the rug, she contemplated the bed, with its luxurious linens neatly arranged by Flora.

Bea turned to Ripley, who stood hesitantly in the doorway, uncertain how much to intrude now that his caper had become a murder. "You say your aunt closed the room immediately after the body was removed?"

"Not *immediately* immediately," he replied, taking a tentative step into the bedchamber. "Matthew did not return from the heath until twelve-thirty, which was a few minutes after the body had been moved to the cellar, and he was distraught to learn what had transpired in his absence. So he had a cup of tea to settle his nerves. *Then* he rose and said he might as well start moving his things. I could not permit that to stand, not with my sincere and abiding affection for the room's splendor, so I said, 'Well, maybe *I* might as well start moving *my* things.' Because there was no reason *he* should automatically get the best room in the house. Then he made several self-important remarks about his position as Grandfather's heir, and I made several cutting comments in regards to his sense of style because he just wanted the room for its size and because it has a sitting room in addition to the dressing room. I wanted it because my elegance complements its beauty. And just as it was to come to fisticuffs, Aunt Celia chastised us both for demeaning the memory of her father—which, between you and me, was a little unfair because I was honoring it by paying homage his impeccable taste. Then she marched upstairs, told Mary to stop what she was doing and ordered her to leave the room. Then she gathered the whole household and announced the room was closed to everybody. Anyone caught inside would be turned out without notice and that included members of the family."

"Do you think the prohibition was obeyed?" Bea asked.

Emboldened by the follow-up query, he walked further into the room until he was standing beside her. "It is impossible to say because the door was not locked or guarded, but I do not know why anyone would disobey it. Unless someone had a particular reason to—"

He gasped in shock and looked around warily, as if expecting to see the killer crouching in the corner. Then in barely a whisper, he said, "You think the murderer came back?"

"It would not be the first time," Bea replied, watching as

AN EXTRAVAGANT DUPLICITY

Kesgrave pulled back the linens on the bed. He had no expectation of finding anything after Flora's exhaustive search, and yet he felt compelled to look for himself. "What we are interested in now is your grandfather's sleeping cap."

At this seeming non sequitur, Ripley shuddered. "You should not be, your grace, for it was a hideous thing: molted green with an orange tassel. I do not know where he got it, but I cannot believe it was from anyone who wished him well. If you are compiling a list of suspects, I suggest you start there instead of with me," he said, laughing at his own sally but it was a half-hearted sound.

"Did he wear it regularly?" she asked, uninterested in his fashion critique.

Taken aback by the query, Ripley stammered that he could not be expected to know such an intimate detail of his grandfather's life, and Bea, noting the tight pull of his shoulders, was amused by the stiff response. He had expected a murder investigation to be intrusive but not personal.

"Mary might know," he offered.

Thanking him for the helpful suggestion, quite possibly his first, she strode to the hallway, summoned a footman and requested the maid's presence in Mr. Dugmore's bedchamber. Then she returned to the room and asked Ripley where his grandfather kept the letters from his mother.

"Over here," he said, leading her to a bow-front bookcase —also in that deep rich mahogany—to the left of the fireplace and opening the top drawer. He extracted a thick packet of letters, which he handed to her. "Grandfather was not very clever when it came to concealing things. I found my mother's missives literally in the first place I looked. That said, I could not locate the note from the crony anywhere, which makes me suspect the information was conveyed in person. Although Grandfather did not get around town as much in recent weeks because of his gout, which seemed to have worsened, he still visited his club every afternoon."

Flipping through the assortment of cream-colored sheets, Bea pulled out one at random and read it. The dowager viscountess began by commiserating with her father on his ailments: Although she did not suffer from gout herself, she had recently injured her foot in a riding accident and knew what it was like to have one's mobility limited. Then she observed how much easier the pain would be to endure if she had her son nearby to comfort her. The next nine ... ten ... no, eleven lines were devoted to bolstering this observation with specific examples of how Ripley's presence would ease her suffering. Then she ended on a plea for him to send her beloved boy home at once.

She folded the letter and returned it to the stack as Kesgrave disappeared through a doorway, presumably to look for the nightcap in the dressing room.

"There is no point in reading any of the other letters," his lordship said wearily, "for if you have read one, you have read them all. All twenty-two are the same. Only her reason why I must return changes, although of late she has started to repeat herself. She cites an ant infestation twice."

"I see," Bea said softly, bearing a greater understanding of his desperation to establish himself in London. With his mother beseeching him to return on a daily basis, his sojourn in the capital felt like a fragile thing, a ladder whose rungs were made of hay.

She returned the letters to him as Mary entered the room.

"You have more questions, your grace?" she asked on a curtsey.

"I do, yes, thank you," Bea said. "You brought Mr. Dugmore his tea every morning?"

Mary nodded. "Absolutely. Not every single morning, because I sometimes have the day off, but most mornings."

"And did Mr. Dugmore wear a nightcap?"

Surprise entered the maid's eyes as she heard the question. It was not the one she had been prepared to answer, which made Bea deeply curious to know what she had been expecting. "Yes."

"Every night?" Bea asked.

She nodded firmly. "Yes, every night, even in the summer. He got cold very easily."

"Was he wearing it on the morning you found him?"

There it was again—surprise—but this time it was accompanied by dawning comprehension. "You're right, your grace, he wasn't. It wasn't on his head. I didn't see it at all."

Ah, that meant she had not looked for it either.

"Thank you, Mary, that will be all unless there was something you wished to discuss?" Bea said.

"No, your grace," the maid said, spinning on her heels as if anxious to leave the room. Then she paused and looked back. "They're saying downstairs that he was killed, Mr. Dugmore. They're saying he was killed, that the fall wasn't natural. Is that true?"

Bea sighed. "I am very much afraid it is. So if you think of anything that might be relevant, I hope you will feel comfortable enough to tell me, either when I am here or at my home."

Mary dipped into another curtsey and murmured, "Yes, your grace," before dashing from the room.

Ripley, displaying some of his old enthusiasm, said, "I reckon you never told the Mayhews' staff to contact you at Kesgrave House. Mr. Twaddle-Thum will be sure to take note of the novelty."

As the wretched gossip took note of everything and cheerfully made up the rest, Bea did not feel as though a response was required. Instead, she decided that Kesgrave's supposition was accurate. The killer had taken the nightcap.

But why?

She thought about the gash.

Whatever transpired in the room, one thing was certain—Dugmore's forehead had crashed into the table with enough force to break skin—and although there was no evidence to support the theory that it was the decisive blow, Bea assumed it was.

Or was *blows* more accurate?

Considering the extent of the wound, multiple bashes seemed likely, and Bea closed her eyes to imagine how the scene might have unfolded. The victim was presumably asleep at the time of the attack, giving his assailant the advantage of surprise. As Dugmore was, by all accounts, old and feeble, it would not require much to overpower him, especially if he was disoriented by the sudden wakening.

And yet there must have been some sort of struggle because that was the only way to account for the missing nightcap. Somehow the garment had been rent or frayed in the tussle, and in its damaged condition it told a story different from the one the killer wanted.

What kind of story could a nightcap tell, she wondered, fluttering her eyes open and gazing at the pier table, with its lovely gilt finish and dried blood. On their previous visit, she had only glanced at the stains, confirming Flora's conclusions, then stood back to allow her cousin to conduct her investigation. Now she drew closer to examine them properly. There were two sets of marks, one near the corner adjacent to the bed and one a few inches away. The latter, which approached the center of the edge, was splotchier than the first, more like a series of small blobs than a smudge, and Bea pictured the fall. She could see Dugmore's head landing against the table there, the skin breaking upon impact, and then rolling to the right as blood splattered toward the middle.

It made sense in its own right.

And yet contemplating the evidence in light of the new theory, she wondered if the stains were a little too far apart to have been caused by a single strike. Perhaps the killer bashed Dugmore's head against the table more than once. Multiple blows would provide plenty of opportunity for the nightcap to get splattered with blood.

Possibly, it was that simple, she thought, feeling the stab of ego again. It was obvious now—from this vantage, the duke's vantage—and although she could not fathom how she had missed it, the fact that she did spoke to just how distracted she was by the cherub.

Peevishly, she shook her head and resolved to correct her mistakes, starting with the murder weapon. She lowered to her knees to inspect the pier table properly. The piece was every bit as lovely as Ripley described, with its finely carved frieze of rosettes and marquetry pateras elegantly rendered in tulipwood, and she could well understand why he wanted to move it to the drawing room, where visitors could sigh over it in envy. It was tucked away here, in Dugmore's bedchamber, overwhelmed by the imposing heaviness of the mahogany. The table was too light, not just in its physical appearance but in its aesthetic feel. It pranced while the furniture around it stamped.

Indeed, the lightness stood out in sharp relief, Bea thought in amusement as she rose to join Kesgrave in the dressing room.

And then she froze, stuck by its discordance.

Why would a man who prized harmony cling to the jarringly mismatched piece?

Bea dropped back to her knees and, staring at the pier table—the lone bright spot in an otherwise coherent room of dark wood and heavy furnishings—considered what value it could serve other than decorative.

Sentimental, she allowed, for the piece had been commissioned by Dugmore's father and might have featured in many fond memories. Perhaps the pier table had sat in the corner of their drawing room, where the men played piquet long into the night.

'Twas possible, yes, but unlikely, and recalling that it had been designed to the elder Dugmore's specifications, she wondered if the attachment was far more practical in nature.

Bea slid forward and ran her fingers gingerly along the side of the table, assessing its dimensions. Despite its delicate appearance, the piece was quite sturdily made, with a thick apron supporting the floral border. She traced the block, following it to the back of the table, where it grew wider as it turned the corner. She rapped her knuckles against the panel and heard a hollowness. Then she knocked on the block before the corner. It was solid.

Feeling more confident in her deduction, she pulled the table farther from the wall and scrutinized its back, noting that the craftsmanship, while still excellent, was a little less perfect. Whereas it was impossible to detect a seam in the front, one could detect—just barely—the line where the frieze met the foliate border.

She tapped the wood again.

Still hollow.

Amazing.

Her tone deliberately mild, Bea called to Kesgrave in the dressing room, "What were you saying about secret compartments, your grace?"

He passed through the doorway with a startled expression, which promptly turned into a grin as he noted her position next to the table. Bea scooted to the side to allow him access, then pointed to the thin seam along the top of the frieze.

"Here," she said.

Intrigued, he struck the wood in several places with

varying degrees of strength, and Ripley, watching this abuse, asked them if it was really necessary to knock so hard.

Or at all.

"It is just that it is a very important piece, in both the development of Chippendale's style as a craftsman and my own family's history," he explained anxiously. "I am certain my great-grandfather would have no need for a secret compartment. Stonebridge House is very modern. It has hardly any priest holes and only one hidden staircase. There is no advantage to be gained from your maltreatment and everything to lose. If you break it—"

He shrieked.

The rosettes garlanding the frieze tipped forward with a click as Kesgrave, locating the mechanism behind the leg, released the latch.

Gaping with astonishment, the viscount said, "By all that is holy, is *that* where he was hiding the mendacious letter from his crony? No wonder I could not find it! I must say, your grace, you are a marvel. I now fear Mr. Twaddle-Thum has not done you justice."

It was not, Bea knew, the right moment to point out the gossip's many inaccuracies, starting with but not limited to his report that she had held the head of the decapitated Mr. Réjane in her hands, but she was sorely tempted to make some small protest. It infuriated her again how little control she had of the public's perception of her.

Fortunately, a hidden cache in the night table of a murdered patriarch was equally compelling and she watched as Kesgrave pulled several documents from the compartment. He sifted through the papers as he handed them to Bea.

Ripley looked eagerly over their shoulders, trying to read the pages or just see what they were. Inhaling sharply, he said, "Is that a will?"

Kesgrave, perusing it briefly, confirmed that it was and noted its date: September 1815.

"That must be an old version because the one in his study desk was from earlier this year," Ripley said, his eyes scrolling the first page of the document before he caught sight of the next item the duke pulled from the compartment.

It was a bill from Hoby.

The viscount gasped. "Good God! Look at that figure! Matthew dares taunt me about the cost of my waistcoat when *that* is what he spends on boots. I cannot believe the hypocrisy!"

As Bea had thus far been denied the pleasure of a pair of Hessians made by the expert shoemaker, she could not speak to the expense. But she did find it interesting that Dugmore had six...no, seven...bills from tradesmen in Matthew's name. She was just as intrigued by the newspaper clippings: two stories about a missing young woman in Northumberland, one from the local *Alnwick Herald* and the other from a larger paper serving the county. Miss Cheever was last spotted walking along the beach near her High Hauxley home, and her family feared she had been swept out to sea and drowned. That had been eighteen months ago.

A small drawing of the woman in question accompanied one of the articles, and Bea noted her delicate features.

"That looks a little bit like Pauline," Ripley said.

Startled, she glanced up. "Excuse me?"

"The girl in the sketch there," he explained with a tilt of his chin. "She looks like Pauline, one of the upstairs maids. Not exactly. Her hair is different and her face is thinner but in a general way, as though they could be sisters. But I am sure it is just a coincidence. Many women have light-colored hair and high foreheads."

Bea was not so certain. It struck her as slightly too coincidental that the victim of a murder was in possession of a story about a missing woman who bore a noticeable resemblance to one of his own servants. If Miss Cheever was hiding from her family, then she would not welcome Dugmore's attention, especially if he had threatened to reveal her location to her parents.

Such a revelation would serve as a powerful incentive to murder.

Moving the clippings to the bottom of the pile, she decided her next interview would be with Pauline.

Ripley drew yet another sudden breath.

Amused by his perpetual amazement, Bea said, "Really, my lord, you are starting to sound like a toad that has been squashed by a carriage."

"I beg your pardon, duchess," he said with a dutiful bow, "but that is a list of my losses down to the farthing. It is an intrusion! An effrontery! How dare anyone make an accurate accounting of my debts! That is such deeply private information that not even I have dared to stay abreast of the total."

As he sounded as confused as he was outraged, Bea assumed the handwriting was not familiar and Ripley confirmed that the tally had not been made by his grandfather. Grabbing the sheet of paper from her hands—and then apologizing profusely for his own boorishness—he flipped it over and read the name at the bottom of the missive.

"Aha! Walberry!" he cried with a hint of triumph. "He is one of Grandfather's oldest cronies. Their friendship goes back decades, to their leading string days. He has a granddaughter six or seven years my senior, and Grandfather said we should make a match of it. I laughed and said I did not know he could be so droll. Obviously, it would not fly. I had just escaped captivity in Shepton Mallet. I would never imprison myself in marriage, especially not with a quiz long in the tooth."

"Apparently, Walberry did not know it was a joke,"

Kesgrave said, reading the letter. "Here he says that your ability to accumulate such an extensive amount of debt so quickly forced him to reconsider your suitability as a husband and he rescinds his approval of the match."

"I like that very much indeed!" Ripley said, his voice stiff with offense. "I did not give *my* approval of the match. I have no intention of marrying before thirty, and when I do agree to take a wife, she will be as fashionable as me, not some ape leader who needs her grandfather to find her a spouse."

It required very little to imagine Ripley making the exact same statement to his grandfather, and Bea wondered how the patriarch received it. The tone of Walberry's letter indicated that the two old men had not considered the viscount's feelings on the matter to be relevant to their negotiation.

Marking the situation as interesting, she scanned the last document in the pile. It was a letter from the head matron of Fortescue's Asylum for Pauper Children promising to cease availing herself of Miss Gaitskill's services in exchange for Mr. Dugmore's generous donation. "While we appreciate your granddaughter's noble impulse to help the less fortunate, we understand how her work with us might limit her future prospects. Therefore, we will happily release her from any obligation to us and consider ourselves well compensated for the inconvenience."

This time the viscount did not gasp, either because he was not shocked by his grandfather's interference in his cousin's life or he was still seething over the dead man's unwelcome intrusion into his own.

Either way, Bea organized the various documents into a neat little stack and suggested they conduct their interviews in the drawing room.

"I assume you want to begin with the maid," Kesgrave said.

"Indeed, yes, she is the most interesting suspect if not the

AN EXTRAVAGANT DUPLICITY

most likely," she replied, returning the documents to the duke, who slipped them into his pocket for safekeeping.

Ripley, seeming to snap suddenly to attention, stared at them in bewilderment. "Do you not want to ask Matthew about his exorbitant bills? Four pounds for a single pair of boots! It is outrageous. I am confident Grandfather took him to task for his extravagance and made the same threat to cut him off, only nobody overheard their argument. I cannot believe that is not a better use of your time than talking to a maid. What can she tell you that Matthew cannot?"

Having witnessed Matthew's earlier contempt for his younger cousin, Bea could understand Ripley's eagerness to see the other man humbled. Nevertheless, she did not conduct her investigations according to the snubbed egos of maligned coxcombs. Naturally, she would find out why Dugmore was in possession of his grandson's bills, but first she wanted to know how Miss Cheever of High Hauxley came to be employed in St. James's Square as an upstairs maid.

"Impossible!" Ripley replied with a firm shake of his head. "Grandfather would never assist a woman in hiding from her family. He abhorred female independence."

Bea assured him that Mr. Dugmore had most likely remained firm in his core principles and any aid or comfort given to the independent female was purely accidental. "The evidence indicates that he did not hire her but rather discovered that she had been hired. Now let us find out what he did with the information."

"But Matthew!" he protested. "The boots!"

Although she promised to talk to his cousin next, the viscount was far from appeased and he muttered sulkily about hypocrisy and profligacy as they returned to the drawing room. He was still grumbling five minutes later, when Pauline appeared in the doorway, her expression at once apprehensive and obsequious. Hesitantly, she took careful little steps, as if crossing a high gorge on a narrow beam, and lowered herself with great reluctance into the chair across from Beatrice and the duke. Her eyes fixed firmly on the floor, she bid them good afternoon in a terrible imitation of a southern accent. The long "a" in her pronunciation of *afternoon* went on for so many seconds Bea feared she was having a fit.

Ripley, finding the display of humility convincing, argued that the girl had clearly been raised in service. "She is not some runaway from the wilds of Northumberland. Can we please turn our attention now to the excessive expenditures of my cousin Matthew? I am eager to see how he will try to evade accountability. He will say something about a Corinthian's values or standards being superior to a dandy's."

Miss Cheever, who was a great deal thinner than the *Alnwick Herald* drawing depicted, with slender shoulders and a slim neck, started at these words but held herself in check, insisting she came from simple folk. "Me mam were a seamstress and me pa fixed carriage wheels. They are gone now. Me whole family is gone."

As she spoke, her accent drifted north, pausing briefly in East London before making the journey to Newcastle.

Gently, Bea said, "There is no reason for pretense, Miss Cheever. We know it is you."

Ashen, Miss Cheever flung herself onto the rug and implored her grace not to send her back. "Please, for the love of all that is good and kind, do not return me to that pit of despair. Please do not, for I shall perish there as surely as I breathe!"

Before Bea could respond to this passionate plea, the door to the drawing room flung open and in strode a man in a fawn-colored coat. He crossed the room in several wide steps, his light-brown brows pulled in a furious expression, which looked slightly out of place on his boyish countenance. "Halt these proceedings at once!" he hollered.

Miss Cheever's whole body froze at the sound of his voice, and then she cried, "No, you must not!"

"I must indeed!" he replied imperiously, dropping to his knees beside her and placing one hand on the back of her trembling shoulder. A lock of brown curly hair fell into his eyes, making him appear even younger. "Nobody, I do not care how illustrious or influential, will return you to that den of horrors while there is still breath in my body."

As Miss Cheever's sobs intensified, Bea contemplated the newcomer. Given his manner and dress, she assumed he was the fourth male cousin: Jesse Parr.

Disgusted by the outburst, Ripley told the other man to pull himself together. "Good God, Jesse, she is a *maid*."

Tightening his other hand into a fist, he exclaimed, "She is not a maid. She is a gently bred young lady, a wretched creature hiding from a monster of a stepfather and ... and ... and my betrothed."

"No!" Miss Cheever shrieked, more wretched than ever as she shrank from Jesse's touch. "I did not agree. I will never agree! I love you far too well to allow you to debase yourself by marrying me. You must let me go."

"Never!" he vowed.

Ripley, whose confusion was resolved by the affecting scene, said, "Oh, I see, Pauline killed Grandfather so she could marry Jesse."

Miss Cheever howled at this accusation just as Jesse leaped to his feet and told his cousin to name his second. The prospect of a duel upset the girl further, and wrapping her arms around her legs as if to curl into a ball, she increased the pitch of her misery. Her wails, seemingly too loud to emerge from such a diminutive frame, could barely be heard over the bickering of the cousins.

Calmly, smoothly, without raising his voice and adding to the fracas, Kesgrave told them all to shut up.

At once, the room fell silent.

Jesse glared at the viscount and lifted his fist as if to deliver a blow, but he too abided by the duke's order.

It was impressive, Bea thought, what a coronet and five hundred years of authority could achieve.

"If you gentlemen are going to join our conversation, then I suggest you take seats," the duke continued. "I am sure Miss Cheever will do the same just as soon as she regains control of herself."

On a ragged breath, Miss Cheever nodded and slowly unfurled her body. Then she rose unsteadily to her feet and lowered into the chair. Although she still looked as though she would dissolve into another bout of tears at any second, she assured the company that she was better. Then she turned to Bea and said she may continue with her interrogation.

"No, she may not," Jesse growled.

The young maid chided him softly, and he fell back into his seat with a snarling apology.

Bea, hoping to reassert her command, assured Miss Cheever that nobody was accusing her of murder, to which Ripley muttered, "I am. A maid with a secret identity seems like a very good suspect to me."

"*You* look like a very good suspect to *me*," Jesse seethed.

Quelling the argument with a pointed look, Bea reiterated that she had no wish to see an innocent young woman stand trial for a murder she did not commit. "I am merely trying to gather information. Let us start by confirming the supposition that you are indeed Miss Cheever of High Hauxley. You ran away from your home to escape your stepfather?"

"*Stepfather* is misrepresenting his villainy," Jesse said, incapable of holding his tongue. "There is nothing paternal about the man. He is a fiend, a veritable beast who dared to raise his fist to my delicate darling. She had no choice but to leave. If she had stayed, he would have ultimately killed her."

Miss Cheever, recoiling at the brutality of the description, conceded that it was nevertheless accurate. "My own mother is a shadow of her former self, and I knew he would do the same to me. He responds with anger to even the slightest display of what he calls spirit. But I am not spirited, your grace. I swear! I have always been a rag doll of a thing, obedient and meek, and still he treated me as if every yes were an act of defiance. I had to escape before he did irreparable harm to me."

"The dear brave girl stole away in the middle of the night," Jesse added fondly. "It was her maid whom was spotted walking along the sea."

Blushing prettily at the approbation in his voice, Miss Cheever said, "She and I have similar builds and she knew I was in mortal danger. I do not know what I would have done without her help. She also enlisted her family. I went to her parents' house that night and they arranged my journey to London. Once I arrived, I visited my old nanny, who helped me find this position. Heddy was resistant at first. She thought a woman of my breeding could not handle the hard work. But I convinced her of the necessity. And I have been here ever since."

"You cannot handle the hard work!" Jesse insisted. "You are wasting away from exhaustion. When you are my wife, you will never lift anything more taxing than a teacup."

Miss Cheever's eyes shone with intolerable brightness for a brief moment, as if she, too, could see the dazzling future dancing before them, then she abruptly turned away, her gaze rigidly focused on her hands. "That cannot be. Your family would never approve."

"Damn their eyes!" her beau said heatedly. "I do not give a fig for their approval. I am my own man!"

Bea, interrupting the affecting exchange before Miss Cheever could reply, asked about the newspaper clipping she had found in the pier table. Its presence indicated that the master of the house knew of her true identity. Did he know of their flirtation as well?

"It is not a flirtation," Jesse snapped. "It is a deep and abiding attachment. We will wed before the month is out."

Miss Cheever's gaunt countenance paled even further at the mention of the *Alnwick Herald,* indicating that she was unaware of Dugmore's interest in her. Anxiously, her voice quivering, she asserted again that she had consented to no such plan. "I cannot allow you to degrade yourself by marrying a maid, nor can I bring myself to be the source of acrimony between you and your family. Mr. Dugmore would not have approved."

"To hell with his approval!" Jesse said, rising angrily and stomping across the few feet that separated them. "Do you think I would allow his petty tyranny and archaic notions about propriety to come between us? It did not matter how many threats he made. My resolution would not falter."

"Threats?" Bea repeated curiously.

Gazing deeply into his beloved's eyes, as if determined to make her agree via the force of his will, he responded with a fleeting glance. "To contact her stepfather."

Miss Cheever cried out.

"No, my love, no," he said soothingly. "I would never have let him put you at risk."

Ripley, also rising suddenly, pointed at his cousin and said, "Oh, dear lord, Jesse did it! Jesse murdered Grandfather to save Pauline."

"Heather!" Jesse barked. "Her name is Heather."

The viscount acknowledged the rebuke with a stiff

apology and said more calmly, "Jesse murdered Grandfather to save Heather."

"Nobody murdered him, you fool," his cousin replied with a scoff of disgust. "He conked his head on the table when he fell. I do not know how you convinced the duke and duchess to take you seriously, but the talk of murder is utter nonsense. You are just seeking the attention of that blathering gossip. Everyone knows it. Matthew does a highly diverting imitation of your paying a call to the *London Daily Gazette* and begging the editor to find you interesting."

Although the notion of his spendthrift Corinthian cousin overtly mocking him had to sting, Ripley did not rise to the provocation. "In fact, it is not nonsense. According to the duchess's deductions, our grandfather was ruthlessly murdered by a member of this family."

"That is not precisely true," Bea clarified. "Kesgrave and I believe Mr. Dugmore was murdered. We have made no determination as to who is responsible. It could be a family member or a servant."

Miss Cheever recoiled as if she had been slapped, and Ripley, interpreting the response as guilt said, "They both did it! Jesse and Pauline killed Grandfather together! It was a conspiracy. Oh, the poor man. He was old and weak and wanted only the best for his family."

"For the last time, her name is Heather," Jesse ground out. "And that is patently false and you know it. Grandfather wanted only what was best for himself and the estates, which meant marrying us off to heiresses. That was what he objected to—not that Miss Cheever had disguised herself as a servant to save her own life but that she does not possess a fortune. He had several prospective brides picked out for me and would not condone my marrying a pauper, which, to be clear, Miss Cheever is not. She has a dowry, not an overly generous one but it is still not nothing. He simply refused to see reason."

"And his refusal to see reason angered you," Bea observed.

"It infuriated me to think he would endanger the life of an innocent girl to appease his own avariciousness," he replied harshly. "I could not believe he would be so cruel."

And yet based on this conversation and the contents of the pier table, Bea rather thought Dugmore would be exactly that cruel. His actions had revealed him to be a man who liked to exert his authority, and it struck her as highly unlikely that he would threaten Miss Cheever without having a particular purpose in mind.

Contemplating his objective, Bea asked, "What did he want in exchange for keeping Miss Cheever's location a secret from her family? That you end the relationship or that you end the relationship and consent to wed one of the prospective brides he picked out?"

Miss Cheever let out a strangled cry at the thought of her beloved marrying another but otherwise remained silent, and Jesse, glaring angrily at Bea, swore it would never have happened.

"That was the deal he offered, but I could not trust him to hold to his end," he said with a cynical sneer, "for he spoke endlessly of integrity and moral rectitude while possessing neither. I am certain he would have sent a missive to Heather's stepfather the moment my betrothal was made public. He felt little sympathy for a child who did not honor her father. That left me with no option but to revise my plan."

"Yes," Ripley said with theatrical relish, revealing how little he comprehended the gravity of the situation. Despite all evidence to the contrary, he still considered his grandfather's murder to be a great romp. "Your plan to kill him!"

"No, you dunderhead," he replied scornfully. "To marry at

once. We were waiting three months for Miss Cheever to reach the age of consent, but now we had no choice but to make a dash for Gretna Green. We were going to leave on Saturday morning."

But Miss Cheever shook her head and repeated that she had never agreed to the plan. "I could not marry you over the objections of your grandfather, not when your reputation is at stake. It would be hard enough to overcome the ton's disgust of your decision; it would be all but impossible without a show of support from your family."

Ripley, nodding vigorously, affirmed that she was right. "Acceptance would have been out of reach once Grandfather disowned you for marrying a maid and thwarting his authority. That is why you killed him. I do not blame you," he added magnanimously. "Given the depth of your feelings, you had no choice but to act rashly, which was why you struck without thinking it through. But for the nightcap, you would have gotten away with it."

Jesse, struggling to hold on to his temper, insisted that none of them knew how his grandfather would have responded to the actual fact of their marriage. "Despite everything, Miss Cheever is a respectable young lady, and to say otherwise would be to imply that our household is in some way immoral, which I do not think Grandfather would have done. Furthermore, I believe the ton would have accepted her as soon as they learned of her tragic past and our family's heroic rescue of her. But you are correct: He *might* have disowned me. That was a possibility, and I was willing to risk it, for a young girl's life is worth more than any inheritance. Can you say the same? Were you willing to allow Grandfather to cut you off for what amounted to little more than high-spirited hijinks? We all heard him threaten to, even Mrs. Keene in the kitchens. I think that is a much more convincing motive for murder, *and* you were seen coming out of Grandfather's bedchamber at six-thirty. Even so, I have not lodged an accusation of murder against you because I know you could never have done it. You are frivolous and fatuous and deuced slippery but not malevolent. No one in our family is."

Feeling as though his cousin had lodged *something* against him—an insinuation if not an outright accusation—Ripley muttered, "He was alive and sleeping peacefully when I left."

Bea, her interest focused elsewhere, confirmed with Miss Cheever that she had no idea her employer knew the truth of her identity.

"None at all," she replied emphatically. "I had very little contact with Mr. Dugmore and would have been astonished if he had addressed me directly. I did not think he even knew who I was. The one time he mentioned me to Mrs. Keene, he called me Irene. If I had suspected he knew the truth, then I would have left here at once. But I truly did not know! And I know you cannot take my word for it, but any of the other maids will swear I was performing my duties from six-thirty to eight-thirty. There is always so much to be done."

"Too much for someone of your delicate constitution!" Jesse asserted fervently.

Miss Cheever fluttered her eyelashes demurely and said, "I cannot imagine how Mr. Dugmore discovered the truth."

"He hired a thief-taker to conduct an investigation into your history," Jesse explained, gripping her hand again lest this information frighten her as well. "The man knew you were from Northumberland because of your accent. With that information, it was not very difficult for him to uncover the whole sordid story."

"But what roused his curiosity?" she asked, her cornflower eyes wide and bewildered. "I was so careful to draw no attention to myself."

"Clearly not careful enough if you drew my cousin's attention," Ridley muttered.

The girl blushed prettily while her suitor openly acknowledged the validity of the criticism. Miss Cheever *was* too beautiful to hide her light under a bushel. His attention had been inexorably drawn and with it his grandfather's. "It is I who had made you vulnerable to these attacks, for I was unable to completely hide my admiration, and I would not blame you if you could not forgive me."

Miss Cheever said that she could sooner not forgive her own heart for beating, and at this nonsensical reply, Jesse dropped to his knees before her. As he pledged his undying love, Bea asked him to relate his movements from six-thirty to eight-thirty on the morning in question.

"Movements?" he repeated, seemingly baffled by the query. "Why would I be moving at that ungodly hour? At six-thirty I was without question in my bed sleeping, where I remained until I was awoken by my valet to start dressing, which was at eight. You can confirm this with Eilish, who begins preparations for my rousing at least two hours before. He is in and out of my bedchamber constantly and would notice if I were absent."

As the compliance of one's servants can be purchased or coerced, Bea insisted on speaking with the valet at once to confirm the story. Although Jesse was taken aback by the request, Ripley had expected nothing less from the Duchess of Kesgrave than an interrogation of the entire staff, and his enthusiasm increased at the prospect of Mr. Twaddle-Thum's reporting. He was slightly standoffish when she excluded him from the conversation, which was brief but decisive—Jesse had indeed been abed until a little after eight—but his spirits improved when she said they would return the next day to interview the members of the family who were not in residence at the moment.

"Yes! You must interrogate Matthew about his fantastically expensive wardrobe. Four pounds for boots! Grandfather could never condone such spendthrift behavior. He had to have threatened to disinherit him, too," Ripley said, adding that he would do everything within his power to ensure his cousin was at home when they called. "If he tries to sprint, I will sit on him."

Beatrice, thanking the viscount for his extravagant offer, gently suggested a milder approach, for she could all too easily imagine Twaddle attributing the subjugation of the poor Corinthian to Her Outrageousness's self-regard rather than his lordship's zealousness.

Chapter Seven

Resting her head against the duke's shoulder as the carriage turned onto Bennett Street, Bea silently acknowledged that she was inordinately fatigued. A bone-weariness had overtaken her the moment she had sat on the bench, and she could not be certain to what to attribute it: the lachrymose scene, the long day, Ripley's overweening high spirits, the cherub.

The last, of course, was the most likely culprit, and yet there was something so draining about a provincial dandy determined to make a name for himself off everyone else's labor.

Kesgrave, appearing to read her thoughts, announced she would need to get a good night's sleep if she was to confront Ripley's shirt points in the morning.

Bea chuckled lightly and reminded him that the boy had been in the city for almost four whole weeks and had yet to achieve social prominence. What else could he do but raise his shirt points as high as his ambitions?"

"Higher, I should think," Kesgrave said wryly.

"Was Nuneaton ever so bad?" she asked, smothering a yawn.

"In regards to his sartorial choices, yes," he said. "I recall one tailcoat in particular that was swathed in so many ribbons and rosettes he looked like the display case at Oddington's. But even with the overwhelming ornamentation, he had a reserved air, an indifference to judgment. One got the sense he was wearing the coat to amuse himself, not others."

"He still has that air," Bea replied.

"He does, yes, which might lead some people to suppose he would happily risk his relationship with Hoby to commission them a pair of boots," he replied languidly. "But they would be wrong. Nuneaton's relationship with his tradesmen is more sacrosanct than mine."

Aghast at his seeming omniscience, she raised her head and stared at him. "How did you know that was what I was thinking?"

"You have not mentioned your need of proper boots in ten days," he explained blandly. "That tells me you ceded the field to come up with another plan of attack. Your options were limited, for your uncle would never consent to the scheme and Hoby would never consent to Russell. Short of seeking a veritable stranger's help, such as Mrs. Palmer's husband, you had no choice but to look to Nuneaton."

How smug he sounded, Bea thought. How pleased he was with his own ability to sift through the evidence and arrive at the only logical conclusion.

It should have annoyed her. She had spent almost two weeks preparing the viscount for the request, offering praise with blatant unsubtlety so that he would know something outrageous was coming and be amused when she finally worked up her nerve to ask it.

And yet it did not.

How could it when it was his displays of pedantry that

beguiled her the most, and thinking how very handsome he was in the shafts of late-afternoon sun that darted in through the windows, she pressed her lips gently against his. He responded at once, snaking his arm around her waist and pulling her closer even as the kiss remained tender.

Neither noticed when the carriage came to a halt in front of Kesgrave House.

Accustomed to their lingering, Jenkins made no attempt to hurry them along and instead called for one of the footmen to bring out carrots for the horses. But Flora, lacking either patience or discretion, afforded them no such courtesy and rapped once on the door before opening it up.

"I am so very sorry," she said quickly, urgently, her shoulders tensing as the sound of hooves echoed up the path. "You must believe me. I was only trying to change the subject. Mama kept asking about Holcroft and she was relentless and I tried everything. Remember the wall in the dining room, the one with the tea splatter that Mama thinks is water damage? I told her that the stain has gotten larger and that I did hope the house did not collapse around us. And Russell with his lessons at Gentleman Jackson's. I mentioned title fights! Usually the mere allusion to boxing is enough to send her off on a tangent for hours. But she remained singularly focused on Holcroft and I had to do something. I could not bear it, so I told her about your plans to make steam engines. I said you were going into trade. And it worked! Only too well. And I am so sorry. You must understand I did not mean for this to happen."

Confounded by Flora's presence in Berkeley Square, Bea felt no embarrassment at being discovered in her husband's embrace. Smoothly, she disentangled herself from the duke as she took note of her cousin's frenzy: the harried expression, the clenched hand gripping the carriage door. The agitation seemed excessive, and although she had no conception what the girl meant by *this,* Bea felt confident it could not be all that terrible.

In the wake of Mr. Holcroft's betrayal, Flora had lost the ability to regulate her emotions and as a consequence responded with immoderate drama to everything. Drawing a deep breath, Bea began to assure her cousin that all was well. There was no need to work herself into a lather.

But the crunch of gravel under the wheel of a carriage caught her attention and she trailed off as another carriage pulled to a halt in the drive.

Out climbed Aunt Vera and Lady Abercrombie.

Seeing their grim expressions, Bea allowed for the possibility that her cousin's response was more appropriate than she had supposed.

While Kesgrave greeted their visitors and led them inside, Flora looped her arm through her cousin's with a pained expression. "I did not intend this, I swear. I thought she would take to her bed or at the very least swoon. Never in a million years did I imagine she would enlist the Countess of Abercrombie's help in dissuading you from your course. You know how strongly she disapproves of her ladyship. As far as Mama is concerned, the woman is the devil incarnate. And yet as blithely as you please, she summoned the carriage to take her to Grosvenor Square. When did she become so daring?" Flora asked crossly as they entered the drawing room, her eyes drawn to her mother, who stared at the various seating options in the extravagant drawing room of the palatial home with her customary timidity. "As bold as brass then and too faint-hearted to choose a chair now. What is she waiting for?"

It was comical, Bea thought, the way her relative's awe of Kesgrave House never diminished. Having visited half a dozen times before, Aunt Vera still entered the drawing room as though its wonders were new to her. Seeming to shrink

AN EXTRAVAGANT DUPLICITY

into herself, she could barely raise her eyes to contemplate the grandeur of the space: its marble columns, its gilded panels, its soaring frescoes.

Dithering over which chair to select, as if there were a material difference between the bergère, settee and chauffeuse, allowed her to narrow her focus to something small and manageable.

At least that was what Bea *thought* was at the root of her aunt's indecisiveness. Bearing in mind her determination to withhold judgment, she acknowledged the cause might be something else entirely.

Perhaps Aunt Vera was inspecting the quality of each cushion to find the one that met her own high standards.

Amused by the notion of her relative finding fault with the magnificence, Bea assured Flora that she had done nothing wrong. "Aunt Vera had to find out some way, and you have spared me the obligation of telling her. Now it is all out in the open."

Flora laughed at this cheerful understanding of the situation and said, "Don't you dare tell me I have done you a favor. That is too big of a plumper even for you."

"But you have," Bea insisted, "for now her ladyship knows as well. It is a bargain, like buying one apple and getting a second for free, and they will distract each other with their disagreements. Although they might be unified in their objection to my entrepreneurial spirit, they still rub together like oil and water. Truly, this is the best possible outcome. And Kesgrave is here to lend his support, which makes the timing of your disclosure especially fortuitous. I would be far less composed if I had to deal with the pair of them on my own."

The duke, as if aware of an expectation to be useful, asked Mrs. Hyde-Clare if she would be so kind as to take the chair next to his. "So that I may better hear your thoughts on the matter."

Aunt Vera, blushing with pleasure, sat down on the embroidered seat just as Joseph carried in the tea tray. He placed it on the table before Lady Abercrombie, who announced that she could not linger.

"Given the constraints on my time, your grace, I trust you will not be difficult," the countess added with sunny optimism.

Flora, insulted on her cousin's behalf, insisted that Bea was never difficult.

Her ladyship contemplated her with a thin smile. "Ah, yes, the little cousin. Your defense of her grace is admirable but unnecessary. As she is the daughter of my dearest friend, I consider myself as a kind of maternal surrogate and would be remiss in my duty if I allowed her to make foolish and reckless mistakes. I had supposed Kesgrave could be relied upon to keep her in line, but it appears as though he has been corrupted."

His lips twitching at the accusation, the duke nodded amiably and said, "Oh, thoroughly."

Aunt Vera, whose flush had darkened to red at Lady Abercrombie's presumption, leaned forward in her seat and identified herself as her grace's *actual* maternal surrogate. "And so it is my obligation first and foremost to dissuade you from sullying our family's good name with this dastardly scheme to engage in trade," she said ardently, then pulled her shoulders back as the audacity of her own presumption struck her. "I mean, yes, the Hyde-Clare name goes back many generations. We have been pillars of the Bexhill Downs community for years. But obviously that pales in comparison to the duke's good—I mean, *excellent*—name. You cannot befoul the Matlock honor by becoming a merchant who deals in steam carriages. The very thought is an abomination. To make the Duke of Kesgrave no better than a cit!"

Her outrage rang clearly in the room, echoing off the

stunning marble, and for one moment Vera sat there, content with her passionate defense of the duke. But it was fleeting, her satisfaction, and within seconds she grimaced and shook her head in agitation as she rushed to explain that *she* did not think that the duke could ever be reduced to a cit. "A transformation of that magnitude is not possible, for no alchemist can turn gold into a base metal. Which is not to say you're gold, your grace," she hastily amended, as if he would take issue with being described as something rare, precious and highly valued. "But golden. Yes, you are golden and I would hate to see goldenness tarnished by cinder and ash."

"Cinder and ash?" Bea repeated, amused by her relative's understanding of the situation. "Aunt Vera, it is not as though I will be forging the steam carriages myself."

"Won't you?" Kesgrave murmured.

"We will hire men to oversee the manufacture," she continued as if the duke had not spoken. "If that is the source of your concern, then I hope that will put your mind at ease."

"I was speaking metaphorically," her aunt insisted. "*Metaphorical* cinder, *metaphorical* ash. I did not imagine that the duke in his lovely coat would personally hammer iron grills in the furnaces—which is not to say that I don't think he *could* hammer iron grills in the furnaces. I am certain he would do it with the same elegance and expertise he does everything else, and I for one would be honored to use any grill he made."

"Your confidence means the world to me," Kesgrave said solemnly.

Aunt Vera simpered.

Bea bit back an impatient sigh and reiterated that she and the duke would primarily hold the patents and oversee its manufacture in only the most general way. "It is little different from owning shares in a mine, for example. That is quite common, is it not? I am sure you and Uncle Horace own shares in some enterprises. I believe our neighbor on Bexhill Downs owns a sawmill. It is no different."

"And a cider press," Flora added. "Mr. Hughes also operates a cider press."

Aunt Vera, having no ready response to these observations, instructed Bea to think of the dowager. "Just a few weeks ago her lone surviving son was killed over a patent dispute and now you are embroiling her grandson in the same wretched business. She would be inconsolable if something happened to him."

Although Bea was sorely tempted to address the irrationality of believing the possession of a patent was in and of itself deadly, she neatly skirted the issue by explaining she had already received the dowager's blessing. "She had no qualms about our ownership as long as we do not name any of the prototypes or models after a member of her family."

"There goes the Dazzling Damian," Flora said with an impertinent grin.

"I am as disappointed as you are," the duke assured her.

Quelled by her niece's arguments, for the girl had an answer for everything, Vera sent Lady Abercrombie a pleading look. She might wrangle with the peeress over maternal surrogacy, which was absurd, of course, for she had overseen the orphan's care and expense for twenty years and the other woman had shown mild interest for approximately four months, but she recognized a superior tactician. Lady Abercrombie had outwitted many of the country's finest male minds. Surely, she could make one former spinster see reason.

Her ladyship, who had accepted a cup of tea all the while proclaiming she could not tarry long enough to enjoy it, assured Bea that she empathized with her plight. "I have read your mother's letters too and know her fondness for the Phillips steam engine. Your fascination stems from hers. Building these machines makes you feel as though a small piece of her were still alive. I understand that, my dear, for it is precisely how I feel when I am with you. But as lovely as that is and as sympathetic as I am, I must beg you to give a little consideration to me."

As the beautiful widow had a tendency to see herself as the sun around which all planets orbited, Bea was not surprised that she would place herself in the middle of the fracas. If anything, she was curious how the other woman would justify the positioning.

Amused by the prospect, she said, "To you?"

"Yes, my dear, to me," her ladyship affirmed without a trace of irony or self-awareness. "*I* am the one who expended all her credit bringing you into fashion. A twenty-six-year-old spinster with unremarkable features and little conversation! It is an accomplishment unmatched in modern times. And I did it despite the seemingly insurmountable obstacles you put in my path. When you refused to give up your investigative habit, I did not try to dissuade you. I said, 'Very well, my dear, you may have your little eccentricity,' and I devised a scheme that allowed you to succeed even with your limitations. And, la, you are the toast of the season just as I promised. I have kept to my end of the agreement, and I must insist that you keep to yours."

If Bea was slightly unsettled to discover she had entered into a sort of Faustian bargain with the countess, she was also deeply intrigued by its terms. "My end?" she asked.

"To hold to investigating as your eccentricity," she replied as if explaining something very simple to a small child. "You insisted that society accept you for your strange habit, and I made sure that condition was met. Thanks to my interventions, you are adored for your cleverness and admired for your deductive skills. It is all that a twenty-six-year-old spinster with a brazen curiosity could desire. And now you turn around and insist that I make you popular as a tradesman as well. It is not a fair request, your grace, and I reject it."

Although Bea knew she was not engaged in a rational conversation wherein the principles of logic held, she made a sincere effort to reason with Lady Abercrombie. "I do not insist on anything. As you noted, you have fulfilled the terms of our contract and are released from further obligation."

Charmed by the naiveté of the statement, the countess trilled fondly and called Bea a darling girl. "One cannot simply be *released* from a moral obligation. One answers to a higher authority. Only think of it: What kind of maternal surrogate would I be if I stood back and allowed you to undo all my hard work? It is not just what I owe you but also what I owe myself. Clara would support me in this. She would not allow me to abandon my responsibility at the moment you need me the most."

It was like being in a play, Bea thought, noting the elegant arc of the countess's arm as she pressed the back of her hand against her forehead. Raising her chin to a flattering angle, her ladyship swept her eyes around the room to see how her audience was receiving the performance.

"I realize this is just a game to you," Bea said. "I am a diversion, like your lion cub, but more entertaining."

The charge, far from insulting the countess, amused her out of her histrionics and she laughed with genuine mirth. "No, my dear, you are not. Are you more ferocious than little Henry? Yes, without question. But not more diverting, especially on occasions like this when you are determined to be stubborn. Except for the time he refused to relieve himself on Cuthbert's shoes, despite my repeated requests, Henry has never thwarted my authority."

Poor Lady Abercrombie, surrounded by wild creatures who refused to do her bidding!

Bea, deciding to change tactics, apologized for causing the

countess so much distress and said that based on her concerns—and Aunt Vera's as well—she would not take out a notice in the *Tribune* announcing the new venture.

Her aunt yelped and recoiled in the chair as if a mouse had scurried across her toes. Then she waved a hand in front of her face as if in genuine danger of fainting. Her breath ragged, she said, "You are teasing! You cannot truly mean to do something so despicable."

"I had intended to preempt Mr. Twaddle-Thum's interest by making the information widely known myself in a rival paper," Bea explained extemporaneously, although the more she thought about the plan, the more it appealed to her. "If I openly acknowledge it, then what is there for him to uncover? But thanks to your and the countess's thoughtful intervention, I see the fault in my logic and resolve to say nothing about it to anyone. It will be our little secret, known only to the five of us and the dowager."

"Seven, counting Stephens," Kesgrave added helpfully.

"You are correct, yes," Bea said with an abrupt nod. "We cannot forget Stephens."

"Stephens?" Aunt Vera said with shrill surprise. "Who is Stephens?"

"The duke's steward," Bea replied promptly. "He is the soul of discretion. Kesgrave trusts him implicitly, but if you have doubts, I am sure the duke will be happy to hear them."

Aunt Vera turned bright pink at the implication that she would harbor doubt about any aspects of the duke's life—save for his choice of bride, of course, which was well documented —and chirped, "No, none at all!"

Lady Abercrombie watched this exchange with a moue of annoyance. "I cannot believe, Kesgrave, that you are indulging this nonsense. You could crush it with a single word."

Kesgrave smiled faintly and asked with seeming sincerity, "Why would I want to crush anything related to Bea?"

"You see, *that* is a relationship," Flora said, gesturing toward the duke as she bounded to her feet. "Implicit trust! Total honesty! Kesgrave would never manipulate Bea's tender heart with a facile story about running to the side of his grieving father or manufacture an argument over the time she is spending with Viscount Nuneaton in order to make her feel as though she had done something horribly wrong when all she did was go driving in Hyde Park in a carriage—a carriage, by the way, that was not as lovely as a certain mustard-colored curricle, which I would have pointed out if I had just been given the chance."

Flora's anger deepened as she detailed the injustices she had been forced to endure, and Aunt Vera watched her daughter march across the room and back again with growing confusion.

"But the duke does not have a father," she murmured quietly, as if to herself. "I am sure Flora knows that."

"Look what you have done, Bea, with your antics," Lady Abercrombie said, shaking her head with exaggerated sadness. "You have broken your little cousin's brainbox. Do change course before your aunt's is damaged as well. As her mind is already so fragile, it will take very little to wreck it completely."

Aunt Vera, either resolving to take the virtuous path or not realizing there was another option, defended her daughter by saying she had recently suffered a grave romantical disappointment. "The particulars of it are unknown to me, but even in her distress she is still worried about her dear cousin. I just wish Bea would cease this madness for her benefit if not for Kesgrave's."

But of course the duke's need was greater and she immediately apologized for discounting his suffering, which was clearly quite acute.

In fact, it was not.

Kesgrave's expression was mild, and if he was worried about anything, it was the Axminster, for Flora appeared determined to wear a hole in it with her pacing.

"It goes without saying that I would not demand trust without giving it in return," her cousin continued furiously. "If he had said one word—one single solitary word about it—I would have fallen in line at once. If he had instructed me to jump off a gangplank into a shark-infested sea, I would have leaped into the water without pestering him with a dozen questions."

Her mother blanched at this declaration of absolute faith and said, "I hope you would pester him with at least *one* question."

Disgusted, Lady Abercrombie rose to her feet and congratulated Bea on routing her. "It is an accomplishment few can claim, only my late husband and your mother. I will support you in your efforts to set yourself up as a tradesman."

Bea was tempted to demur. She understood, yes, how shocking it was for a man of Kesgrave's standing to dirty his hands with trade, but the argument regarding sawmills and cider presses was valid. The successful stewardship of a large estate required the owner to oversee the management of a host of enterprises that bore a striking resemblance to a manufactory—at least in spirit. With that in mind, she felt confident Kesgrave's reputation could withstand whatever mild scandal the venture kicked up.

Or, rather, whatever Mr. Twaddle-Thum kicked up.

He would inevitably write a profusion of gleeful columns deriding the undertaking, and even as she felt a wave of exhaustion overcome her at the prospect, she wondered why she still cared. His dispatch on rout cakes had been instructive, and it was well past time she learned its lesson: It did not matter what she did. Her actions were meaningless. If she spent an entire day staring at the stain in her aunt's dining room, Twaddle would hold her up as the embodiment of indolence. If she devoted herself to emptying chamber pots for veterans of the Peninsula War, he would mock the ostentation of her charity.

Twaddle would twitter regardless.

There was comfort in that, she supposed, because it revealed the futility of worrying.

Even so, she did not refuse Lady Abercrombie's help. The other woman was self-absorbed and myopic but also kind and well-meaning. She had paid Bea the compliment of her attention when the rest of the ton refused to acknowledge her existence, and if the attention was given solely out of a fondness for the girl's late mother, then it was still more than her own relatives had done.

Consequently, she would submit to whatever scheme the widow deemed necessary to save the Matlock name from disgrace.

A dinner party, it appeared, was the curative she had in mind.

Of course it was, Bea thought in amusement. The countess's success with her murder mystery dinner party play—which she somehow considered a triumph despite her lover being stabbed to death after the dessert course—had affirmed for her what she had always known: A good old-fashioned English dinner party was the remedy to all problems.

"It will have an industrial theme woven throughout the evening," Lady Abercrombie said as Bea escorted her to the door. "The particulars escape me, but I am sure my chef could devise some way to incorporate ash into the meal—*saumon à la suie* or *carottes en sauce à la cendre*. And the modiste! I am certain Madame Bélanger is clever enough to come up with a style involving soot. It will be glorious, I am sure, and the entire beau monde will clamor to ape the fashion. Yes, all will be well, my dear."

Invigorated by the challenge, her ladyship posited a cake molded into the shape of a steam engine with gentle billows of smoke wafting from its fume.

It would require great expertise, and with the most obvious candidate removed from contention by a spiteful fishwife, she was not certain any living pâtissier had the proficiency required to make it.

"La! I shall figure it out," she said confidently as they walked down the steps to the drive. "You must not worry about a thing."

Naturally, Bea felt a frisson of alarm at these words but decided it was unnecessary. Given the complexity of the situation, she and Kesgrave were many months, if not a full year, away from establishing a manufactory.

As her ladyship climbed into the Hyde-Clare carriage, she asked Bea to convey her apologies to her relative for taking the vehicle. "It is just that I find your aunt intolerable and would rather not spend more time in her company than necessary. I trust you will explain that to her."

"I am sure she will be gratified to hear it," Bea replied satirically.

Alas, Aunt Vera was not.

Grasping her hands together, she despaired of ever returning to her home, for she could not bring herself to consent to either of the proposed solutions. Taking the duke's carriage was out of the question because the conveyance was too grand for the meagerness of the errand, and the distance to Portman Square was too great to traverse on foot.

Flora, whose tirade over Holcroft's treatment had devolved into a muttered lament about his deplorable lack of faith in her sex ("God forbid that I, a mere female, be given dominion over my own life and decisions"), broke off as she looked at her mother in confusion. "But it is not even a full mile. I walked here in less than twenty minutes."

Her complaint validated by this observation, Aunt Vera nevertheless allowed herself to be persuaded to go by foot when the third option—the duke himself hailing a hack—proved intolerable.

After her relatives left, Bea tossed herself onto the settee with a hefty sigh and congratulated Kesgrave on his ploy. "Nothing mortifies my aunt more than allowing you to perform a service for her."

Accepting the compliment with a dip of his head, he sat down next to her. "I think it is time for you to resolve the matter between your cousin and Holcroft."

"*I* resolve it?" Bea asked, confounded by the notion. "I would never presume to insert myself into a situation about which my thoughts have not been explicitly requested."

Kesgrave, smiling faintly, said, "Mrs. Mayhew will be relieved to hear it."

"On that occasion my assistance was specifically sought," she reminded him. "Joseph came to me with his concerns."

"And Otley?" he asked. "On that occasion, your assistance was specifically refused."

"I was morally obligated to discover the truth," she said, recalling the way the murdered spice trader had looked in the darkened library at Lakeview Hall, his head bashed and bleeding in the moonlight. "As Lady Abercrombie said, one cannot be released from a moral obligation."

At the mention of the countess, the duke winced and said, "Then do please consider yourself morally obligated to spare us further scenes with your aunt *and* Tilly."

"I am sure we are safe from that," Bea said confidently. "The look on Aunt Vera's face when she realized her ladyship had stolen her carriage was enough to convince me she will not ally herself with her again. And I think my cousin learned her lesson as well. She was embarrassed by her own behavior."

Kesgrave, who had been present for the entire rant, which had included several invectives that made the girl's mother cringe in horror, begged to disagree. "She seemed indifferent to public condemnation as she furiously proclaimed her right to self-determination."

Detecting censure in the comment, she felt compelled to defend her cousin by pointing out that the claim was well justified. "It *is* infuriating to have one's options curtailed by a happenstance of birth," she said, aware that it was a concept few men could grasp. Doing so required them to view women as fully human, not merely as appendages or brood mares.

Ah, yes, brood mares, she thought sourly, annoyed that a conversation about Flora's quarrel with Holcroft had somehow led to thoughts about breeding.

But it had and she recognized the moment for what it was: the ideal opportunity to mention the cherub. They were alone, she had the duke's attention, and the word *birth* had already been uttered.

Conditions could not be any more propitious.

Just say it: I am with child, your grace.

But as easily as the words echoed in her head, as smoothly as they tripped off her imaginary tongue, she simply could not bring herself to do it.

It was irrational, this fear, for she knew her strange investigative bent was not the reason Kesgrave loved her. He had been very clear about the things that had drawn him to her: her sharp mind, her quick wit, the sparkle in her eyes when she was about to say something impertinent. Those traits had nothing to do with murder, and he stared in bemusement as much for her opinion of *The Vicar of Wakefield* as for her skill in deciphering clues.

And yet he would not have known she existed if not for

Mr. Otley's bloody corpse. If she had never wandered into the library at Lakeview Hall at two in the morning to find something to read, then he would have forever remained the intolerable duke across the table at whom she longed to throw eels *à la tartare*.

More to the point, was this unnerving truth: But for Mr. Otley's bloody corpse, *she* would never have known that Bea either. The audacity that had enthralled and appalled him in equal measure was an artifact of her terror. Fleetingly, heartrendingly, she had believed her life was over—her narrow little life, with its docility and muteness.

That moment had changed everything.

And now this moment would change everything again, and because she was not ready for it, had not prepared her speech or fortified her defenses, she remained silent. Instead, she grappled for a benign comment to make and settled on Dugmore's will, which Kesgrave had slipped in his pocket along with the other hidden papers to keep safe.

Her tone bland despite the turmoil roiling her emotions, she asked to see the document.

He produced it at once, adding that he had merely glanced at it. "I had meant to read it once we returned, but Flora waylaid us. To get a full understanding of the differences, we will have to compare the two wills side by side. I think, however, we can get a general idea by examining the behests told to us by Ripley. Start with the eldest grandson."

"Thank you, your grace," Bea murmured, amused by his compulsion to provide detailed instructions for something patently obvious. How else did he think she would gain useful information from the document? "And after Matthew, I shall proceed to Clifford, the next eldest grandchild, shall I?"

"Only if you wish to be orderly about it," he replied mildly, refusing to rise to the bait. "If you find chaos to be

AN EXTRAVAGANT DUPLICITY

more conducive to your process, then you must proceed that way. I would never presume to curtail your options."

It was curious, indeed it was, the way this comment affected Bea, how it caused her heart to trip, how it made her stomach flip. His tone was wry, facetious, perhaps even a little defensive, but all she heard was generosity and understanding.

Because it was the truth: Kesgrave did not curtail her options.

Far from limiting her activities, he chose instead to expand them.

Grimly, a sour little voice reminded her it was only a matter of time. As soon as the duke learned of her condition, the curtailment would begin.

But Bea was tired of it, the dourness that hovered over her like a gloomy cloud, and determined to banish the darkness with light, she launched herself at him, causing the papers to flutter to the floor.

It was a good long while before they discovered the only discernable difference in the two documents was Melody's inheritance.

Chapter Eight

When Bea and Kesgrave arrived in St. James's Square the following morning a little before nine-thirty, they found Viscount Ripley standing outside the drawing room door, a disgruntled expression on his youthful face. Although the height of his shirt points—creeping slightly up his cheeks—indicated that the day had started ordinarily enough, the disheveled state of his cravat spoke of disagreement and strife. Formerly the Waterfall, it was now a lesser version of itself: the Dribble, perhaps, or the Drip.

His lordship began to shake his head the moment he saw them and apologized in a frenzied rush for not being able to carry out her request. "Matthew and Clifford are inside. I succeeded in detaining them before they left the house this morning, although Clifford insists he was not going anywhere—a blatant falsehood, for he had his hat and riding crop in his grasp. As expected, I had to use physical force to keep Matthew here, for he had no intention of abiding by your wishes, your grace. I conveyed to him your interest in interviewing him as soon as possible and he said your preferences were of no consequence to him. No consequence, your grace!" he repeated, a hint of shrillness entering his tone as he swept a hand through his hair, an indication of his frustration. "But you must not worry that I sat on him. Mindful of your advice, I secured him to his chair with cord. I must admit, he did not take to that very well, but Clifford found it vastly amusing and called me 'old sport,' which is the nicest thing he has ever said to me."

Binding the gentleman with rope was not quite the improvement Ripley thought it was, and Bea flinched, imagining the description Twaddle would offer: Her Outrageousness's antics took a swashbuckling turn on Tuesday, when she lashed a suspect to a chair like a pirate on the high seas. Ahoy!

Nevertheless, she thanked the viscount for his diligence and asked where cousin Matthew was now. "Not still tied up, I hope."

The shake of Ripley's head was reassuring. "Once he realized the extent I would go to ensure he remained, he agreed to stay without restraints. He is in the drawing room with Clifford. They are both eager to discuss Grandfather's murder with you. I am ashamed to admit, however, that while I was tussling with Matthew in the breakfast room, Melody and Aunt Celia slipped out unnoticed. Unlike Matthew, I am certain they mean no disrespect. They are just overly diligent in their obligation to the orphans at Fortescue's. Although the head matron employs a full staff to take care of them, Melody seems to think she is the only thing standing between the dirty mites and starvation. I would find the attitude mawkish if she weren't my cousin. That Grandfather had any patience for it is a—"

He broke off as the door suddenly swung open and Matthew stood on the threshold with a piercing scowl. "You dolt, forcing me to cool my heels despite several pressing engagements and then squandering precious moments as you blather about nothing!"

But of course explaining his *murdered* grandfather's opinions about various members of his family was not blathering, and Ripley took a step toward his cousin as if to engage in fisticuffs.

Laughing without humor, Matthew said, "You would like that, wouldn't you, if I stooped to brawling in the corridor. Your Mr. Twaddle-Thum would be sure to take notice of you then. Well, unlike the duke and duchess, I will not allow you to exploit my position to increase your fame."

Although Bea preferred to believe she and Kesgrave had been manipulated by facts rather than the viscount, there could be no denying the sentiment. Nevertheless, she complimented Matthew on his imperviousness and thanked him for taking the time to answer some questions.

Sighing heavily, Matthew asked if it was really necessary. "I swear we had this exact same conversation yesterday, and you conceded that it was just my nodcock cousin trying to get that officious busybody's attention. And yet here you are again, insisting it was murder. My grandfather was a frail old man with unsteady balance, thanks to his ailments, and he fell. It is no great mystery what happened."

"*You* are the nodcock, for I explained all this!" Ripley replied, glancing at Bea as if to apologize for his cousin's obtuseness. "I told him about the missing nightcap and he asked me what game I was playing, as if I had taken it myself! And then I tried to open the secret compartment to show it to him but could not figure out the mechanism!"

"Is that why you were crawling under the table?" Matthew drawled. "Clifford and I could not figure out what you were doing. Clifford thought you were looking for your quizzing glass, but I said you had ceased to wear one after Dankworth asked you if you were hoping to find your good sense with it."

Ripley straightened his back in insult and said coldly, "No, he asked if I could find *his* good sense because it had just been knocked out of him by the sight of Miss Petworth, whose beauty is so extraordinary it strikes men dumb."

"How appropriate," Matthew said kindly, "as *dumb* nicely sums up this conversation."

Even as his lordship inhaled sharply to respond—and no doubt further prove his cousin's point—Bea jumped in to explain that she and the duke now believed Mr. Dugmore had been murdered based on the missing nightcap. Then she suggested they continue the discussion in the drawing room. "Unless you are comfortable with the prospect of this conversation appearing verbatim in the *London Daily Gazette*. I do not presume to know anything about Twaddle's methods other than the fact that he is thorough."

"Very well," Matthew replied, leading the way.

As soon as they were settled, Bea added that the compartment was not a figment of Ripley's imagination but an actual depository containing several documents deemed significant by his grandfather. "Among them were tradesmen bills in your name, Mr. Gaitskill. We would like you to tell us about those debts."

"Yes," Ripley said with a broad smile, his stance relaxing as he rested one shoulder against the wall, as if settling in for a long conversation, "tell us about them, Mr. Gaitskill. Your financial situation is little better than mine, for your father was also a wastrel. How can you afford to spend so much money on waistcoats?"

Stiffly, his cousin responded that he would do no such thing. "The pecuniary arrangement between a man and his tailor is sacred."

"What about between a man and his bootmaker?" his lordship asked goadingly. "Or between a man and his haberdasher? As you can see, it is quite a large stack, at least an inch thick. Would you not agree, your grace?"

Matthew scowled darkly and bit back whatever angry retort rose to his lips. Then, addressing Bea and the duke, he announced he would not say another word in the presence of his cousins. "The expenditures I make to ensure I turn myself out in a manner that is above reproach are themselves above reproach. I refuse to answer for them and will absolutely not say a word in the presence of a preening provincial whose understanding of elegance is to add another gold tassel to his waistcoat."

Naturally, this was a deeply offensive notion to the viscount, who had never sported a waistcoat bearing a single tassel in his life. The very idea was laughable, for only but the most ignorant cawker knew tassels belonged on a greatcoat.

Sneering lightly, Matthew thanked Ripley for illustrating his point.

When his lordship could not be prevailed upon to leave the room, Kesgrave suggested they move their conversation elsewhere. Matthew said they could talk in his grandfather's study, which was at the end of the hall, and as he led them there Ripley called to their departing backs, "I shall just interrogate Clifford, then, shall I?"

The study was a square room with heavy damask curtains and simple wood furniture, all in pristine condition, and Bea noted the scent of tobacco as she entered. She and Kesgrave sat down at Matthew's urging, but their host remained standing as he launched into an explanation.

"You must understand: My grandfather had very old-fashioned ideas. He could not accept that things had changed in the past fifty years, especially prices. He still thought a pair of boots should cost what they did in 1766 and had no appreciation for the superior quality provided by a man of Hoby's skill and experience. He got his own boots from a cobbler in the village near his home. Other than artifacts of my grandfather's antiquated ideas, the bills can hold no interest."

Matthew pressed the lower part of his back against the desk as he spoke, the palms of his hands pressed flat on its surface and one leg crossed over the other. His position allowed him to retain the advantage of height, and Bea, tilting her chin up slightly to look up at him, wondered why he felt the need to employ the tactic.

Presumably, he hoped to intimidate them.

Bea found the impulse fascinating, for nothing he had said was remarkable. Only the day before, Ripley had lodged a similar complaint against their grandfather. And yet the two men had had wildly divergent experiences. Dugmore threatened disinheritance for the viscount's excessive debts while settling them for Matthew. It was the latter action that she found more puzzling, for it implied tacit approval of the expenditure.

Gambling was verboten, but turning oneself out in the first stare was permitted.

She recalled what Matthew had said previously regarding his grandfather's code: *He believed a man should suffer the consequences of his actions.*

Presumably, then, paying deeply for quality clothing was not an indulgence but a necessity. Maybe so, but yesterday Matthew had scathingly derided the viscount's desperation for the ton's approval. As his own preoccupation with his appearance struck her as equally vain, she found it difficult to believe Dugmore perceived a difference. A man with old-fashioned notions was not likely to be flexible in applying them.

So why had he paid the tradesmen on Matthew's behalf?

Rather than speculate about the reason, she asked him.

"It was all Ripley's doing!" Matthew spat. "Grandfather did not mind my debts until my cousin came along and got himself in twice as deep. Then all of a sudden he was worried that the whole lot of us were degenerate spendthrifts. It was infuriating, to have my bills examined like the veriest greenhorn who did not know a morning coat from a riding coat. Needless to say, I submitted without complaint out of esteem for my grandfather. Just because he did not respect excellent tailoring did not mean I lacked respect for him."

Although the answer contained several interesting details, it skirted the actual question, which Bea resolved to ask again. Before she could, however, the duke noted that Dugmore appeared to have a highly developed appreciation for tailoring. "Judging by the clothes in his dressing room, that is," Kesgrave said. "The tailcoat I saw was as good as anything Weston has ever turned out."

"Is that so?" Bea asked thoughtfully, unaware that such a thing could be detected at a glance. "That indicates to me that Mr. Dugmore's objections were not as strenuous as you would have us believe. Or they were but the subject was different. I am still curious as to why your grandfather paid your bills with the tradesmen while insisting his lordship settle his own debts. He sought to control your cousin Jesse's behavior with the information he had kept in the pier table's compartment. Are you sure, Mr. Gaitskill, that he made no attempt to influence yours?"

Arching his back slightly against the desk, he assured her he was positive. "I think I would have noticed if my own grandfather tried to force me to do something. And what would he have forced me to do?" he asked, laughing lightly in contempt as he continued to consider the notion, as absurd as it was. "I have satisfied all his requirements. I know all the best people and belong to all the right clubs. I am an excellent whip hand, a skilled boxer, an expert marksman, a conscientious landlord and a moderate gambler. I am everything my grandfather was at the age of thirty-three. He had no complaints."

In fact he was not, Bea thought, noting the one credit his recitation lacked. "You have no wife."

A muscle in his cheek jumped as he smiled thinly and said with withering condescension, "As is typically the case for unmarried men, your grace."

"That is true, yes," she agreed mildly, not entirely sure why the distinction struck her as significant.

But it did.

In some way she did not yet understand, his marital status pertained to the conversation. His snide response proved it.

Contemplating it further, she reminded him that it was he who had raised the issue by claiming to have mimicked all his grandfather's achievements. "You said you were everything Mr. Dugmore was by the same age, but that is not accurate. He was married with three daughters by the time he was thirty-three, and I find it difficult to believe that a man whom both you and your cousin described as old-fashioned had no issue with your unmarried state. Did he never express a preference for you to wed?"

Matthew shifted his position, rounding his shoulders as he crossed his arms in front of his chest. "He expressed *some* preference, but he trusted me to make the right decision."

Bea recalled Dugmore's objection to his other grandson aligning with a waifish runaway who had descended into service to hide from her family and wondered if the old man displayed that level of trust in anyone. "Did he really?"

For a moment he glared at her, his pose standoffish as his grimace deepened into a scowl. Then he lowered his gaze and mumbled, "Fine, yes, he wanted me to marry. He hoped I would make a match of it with Lucinda Steed, the daughter of my neighbor in Warwickshire. Miss Steed and I have spoken only a handful of times, but she is young and biddable and rich—everything a wife should be, according to my grandfather. I promised to take it under advisement but that was not enough for him. He insisted I propose before a week had passed and held my debts over me as a threat."

He paused, as if he had provided enough information, but of course he had left out the most important part.

"A threat how?" Bea asked.

Red stained Matthew's cheeks as he replied abashedly, "Debtors' prison. That is right, your grace, my own grandfather threatened to send me to debtors' prison for my unpaid tradesmen bills if I did not propose to the girl by the end of the week."

"How did you respond?" she asked.

"I refused," he said stiffly. "Even if I had been inclined to propose to Miss Steed, which I was not, for she is a little beetle of a thing, all rounded and spindly, with large eyes, I could not allow him to run roughshod over me. It would have only made him more of a tyrant."

"*More* of a tyrant," Bea repeated with a curious lift of her brow. "Was he already much of one?"

Matthew glowered at her with intense dislike, as if she had deliberately tricked him into making an unintended disclosure. Then he smoothed his features and insisted that his grandfather was merely set in his ways. "As, I daresay, most men his age are. And I knew he meant no harm. He just wanted to see his grandchildren settled, which is not remarkable. I believe it is the goal of all patriarchs."

"I would imagine a stint in debtors' prison would be quite harmful to a man of your taste and proclivities," Bea observed.

"Well, he would never have done it, would he?" he asked, shaking his head with disbelief. "Consigning his own grandson to debtors' prison is arguably a greater sin than being consigned to debtors' prison. The whole family would be shamed if he followed through on his threat, he most of all, and I told him to do it if he must. I would never bend to extortion. And, frankly, I think it would have given him a disgust of me if I had. He might have resented my refusal to conform to his wishes, but he respected my independence more. He appreciated that I was my own man, not a squeak and squawk like Clifford."

Although this assessment did not vary much from Ripley's, his tone conveyed a greater disgust. "A squeak and squawk?"

"A mouse with no pluck," Matthew explained. "Clifford would do anything he asked. That is why he spied for him, running back to his side with tales about all of us. The only way Grandfather could know I would never propose to Miss Steed of my own volition was Clifford told him after he read my correspondence to my...to...my..."

Trailing off, he darted a look at Kesgrave that was as awkward as it was apologetic. Then he coughed uneasily and continued. "Regardless, I should never have put it in writing. And that was my mistake. But a man should be able to write a missive to his...his...er, write a missive to *anyone* without fear of it being read without permission. I cannot imagine how he lives with himself, the craven toady. If I thought your preposterous theory about my grandfather's death had any merit at all, I would point you toward Clifford. I can only assume he is as disgusted with himself as we are with him, and killing our grandfather might have been the only way he could free himself from his oppressive presence."

Bea, who had developed a deep appreciation for heavy-handed allegations during her brief tenure as an investigator, thought this charge was among the clumsiest she had ever heard, not the least because it revealed more about the accuser than the accused.

Whatever antipathy his cousin may or may not hold against Mr. Dugmore, Matthew resented his grandfather's authority. It led her to suppose he was not quite as sanguine about the possibility of going to debtors' prison as he strove to appear. If his grandfather was genuinely tyrannical, then he might not care as much about the family's reputation as Matthew claimed.

Pressing him on his relationship with his grandfather, however, yielded no satisfying answers, for he refused to acknowledge any significant points of disagreement other than Miss Steed. Instead, he took considerable pains to convince Bea that their dispute over his pending nuptials was equally as minor.

"I am confident my grandfather would have gotten over his disappointment within a week or two and settled on another cause to champion," Matthew said with airy determination. "At his age, nothing held his attention for long. Look at the matter with my sister. For months he tried to press her into marriage, and then he turned around and left her a comfortable living. I know it would have been the same for me. Miss Steed was merely a passing fancy."

Although Ripley had made a similar remark regarding the fleeting nature of his grandfather's rages, Bea could not believe it applied to extortion schemes, which required an expenditure of time and money. Given the lengths to which he had gone, she thought it was likely he would not have abandoned the effort at the first sign of resistance.

Would he have gone as far as harming the entire family's reputation?

Bea could not say, but if Matthew believed his grandfather was too stubborn to relent, then he would have an excellent reason to want him dead. Caught between debtors' prison and the parson's mousetrap, he may have decided that helping an old man attain his heavenly reward a few years ahead of schedule was a viable solution.

Possibly, another relative felt the same. If one of the cousins knew of the threat and feared Matthew would not submit, they might have decided killing Dugmore was a way of ending the stalemate without tarnishing the family name.

If that was the motive, Bea thought with amusement, then Ripley was not in contention, for he seemed ready and willing to suffer any degradation as long as it increased his popularity.

And Jesse—he was determined to bring a different kind of shame onto the family.

That left Melody, Clifford, and Mrs. Gaitskill.

Actually, no, not Melody, for any woman who preferred the toils of an orphan asylum to marriage had little care for society's judgments.

Before summoning her next interview subject, she asked Matthew to detail his movements on the morning his grandfather died. Although it was a mundane request, he took great exception to it, casting an offended look at Kesgrave and asking if it was really necessary.

"It is, yes," Bea said. "And do not leave out the name of the friend with whom you went fishing so we may confirm your story."

Further affronted by the notion that his actions had to not only be established but also corroborated, he launched into a detailed account of his every movement starting nine hours earlier, when he and his friend Hogan—that was, Kyle Hogan, of Lindmore Street—decided to go angling on Hampstead Heath. He included what he had been drinking during the conversation (claret), where he went after it concluded (Mrs. Haspel's rout) and when he returned home to ensure he was properly rested for the outing (1:30). An elaborate description of the fortifying breakfast he consumed followed.

As presumably the point of the performance was to try her and Kesgrave's patience, Bea smiled blandly throughout the recitation and thanked him for being so thorough. "I wish every suspect we interviewed were as meticulous."

He glowered at the characterization but did not protest.

Ignoring his petulance, Bea asked him to send in Clifford next and as soon as he left, she asked Kesgrave if he knew Mr. Hogan.

"I do not, no," he replied, adding that few of his acquaintance cherished a fondness for fishing, especially at so uncivilized an hour. "I assume Gaitskill will remain on your list until you have your minion confirm his story with Hogan."

Amused by his description, she swore she had never regarded Flora in such a subsidiary light. "If anything, she is an associate. And given her surliness over Holcroft's treatment, I expect she would argue fiercely about being assigned work for her own investigation. Recall, we are here on her sufferance."

"I was referring to Joseph," Kesgrave explained.

Although initially overwhelmed by the prospect of overseeing a domestic staff as large as the one Kesgrave House required, she had of late discovered its value. Employing a quartet of footmen allowed her to confirm several pieces of information at once as well as keep watch on establishments relevant to her investigation. Two weeks ago, she had tasked Joseph with infiltrating a charity that helped widows and orphans to gather intelligence on its governors.

Well, not *infiltrate*.

Far simpler, the assignment had been merely to interview various supervisors to get a general sense of their honesty and ascertain if any of them seemed likely to explode an inventor to gain possession of his patents.

It was Joseph himself who used the word *infiltrate* when boasting of the undertaking with the other servants belowstairs, according to Bea's maid.

"Oh, I see, yes," she replied. "In that case, it is minions, plural, for others on the staff have signaled their willingness to participate in future infiltrations."

Kesgrave nodded as if something suddenly made sense to him and asked if that was why Edward had delivered the breakfast tray the day before with a patch over his right eye.

"No," she said firmly. "That was the result of an unfortunate encounter with a wayward broomstick. His vision is unharmed, but the injury is unsightly. Lily says one of the kitchen maids fainted when she saw it. But it *is* why James was rolling his *r*'s while serving dinner on Tuesday."

Here, too, the duke appreciated the explanation, for he had noticed the change in diction and wondered why the first footman had suddenly developed a lisp.

"Oh, dear," Bea said, incapable of smothering the giggle that rose to her lips. "James will be distraught to know his efforts at a brogue failed so spectacularly."

"Let us hope he never finds out," Kesgrave said with a visible shudder.

His genuine aversion to giving offense to his own servants was one of the most fascinating things about him, for a man of his wealth and lineage should have been above considering the feelings of his staff.

Indeed, he should have been above considering the feelings of anyone.

From the very first breath he drew, obedience had been owed to him, and deference on that scale, compulsory and expected, frequently bred tyranny.

And how could it not, Bea thought, for anyone accustomed to compliance would feel thwarted by even the slightest challenge to his authority. That the duke did not default constantly to his importance, that he did not stand endlessly on his consequence, was the most persuasive indication of his decency. He had his moments of pomposity, instances of pontification during which he held forth on any number of topics in stultifying detail, but they were tedious, not cruel.

Struck by it now, she realized then what a wonderful father he would make. Engrossed by her own anxieties, she had not contemplated it in such simple terms, but, oh, yes, he would be very good with the cherub.

Noting the arrested expression on her face, he said, "I do not think you should be surprised to learn I have no desire to impugn the theatrical skills of the staff."

"No," she said softly, "I should not be surprised."

Now he looked at her curiously, bewildered, she assumed, by the strange earnestness of the response. Usually she replied to such provocation in kind, teasing him about his irrational fear of his household descending into chaos.

Disconcerted by his intuitiveness, she tried to think of something to say that would draw attention away from herself, and it was with heartfelt gratitude that she heard Clifford knock on the door.

Chapter Nine

Clifford perched hesitantly on the threshold.

"Matthew said you wished to speak to me, but if I am interrupting, I am happy to come back," he offered with a pained expression. Tall and wafer-thin, he held himself awkwardly, his shoulders pulled together as if to avoid knocking into an approaching person or a nearby object. Despite the look of severe discomfort, his countenance was appealing and benign, with dark brown eyes and full lips. "I have nothing pressing to do today and can wait as long as you require."

Bea, assuring him that was not necessary, waved him into the room. "Do come in and take a seat. We have some questions about your grandfather."

Clifford hovered in the doorway for a few more seconds, seemingly uncertain about following her instructions, then stepped into the study. After eyeing the limited seating options, he sat down in a high-back chair and hunched his shoulders. "I am really not sure what I can add to our conversation from yesterday. Ripley has been rambling on about secret compartments and murder, but I am convinced he misunderstood something."

Assuredly, she told him his lordship had not. "Based on the evidence we have found, including a secret compartment in your grandfather's pier table, we have concluded he was in fact murdered."

"I still cannot believe it," he said, shaking his head. "To think a member of the family harmed Grandfather. ... It is impossible! Furthermore, it does not make sense. None of us had any reason to wish him harm. He was beloved by all. It had to have been a servant. One never knows what resentments the staff hold. That is the only explanation that makes sense."

Based on her conversations with the three other male cousins, Bea could be persuaded to believe the victim was respected by his family—though in reality he seemed more feared than anything else. Beloved, however, was too much of a stretch, and she wondered why he would make such a blatantly false statement.

To protect his brother, perhaps.

Drawing attention to that possibility, she said, "Nobody? Not even Jesse?"

Although he fidgeted uneasily in his seat, his voice was firm as he asserted his brother had no quarrel with their grandfather. They agreed on every point. But he could hold the pose for only a few seconds, then he relented and admitted that there had been some wretched business with one of the servants. He was certain, however, that it was merely a misunderstanding. "I mean, what else could it be? Jesse is too kind to dally with a maid and too mindful of his position to degrade it by seducing a member of the staff. If he displayed any interest in the girl at all, it was only to tweak Grandfather's nose for daring to arrange a marriage for him."

It was, Bea decided, a facile attempt at a lie, and she

wondered why he made it. Even if he was not the recipient of confidences from his brother, which, given the general assumption that the young man spied for his grandfather, was likely, he had to know by now that Jesse's feelings for Miss Cheever were in earnest. Ripley would not have maintained a discreet silence regarding the shocking scene he had witnessed.

Curious to see where it led, she did not contradict the fiction. "You believe Jesse resented your grandfather's efforts on his behalf?"

"How could he not resent it?" Clifford asked heatedly. "Grandfather presented him with what he described as wife candidates and told him to choose one. They were all suitable women, presentable, wealthy and docile creatures befitting the Dugmore line. It was past time, he said, that Jesse married and started a brood. That was two weeks ago now, and it is why Jesse created the uproar with the maid. He wanted to show Grandfather that he was his own man and would tryst with whomever he wanted however unsuitable. I assume he told Pauline what the game was because he is honest in his dealings."

His determination to hold to what was blatantly a falsehood fascinated Bea. She knew he did not believe it, and she knew that he knew that she did not believe it. That indicated he had some motive other than to deliberately mislead her, and since his words only sharpened her interest in Jesse, she assumed he felt comfortable casting suspicion on his brother because he knew the other man had a witness who had placed him in his bedchamber at the time of the murder.

As she contemplated the reason he would make such an effort to draw attention away from himself, she began with the obvious one. "Tell me, Mr. Parr, how old are you?"

His expression was tight as he replied, "Twenty-seven."

"Two years older than your brother," she said.

"Fourteen months, to be exact, so more like one," he said.

It was revealing, the clarification, for it made plain that he understood the implication of the question, and she interpreted it as confirmation that his grandfather had subjected him to the same treatment as Jesse and Matthew.

And yet there was no document in the secret compartment that Dugmore could have used to compel his compliance.

Indeed, there was nothing in the secret compartment that pertained to Clifford at all.

Bea found that interesting.

Leaning forward with an air of intimacy, she said, "Tell me, Mr. Parr, what did you take from the pier table?"

He fluttered his lashes.

Like an Incomparable receiving a compliment on her unsurpassed beauty, he simpered with lavish modesty and insisted he had *no idea* what she was talking about. Even as she regarded him with frank disbelief, he remained determined to brazen it out, even going so far as to ask what she meant.

He was, Bea thought, a hairsbreadth away from saying, "What pier table?"

But he managed to hold himself back. Recognizing the futility of denial, he swung his fist as if to pound the table and swore fiercely for several seconds, displaying an impressive vocabulary of oaths and profanities. When he ran out of expletives, he said with surprising composure, "I know this looks bad for me, but you must believe me when I say he was sleeping when I left. Because he was! I never touched him. I only touched the table. I swear it!"

Having failed to anticipate such a revealing answer, she opened her eyes wide in surprise. "You removed coercive information from the compartment on the eve of the murder?"

Clifford's expression turned stormy as he exclaimed, "I had no choice! I *had* to retrieve them at the first opportunity. If they fell into the wrong hands, it would spell disaster for me. How could I have known he would be killed a few hours later? It is a terrible turn of events. I could have strangled Ripley when I found out what he did. The damned fool, always trying to stir up trouble! I was so relieved when your party left yesterday, and to have you return with all this talk of murder, it is very upsetting. If you are so determined to find a killer, I am telling you to look among the staff. They are the only ones who could have done it."

If he hoped to distract her from the documents he took from the pier table, then he would be sadly disappointed. That being the case, she did not mind indulging his efforts briefly and asked whom he suspected.

Taken aback by the question, he had no ready answer and turned to look at the duke, as if expecting him to list servants from whom he could choose. After several seconds, he finally said, "I have no idea and that is precisely the problem! Can anyone ever really know a servant? They live such secretive lives. We do not know what they are thinking, what they are feeling. Any one of them could harbor resentments so deep we cannot even imagine. You must interview them all, starting with Pauline. Being a woman, she would cherish dreams of uniting with my brother even though he had told her it was impossible. The female mind is intractable."

Although Bea had expected an argument with more substance, she was never surprised to receive an answer that was two parts misogyny and one part nonsense. "We have confirmed Miss Cheever's alibi with half a dozen people, but do let me know if someone else in particular occurs to you. In the meantime, I would like to return to the documents contained in your grandfather's secret compartment. You said 'they,' plural. He had more than one document that could be used to influence your behavior?"

Clifford sniggered at her use of the word *influence,* calling it a weak description of his grandfather's objective. "He wanted to *control* my behavior. As you have intuited, he thought it was past time that I marry as well and as he held letters attesting to a faux pas in my youth, he could pretty much compel me to do anything he desired."

She recognized the description as an attempt to understate the severity of his indiscretion and asked to what the letters attested.

Incapable of looking either her or the duke in the eye, he pressed his chin against his chest and pleaded with her not to make him say it. "Please! If I speak the words, they will be out there in the world and everyone will learn the truth. I do not know how it will happen, but the infernal Twaddle will find out, and I will be destroyed. Please! I promise you it has nothing to do with my grandfather's death. Nothing at all!"

It was, Bea thought, a reasonable objection. Unable to figure out how the detestable gossip managed to uncover so many intimate details of her own life, she could not offer any guarantee that he would not find out about Clifford's. Twaddle had access to locked rooms and private conversations, and although his methods were just well-honed and meticulous, they felt mystical. Sitting there, in the study in St. James's Square, she knew there was always a possibility that their conversation could appear word for word in the *London Daily Gazette*.

The conundrum either did not occur to Kesgrave or present an issue for him, as he unstintingly offered Clifford his assurances that his secret would not leave the room. "Say it quickly and be done with it."

Responding to the authority in the duke's voice, he complied. "I cheated at cards. It was just the one time. An impulse of youth, reckless and stupid. I was barely out of leading strings and desperate to buy a commission. My mother would not help me because Father died in battle, and Grandfather said the army was for fools and climbers. But I was so close to having enough money to secure a rank in the infantry and I—" He broke off, unable to finish the sentence. His head hanging low again with the disgrace of it all, he mumbled, "Grandfather hushed it up, paying handsomely to ensure everyone's silence, but not before attaining letters from all the participants attesting to my despicable behavior."

As these testaments were clearly the documents he had taken from the table, it required little imagination to figure out what he had done with them. Nevertheless, she asked and received confirmation that he had burned the incriminating evidence immediately.

Now she had no way to prove that his story was true.

But did she need to?

Dugmore's pattern was known to her now, and even if the documentation was not as Clifford claimed, it was still leverage to be exploited by the patriarch to achieve his own ends. Ultimately, all that mattered was how he would use the information—and that had already been made clear.

"How long did you have to propose to your wife candidates?" she asked.

He jeered at her use of the plural. "Unlike Jesse, whom Grandfather always loved more despite my efforts to ingratiate myself, I was given just the one candidate: Adelaide Farnsworth. She is a dull-witted harpy with a fat dowry whose family owns a shipping company. Despite his manipulations, I resolved to keep an open mind and met Miss Farnsworth in Hyde Park for a walk. She is horrible. All she talked about was the price of sugar and how to change a horse's shoe. She knew nothing practical and was completely incapable of making intelligent conversation. And she had spots! One horrible one on her chin that was impossible to ignore. The whole experience was intolerable, but Grandfather did not care. I had five more days to either resign myself to an excruciating fate or face social ruin."

Although the prospective bride sounded reassuringly sensible to Bea, she understood that was not the young man's perspective. Trapped with no way to escape, he had to act.

But did he stop at stealing the documents?

The timing of the two events could not be ignored, for it was difficult to believe that it was mere coincidence: the latenight foray just happening to coincide with the murder. If his grandfather had woken up while he was searching the table, then Clifford might have bashed his head against the table in panic.

Or it might have been a premeditated decision, knowing a man as relentless as Dugmore would not accept being outmaneuvered by his grandson. With his first scheme failing, he would concoct another or try the same one again. The men against whom Clifford had cheated had the same tale to tell and could more likely than not be persuaded to record it again for further compensation.

There really was only one way to stop a man of Dugmore's resources and determination, and Bea wondered if Clifford had the stomach for it. Sleeping, the victim would have looked frail.

Did that vulnerability make him easier or harder to kill?

Standing there, his candle illuminating the narrow gap along the side of the table, he might have realized how effortless it would be. Having never contemplated it before, the idea might have wormed its way insidiously through his consciousness, taunting him with the simplicity of the resolution, as he stared down at the sleeping man.

One bash against the wood and it would all go away.

Again, Bea considered the timing.

AN EXTRAVAGANT DUPLICITY

"How long have you known about the secret compartment?" she asked.

"I just found out!" he exclaimed. "I had no idea the table had a false side until Wednesday night, but once I knew it did, I had to act. It was all I could think about, the letters being in the table, and I could not sit still until they were in my possession. I was so afraid that if I waited, the opportunity would pass. Grandfather would realize in the morning he had not shut the compartment properly and move its contents to another, even more secure place."

"And that is how you found out about it?" she asked.

"Grandfather did not latch it properly, and when I went to his bedchamber to apologize for losing my temper earlier, I noticed the gap between the panel and the table," he said. "It was so shocking, I lost my train of thought and sputtered inelegantly through several sentences. Fortunately, he was too tired to notice."

Given Matthew's derisive description of his cousin's interminable toadying, she was taken aback to learn he had done something requiring an apology. She had assumed he displayed allegiance at all times and seethed silently. "What were you apologizing for?"

Tilting his head down in embarrassment, he admitted that he had called his grandfather a doddering old fool. "But I had just had a walk with Miss Farnsworth that very afternoon, and we were clearly not suited. Her interests were so insipid, and she knew nothing about military history and could not name a single commander of the British Army other than Wellington. I told him only a doddering old fool could think we should make a match of it. And clearly, his mental faculties *were* on the wane. Otherwise, he would never have proposed the match or left a house to Melody or put up with Ripley's nonsense. If he were as sharp as he was even a year ago, he would have sent Ripley packing after his first escapade, not made repeated threats that were ignored. It is infuriating what he is allowed to get away with!"

Bea waited for him to finish his rant and said, "On the night before the murder, you were very angry with him."

"You make it sound so nefarious," he said petulantly, glaring at her with intense dislike, "as if there were something particular about *that* evening. Grandfather was a domineering tyrant who wanted everything his own way and cared not a fig for the hopes and wishes of anyone around him—I was *always* angry with him."

Bea, loath to quarrel with a suspect, refrained from pointing out that it was he who made it sound nefarious. With every word he said, he sharpened his motive for murder.

"And because I was always angry at him," Clifford continued, "I was in effect never angry at him. It was a customary sensation, one I hardly noticed. But it was a mistake to let him see it. I was just ... I was not myself after spending an hour with Miss Farnsworth. For years, I had done everything in my power to please him, even spying on my cousins on his behalf, and it was devastating to have him treat me like the rest of them. I thought he valued my loyalty, that we had formed a partnership of sorts, but in the end it made no difference. I received the same treatment as everyone else. Worse! Jesse was given three options while I was provided with just the one! As angry as I was, I knew if I was to have any hope of evading Miss Farnsworth, then I would have to undo the damage by apologizing for my tantrum. By the time I calmed down and sought him out for an apology, he was in his rooms, readying for bed. That was when I noticed the gap in the table."

"You had been looking for the letters for some time and thought you had finally found them?" she asked.

With a wry twist of the lips, he admitted he had not even

tried. "I knew he would never leave them in a place where I or anyone could find them. The old man was too crafty. That is why I knew I had to act at once. Leaving the latch undone was the first mistake he had ever made, and I had to take advantage of it. There was no time to lose. So I waited until one, when I was sure he would be asleep, and slipped into his room to examine the table. And it was still there, the gap. I was so relieved! I had been terrified Grandfather would realize his mistake and rectify it before I had a chance to save myself."

"So you took your letters and left?" she asked.

Nodding brusquely, he said, "Precisely. I took my letters and scurried from the bedchamber as quickly as possible."

Bea found it difficult to believe he had his hand in his grandfather's storehouse of secrets and did not rummage around even a little. "You did not look at the other documents in the compartment?"

He laughed with genuine amusement, his countenance lightening with mirth. "Your grace, I just said I *scurried* from the bedchamber. Does that strike you as the sort of man who has the constitutional fortitude to linger at his grandfather's bedside and peruse documents? I wanted to get out of the room as quickly as possible, so I found the letters and ran. It was actually rather easy because they were tied together as a single packet."

The explanation made sense. Fearful of being caught in the act of trespassing and larceny, he had expended only the minimum amount of time required to accomplish his goal.

And yet she remained skeptical. "Knowing what you do about your grandfather's penchant for blackmail, you were not tempted to learn what information he held over their heads?"

"I was hugely tempted!" he insisted, his lean visage sharpening with eagerness. "Of course I wanted to know what terrible things the others had done! Matthew is a smug customer, and I would love to be able to knock him down a peg. The pleasure of seeing humiliation or embarrassment on his cocky face would be—"

Clifford shook his head, unable to articulate the joy it would bring him. "But Grandfather was groaning and tossing, and I was terrified that even the light from the lone candle would wake him. I kept imagining his fury if he found me there, on my knees, next to his table, my hand in his secret compartment. I do not know what he would have done, how he would have punished me, but I am certain it would have been devastating. Printing the letters in the dailies would not have been the end of it. He would have done that and worse."

"What about the family name?" she said, recalling Matthew's assertion that Dugmore would never do anything to harm it.

"It meant nothing if he couldn't control it," he replied. "If we could not be brought to heel, then he had no use for us. And our only use for him was enriching the family through advantageous marriages. Knowing how little he valued me, I wasted no time. I just found the papers, secured the latch and left. By the time I returned to my bedchamber, I was shaking like a leaf. It did not stop until after the letters were ash in the fireplace. Then I knew I was safe."

"But were you?" Kesgrave asked thoughtfully. "Or was it only a reprieve? As soon as Dugmore inspected the contents of his compartment, he would know what you had done. By taking only the documents that related to you, you revealed your culpability."

Clifford flinched at the observation, then smiled grimly. "Congratulations, your grace, for being so very clever. You have the advantage over me, for I did not realize that until after I was in bed. Worn to a nub by anxiety, I expected to fall to sleep immediately but instead my mind whirled with speculation. What would happen when Grandfather looked into his cache and found my letters gone? It was only then that I realized how badly I had miscalculated."

Struck by the timing again, Bea reminded herself that his own testimony was the only proof she had that he had made the foray at one in the morning. In actuality, he could have sneaked into the room after Ripley left, especially if it was his second visit, after realizing his mistake. "Did you consider going back for the rest?"

He laughed again, but the sound contained no humor, only contempt. "Not even once! It took all my courage to sneak into the room the first time, and I could not bear the thought of going in there again. You see, that is how little pluck I have! I kept telling myself I should, and yet it seemed foolish to push my luck. So rather than do something, I worried myself into a lather and eventually fell asleep around three. And then I was awakened a few hours later by Matthew making an infernal racket because he could not find his favorite fishing pole. I tried to fall back asleep but was too anxious. I kept picturing the moment Grandfather discovered the theft and tried to decide how I should respond. Deny it? Admit it? Blame it on the servants? Since it was useless, I climbed out of bed even though I was exhausted, and went down to the breakfast room and tried to distract myself with the newspaper. It did not work, but I stayed at it until I heard Mary scream. I am ashamed to admit that when I understood what had happened my first response was relief that he would never know what I had done. And then I was overcome with repugnance for thinking of myself."

Tears sprang to his eyes and he wiped them away with his hands, which were clenched in fists. She did not doubt that his grief was real; she merely wondered at the cause. Killing one's grandfather would inevitably engender strong emotion, including pain and regret.

Sniffling, Clifford apologized for the outburst, which he struggled to contain. "It has been a difficult couple of days. Grandfather's death, then Ripley's antics, then this inconceivable claim that he was murdered. To be completely honest, I have no idea what to think anymore other than to tell you with absolute certainty that my cousins are not capable of this, not even Matthew. I hope you will keep that in mind."

Bea, assuring him that she kept everything in mind, realized he was the only cousin to whom she had spoken to show sadness at Dugmore's death.

Again, that could be remorse or guilt.

She thanked him for his time, and when Clifford suggested they talk to the servants next, explained that they planned to interview Mrs. Gaitskill and her daughter.

"But they are at the home for indigent and orphaned children," he said, as if the establishment was dozens of miles away and not just on the other side of the river. "They take their work very seriously and won't appreciate the interruption. I really think it would be better if you stayed here and talked to the staff."

"Thank you but no," she said firmly.

Although she would never rule out any theory, especially not so early in her process, she knew some things were more probable than others. In this case, it seemed likelier that the perpetrator was one of the half dozen family members the victim was trying to control through coercive means. The fact that so many of them had seemingly irrefutable alibis was an obstacle to that theory, but she had learned from the Mayhew investigation that time was not quite the immutable marker she had thought it was. Events could be manipulated in unexpected ways, and until she was convinced that was not the case here, the family would remain her primary focus.

With that in mind, she directed Jenkins to take her and the duke to Lambeth.

Chapter Ten

Orphan asylums terrified Beatrice Hyde-Clare.

Stricken with grief, overcome with despair, her little fingers clutching the silk of her mother's worn glove, she had been deposited at 19 Portman Square and told how lucky she was.

Repeatedly, the solicitor who had been charged with her transport congratulated her on possessing an aunt and uncle whose generosity was so immense they willingly accepted the endless burden of her presence.

They could have refused, he explained as the carriage traversed the great distance from Ashurst Wood to London, and consigned her to an asylum for orphans.

Over and over, mile after mile, he marveled at her good fortune and cautioned her against indulging in any juvenile behavior that might induce her relatives to reconsider. "You are there on sufferance," he said cheerfully. "So modulate your actions, keep your thoughts to yourself and agree to every request. Do not give them cause to change their mind. Trust me, young lady, you do not want to go to an orphan asylum.

They will starve you and beat you and put you to work in a coal mine."

Five years old and surrounded by strangers, she had taken every single word he said to heart, smothering her anguish, swallowing her anger, until the only thing she was capable of feeling was fear. At night she would lie in bed, her legs curled against her chest, her mind struggling to comprehend the gloomy abyss of a mine, and tell herself how lucky she was.

None of it mattered, how she was treated—her aunt's coldness, her uncle's indifference, her cousin's maliciousness.

She was not starved.

She was not beaten.

She was not consigned to a narrow shaft as black as night.

To their credit, her family never implied that disobedience would be met with expulsion, and although Aunt Vera would sometimes ramble incoherently into praise for her own overweening munificence, her relatives did not require her to be permanently grateful for their charity.

Even so, as an orphan, she could not help but feel as though she had one foot in the asylum and that even the gentlest brush of a shoulder against her own would be enough to push her into it entirely.

Always, always, Bea expected the fall, into the deep, dark abyss.

The fear lessened as she grew older, for she was clever enough to figure out ways to make herself useful and she knew Aunt Vera had come to depend upon her good sense. Scatterbrained and apprehensive, her relative possessed very little of her own. But it was only when Bea learned that she was to have a season like any other genteel young lady of her rank and breeding that she realized she had never been in danger. The asylum was merely the beast at the door whose petrifying growl was revealed to be nothing more than a particularly fierce wind.

Truly, she had had no reason to be afraid.

And yet Bea could not suppress the quiver of disquiet she felt as she contemplated the imposing immensity of Fortescue's Asylum for Pauper Children, its gray towers looming over the landscape and bathing the small rose garden in murk. Everything about the building felt old and ominous, as if it belonged on an isolated cliff somewhere in a Horace Walpole novel.

She was being fanciful, she knew, imagining she was standing before some Gothic bastion, like the castle of Otranto, and yet Kesgrave was struck by it as well. Silently, he examined the menacing structure, his eyes focused on the doorway, where a woman in a poke bonnet had emerged. Tall and thin, her willowy frame swathed in muted colors, she appeared to be a matron, and although Bea and the duke were obviously visitors of wealth and prestige, she did not stop to welcome them.

The inhospitality felt appropriate to the setting.

Straightening her shoulders, Bea said, "We should go in."

Some aspect of her distress must have communicated itself to him because he looked at her then, his eyes slightly surprised. "We should, yes."

Realizing she had unintentionally laid bare the ugliest part of herself—the terrified little girl with nothing to cling to except a thin slip of silk—was embarrassing for Bea. She rarely allowed herself to think about that interminable journey with Mr. Montrose, his jolly cheeks stretched into an overly bright smile as he babbled about deprivations narrowly missed, and was not entirely surprised that recalling it now unnerved her in unexpected ways.

Willfully suppressed memories were always the sharpest.

Seeking to place her disquiet in a larger context, Bea noted that all orphans must fear being deposited in such a sinister-looking home. "One does not have to turn to Gothic literature to find reports of the horrors. Just a few years ago, the *London Daily Gazette* published a series of articles revealing the cruel living conditions in an asylum near Spitalfields Market. The children were whipped regularly and the boys were sent to work in the blacking factory nearby for no pay. And the girls! It does not bear repeating what happened to some of the girls other than to say it was barbaric. I am glad, to be sure, that the *Gazette* exposed the abuse, for it is good to recall the paper has some use other than as an outlet for the despicable Twaddle, but the story made one aware of the extent of the problem, which makes it hard to stand against despair. I am sure not every orphan asylum is a dark pit—this one, for example, must be fine enough if Miss Gaitskill and her mother can bear to spend time here—and yet I cannot shake the sense that the institution itself should be shut down and a new model established. Now *that* is something we should assign to Mr. Stephens. With his meticulous eye for detail and aptitude for solving problems, he would devise a new system in a matter of months. You really should present the idea to him rather than—"

Kesgrave, grasping both her shoulders, said her name sharply, making her realize belatedly that he had been trying to interrupt her speech for some time.

Baffled, she stared up at him, her lips pressed together as she tried to remember what she had been saying.

She could not recall, which was strange, for she had a habit of remembering everything everybody said, not just herself.

Loosening his grip, the duke announced that he was going to say something very upsetting. "I need you to know that I adore you and it is only because I hold you in such high esteem that I am making this highly disturbing remark. Do you understand?"

Bea, observing the sobriety on his face, nodded her head

slowly. She could not imagine what horrible thing he was about to say, and her curiosity outweighed her concern.

Presumably, it pertained to the investigation.

They were in pursuit of a murderer, after all.

Bluntly, he said, "You sound like your aunt."

Startled, she stared at him blankly for a moment before replying with confusion. "My aunt?"

"You are rambling in that disjointed way of hers, veering from one thought to the next without coherence," he said matter-of-factly, his brows drawn tightly in a worried frown. "Having never heard anything like it from you before, I am left to conclude you are unsettled by the prospect of entering an asylum for orphans. You do not have to. You are the Duchess of Kesgrave and short of the royal family, you can summon any person in the country to your home—and even then, you are well within your rights to beckon the Duke of Cumberland and Teviotdale, as my father oversaw his convalescence when he returned from France with grievous injuries he suffered during Battle of Tourcoing, and the Duke of Sussex, who has borrowed liberally from my library. Cumberland and Teviotdale's wife, Frederica, too, is fair game, as well as the princesses who are as yet unmarried: Augusta Sophia, Elizabeth, Mary and Sophia."

He had done it on purpose, Bea knew, descended into pedantry in an effort to quiet her nerves. He knew how much she appreciated his love of precision, for she never missed an opportunity to tease him about it, and as she listened to him list royal family members, she felt the knot in her belly begin to loosen.

No, not loosen, she thought as she contemplated his proposal. It unwound entirely, for the picture he presented was utterly absurd. However much impudence Miss Hyde-Clare did possess—and it was certainly more than either she or her relatives or even Mr. Montrose had ever conceived—it still fell well short of the amount required to demand the presence of any of King George's children, let alone one who stood accused of slaying his own valet.

But the suggestion, for all its ridiculousness, displayed a level of perception she had never anticipated. It was one thing for the duke to understand the emotions she knew she was feeling and quite another for him to comprehend the ones she herself did not.

Profoundly grateful, she nevertheless managed a playful smile and apologized for worrying him unduly. "As the prospect of turning into my aunt Vera is a literal nightmare of mine—and I can remember precisely what I consumed at the meal directly preceding the dream, for I have resolved never to eat sweetbreads again—I can only imagine how troubling the transformation would be for you. But I am recalled to my senses now and prepared to resume our investigation," she said firmly, taking a step toward the gloomy building.

And it was true.

Having overcome her apprehension, she was eager to interview Mrs. Gaitskill and her daughter. The unlikely setting, so inhospitable at first glance, might aid in the questioning by making the respondents impatient to be done.

Impatient people were frequently careless.

Kesgrave, however, deftly seized her arm and tugged her back to his side. Linking his fingers through hers, he gently swept a lock of hair from her forehead and announced that he was not. "Prepared, that is. Although I won't pretend that I did not find your descent into Vera-like babble deeply unnerving, I am more troubled by its cause. Were you placed in an orphan asylum after your parents' death? I had thought you were brought immediately to the Hyde-Clares."

Horrified, Bea tilted her eyes down to examine their clasped hands as color suffused her cheeks.

She appreciated his concern.

Of course she did!

Twenty years in her relatives' home had taught her how easy it was for a husband to brush off his wife's feelings. Uncle Horace did it every day, pretending not to notice Aunt Vera's distress so as not to be required to deal with it. Determinedly, he kept his eyes focused on the thing before him, be it the newspaper or a joint of beef, and feigned obliviousness to the poor woman fretfully wringing her hands.

This response made sense to Bea, for she knew how exhausting it was to navigate her own emotions, and refusing to tend to another person's—especially a female person's—seemed like precisely the sort of privilege men would reserve for themselves. In contrast, Kesgrave was willing to not only address her feelings but also draw them out.

Clearly, he did not consider her anguish to be a bothersome annoyance.

It was a reassuring trait in a husband, to be sure, but all she could think was how wretched she must look to have elicited his concern. A month ago she had stood without flinching across from a vicious brute who had battered so many people to death with a hammer he had earned the nickname the Bludgeon. A few weeks before that she had driven a magnifying glass into the eye of a vengeful earl to repel his attack.

Again and again, she had confronted genuine threats.

And yet it was this grim building, this hulking gray edifice, with its worn stones, dark turrets, and haunting allusions to an alternate history, that eviscerated her.

Nothing happened.

It was precisely as Kesgrave said: She had gone from her father's home to her uncle's house. Her material comfort never waned. Her sense of security faltered, yes, but she was provided with food and shelter.

She had not suffered at all.

The fear she felt now was a remnant, a vestige of a little girl's terror.

It was a figment then, Bea thought, and it is a figment now.

But somehow it leveled her.

Irritated by her unwarranted fragility, she tried to think of a lighthearted reply that would change the subject and demonstrate her insouciance.

It could not be the warships.

Randomly dropping the *Goliath* or *Majestic* into a conversation that had nothing to do with either would be an obvious ploy. Kesgrave would see through it immediately.

Her response had to be relevant to the topic under consideration.

Further exceptions among the royal family?

That would work nicely, she thought, and attempted to recall the name of one of the Hanover cousins. It could not be difficult, for King George had eight siblings and there were dozens of relatives racketing about in the family tree.

And yet she drew a blank.

Consequently, she turned her attention to the grandchildren.

The problem was the third generation was remarkably threadbare. Of the king's considerable brood, only Prinny had produced any issue—and just the one daughter at that—unless one counted children born on the wrong side of the blanket.

Was it even fair to describe the offspring as such when Prince Augustus Frederick wed Lady Augusta Murray in St. George's Hanover Square?

Well, yes, because the king had not given his consent, which made the marriage null and void. The proviso was plainly laid out in the *Royal Marriages Act* of 1772.

"Bea?" Kesgrave said softly, his grip on her hand

tightening.

At the increased pressure on her fingers, she blinked in surprise and realized she had not spoken for several seconds.

Or was it a few minutes?

The fact that she could not identify just how long the duke had been waiting for a reply was disconcerting and strange. Usually she was able to think and speak at the same time. Various ideas flew through her head as words, sometimes directly related, sometimes only tangentially, emerged from her mouth.

And now she was silent.

The faint heat in her cheeks intensified.

With wry amusement, she wondered if this befuddled inadequacy was what Aunt Vera felt all the time.

Smiling faintly, she raised her eyes to his and answered his query without evasion or distraction. "I was taken directly to my uncle's house and never suffered the deprivations of an asylum. It was something I did not have to worry about, being deposited on the doorstep of a place like this, but as a child I did not know that. And even if I had been assured of my place within my new family, I would not have considered it secure. My parents had died in a tragic accident. Who was to say it would not happen again? And if my aunt and uncle were killed suddenly, then where would I go? Who would take me in next? There could not be an endless supply of relatives willing to be saddled with a penniless orphan."

In fact, she had not been penniless. Her parents had left her a modest fortune in the form of bonds and shares in valuable companies. But that was also something she did not know as a child.

"So it loomed in the distance, always on the horizon, waiting for me," she continued, gently disentangling her fingers from his as she turned to examine the tall structure. It was really rather benign, with its classical architecture, symmetrical and even, and its gardens struggling to bloom in the weak light of the damp spring. "And something about this building made it real. Briefly, it felt as though the moment I had dreaded my entire life had finally arrived."

Bea expected the confession to deepen her embarrassment, but she felt only relief at being able to articulate her response coherently. The sudden descent into dull-wittedness had been disquieting for her, and she took comfort in the specificity of the circumstance. One was hardly ever confronted with the embodiment of every childhood fear all at once.

Kesgrave, standing beside her so closely his shoulder brushed hers, silently appraised the building for several seconds before speaking. "I will not pretend the insecurities of my childhood are equal to yours, but I will attest to the strange fits and starts of the mind. I once screamed in terror at a meat pie."

Assuming he would offer a bolstering platitude in response, for really what else could one say in reply to such an admission, she was nonetheless unsurprised by this comment. Kesgrave rarely resorted to banalities. "A meat pie?" she asked, tilting her head to glance at him curiously.

"A steak and kidney pie to be precise," he said briskly. "It was during my first week at Eton, while I was still trying to establish myself as an out-and-outer, so you can imagine what shrieking at the sight of a pastry did for my reputation."

"I am sure it secured it," she said confidently.

His lips twitched in confirmation. "Had I not been the future duke, Hartlepool and the fellows would still be calling me Kidney Cry to this day. As it was, it lasted several months."

Bea giggled at the epithet, for she appreciated a well-constructed taunt, and wondered what Mr. Twaddle-Thum would do with the information.

Promptly resurrect it, she decided, not as troubled by the prospect as a fond spouse ought to have been. It was merely that she had endured several weeks of being addressed as Her Outrageousness in print, and it struck her as unfair that the duke had so far escaped the indignity.

The rapacious gossip had been oddly slow in bestowing a sobriquet.

"And what was it about this particular steak and kidney pie that upset you?" she asked. "Did it contain chunks of pineapple?"

Now Kesgrave laughed and retook her hand. "I assure you, the kitchen at Eton never prepared anything as culinarily daring as André's wondrous creations. Everything was always the simplest version of the recipe, including this particular steak and kidney pie, which is almost enough to make anyone scream in horror. If I remember correctly, the kidneys were crunchy. But the reason I screamed was it looked exactly like the pie that almost killed my nanny. Dear Uncle Miles had poisoned it, you see, but Nestor—he was the head groom—had snuck me apple tarts all afternoon so I was not hungry for dinner. Rallie was famished and kidney pie was her favorite, so she ate it. She had barely finished it before her stomach began to churn most violently and she doubled over in pain. I do not recall how old I was when it happened, possibly five, maybe even four. It had slipped my mind, but something about the look of the Eton kidney pie brought it back and in that moment I could hear the horrible gurgling sound Rallie's stomach had made. So I screamed my head off."

Kesgrave did not have to pretend the insecurities of his childhood were equal to hers, Bea thought, because in fact they were so much worse. She had been benignly neglected; he had been deliberately abused.

There was no comparison.

Furious again at his uncle for trying to harm him and his father for allowing it to happen, she regretted more than ever that they were dead. She longed with every fiber in her being to pummel them both with her bare fists.

Like Marlow, she thought, picturing the brute boxer whom the dowager duchess had hired to protect the young dukeling.

She wondered if he ever had the opportunity to land one decisive blow.

"You were how old—thirteen, maybe twelve?" she asked, finding the idea of a caterwauling Kesgrave at once difficult to conceive and incredibly easy to picture. "And away from everything familiar for the first time?"

Kesgrave smiled faintly. "You are trying to excuse my behavior."

"Not excuse," she said. "Explain. Given those two conditions, I think it's reasonable that a vague recollection would burst suddenly into a detailed memory. And given the awe with which all of the beau monde holds you, I can only assume you achieved out-and-outer status quickly enough."

"I challenged the boy with the best seat in the college to a race and rode neck or nothing over the jumps," he said. "I won handily, mostly because Kingsley's horse clipped the first hedge and took a moment to recover his balance. The lower master was most displeased with us and we both took a beating."

He said it so casually, so coolly, as if receiving several wallops on his bare buttocks with a birch rod did not merit even a grimace, and she realized how thoroughly mundane brutality was for him.

At home, at school—it was everywhere.

Ardently, she said, "I do not care if it's tradition. I will not send my son to Eton or Harrow or any college that answers high-spirited behavior with corporal punishment. It is barbaric."

He rejected the notion.

It was apparent, yes, in the way he tightened his shoulders and pressed his lips together, as if to hold back some snide comment, and seeing it, Bea felt her stomach tense.

No, it did more than that.

Her stomach curled into a knot so tight she was unable to draw breath for several seconds because his response was everything she had feared.

Tradition was exerting its pull.

Eton was the bellwether, the first in a long line of archaic institutions that would prevail.

Although she stiffened in anticipation of a harsh reply, he offered no correction or objection. Instead, he advised her with amused condescension to focus her rhetorical vigor on an actual problem, such as convincing him to commission a pair of boots on her behalf with Hoby. "You do not need to wear yourself out with hypotheticals."

It was an infuriating answer—smug, patronizing, laden with centuries of superiority—and yet she would have responded calmly if they had been anywhere else. If they had been in the library at Kesgrave House or even the back parlor, which was reserved for interviews with murderers, she would have replied with aggressive civility, returning contempt for disdain.

But she was not there.

No, she was *here,* in the shadow of a Gothic monstrosity, besieged with fears she did not know she possessed and beset with anxieties that were worse than she had feared, her emotions heightened to an unbearable pitch, and she snapped, "It is not a hypothetical!"

He reared.

Like a horse encountering a wolf or a fence that was too high, Kesgrave pulled back abruptly.

And he gasped

Drawing a deep, rattly breath, the Duke of Kesgrave stared at her utterly flummoxed.

It did not last long.

Bea barely had time to call herself a daft rattlepate before he shook off his astonishment and glared at her with disgruntlement.

"You wretched girl!" he said on a bewildered laugh. "How *dare* you do this to me! We are in the front garden of an orphan asylum in the middle of a murder investigation. I cannot *conceive* of any worse moment to tell me you are increasing."

But there was delight now in his expression, a giddy happiness in his eyes, and she clenched her left hand to try to contain her own pleasure at his pleasure. He was right, after all. They were in a field in the middle of the day for anyone to see, and it would never do for her to tackle him there.

His dignity had suffered enough.

"Why am I surprised?" he asked with a glint of wonder. "I should not be surprised. You proposed to me while sitting on the chest of a killer. Your making the revelation in an appropriate location—that would be the shocking thing. Even this setting is rather mundane for you. I suppose I should just be grateful you did not tell me while we were in the middle of apprehending a culprit. I can see you aiming your flintlock at a suspect, saying with maddening nonchalance, 'By the bye, your grace, I am with child,' and shooting."

Bea, tightening her fist because the impulse to tackle him was so strong, said, "That is fascinating because I *cannot* imagine it, as Prosser still has not let me get off a single shot with a loaded gun and it has been four weeks. I do wish you would talk to him."

She had made this comment to lighten the moment because there was something painful about the unholy glint in his eyes. Like staring at the sun, it hurt to look directly at it, so she tried to avert her gaze with levity. Even so, it was a sincere complaint. After so many weeks of lessons, she was as intimately acquainted with the weapon's recoil as any human could be, and she had asked him repeatedly to communicate her readiness to use gunpowder to her instructor.

It did not work, however.

Far from easing the situation, the introduction of the familiar debate served only to intensify it, for suddenly she found herself wrapped in his arms, his lips pressed against hers in gross indifference to their surroundings: the hundreds of windows overlooking the garden, the scores of children, the dozens of servants.

Just a few minutes ago, the willowy matron had strolled up the walk.

Where was she now?

Bea did not care.

Good God, she could not have cared less if Mr. Twaddle-Thum himself caught sight of them entwined in the front garden of Fortescue's Asylum for Pauper Children, and she succumbed to the heartrendingly tender kiss. It baffled her that something so sweet could cause a swirl of emotions, and even as he lifted his head, she pressed her body closer.

"Are you well?" he asked softly. "Do you have any symptoms? Are you eating enough? Do you need more sleep? Are your ankles swollen? Are you chilly? Are you queasy? Do you need to sit down?"

The flurry of questions undermined whatever good sense she had left, for it revealed how bemused he still was, and although she had thought to give a satirical reply about pulling up a comfortable toadstool like in a fairy story, she instead succumbed to the impulse to kiss him again.

Chapter Eleven

❦

Melody Gaitskill resembled her brother in appearance—same brown hair, jutting chin and appealing eyes—but her disposition varied wildly and she greeted them with seemingly sincere warmth.

"I know you are here to question me and my mother about Grandfather's death," she said as she strolled down the long corridor to meet them. They had been asked to wait by the entrance while one of the maids fetched Miss Gaitskill from the painting parlor. Their claim to be the Duke and Duchess of Kesgrave had been treated with both awe and suspicion. "We should adjourn to the front parlor so that we may talk about matters in private, but I would much rather give you a tour of the asylum. Although we are on fine financial footing, thanks to Lady Petersham, who is our patroness, we could always use more funds. The more money we have, the more children we can help. Alas, London does not want for orphans. The best we can hope to do is keep them out of the workhouse until they are grown."

Although Bea was sympathetic to her plight, she accepted the first option. "It is better suited to our purpose."

AN EXTRAVAGANT DUPLICITY

"I imagine it is," Melody conceded, leading them down the hallway. "It is challenging to conduct any conversation with children underfoot. They are so rambunctious! That is why we have so many classes for them. We try to keep them occupied while equipping them with the skills they need to stay *out* of the workhouse. I teach music and drawing. I am not particularly adept at either, but I possess enough understanding of both to provide foundational principles. I find my art classes to be especially rewarding. At the moment we are studying the classics by re-creating them. It helps the children grasp the basics of art while familiarizing them with its magnificent history. Currently, they are working on Rembrandt's *The Night Watch*."

The inside of the building lacked the elaborate features of the exterior, with unadorned white walls and concrete floors, and the room to which Miss Gaitskill led them was a simple square with practical furniture.

"Please do sit down," she said, indicating to a quartet of wood chairs near the window, their seats decorated with embroidered cushions that were too thin to provide any comfort. "Please make yourself at home. I have asked my mother to join us so she should be here soon, and of course the head matron of the asylum will look in as well. She is also hopeful of engaging your interest."

As Bea was not yet accustomed to being valued for her wealth, her body grew warm at this information and she tilted her eyes toward the window. It looked out onto the lawn where she and the duke had embraced and, wondering how many people had observed them, she felt her embarrassment deepen.

Kesgrave, ascertaining the name of the head matron, said he would be pleased to meet Mrs. Chaffey. "And we will be happy to accompany her on a brief tour after our interview."

"You are too kind," Melody murmured as she herself sat

down. "I feel dreadful about taking advantage of your presence, knowing as I do the circumstances that bring you here. I loved my grandfather tremendously and am enraged at the thought of someone deliberately harming him. He was a tough old campaigner, very stubborn and set in his ways, but also open to reason. Clifford says it is one of the servants, but I cannot believe any one of them would harm Grandfather. He was a good employer—exacting but fair."

As Dugmore had ceded to his granddaughter's wishes, Bea was not surprised to learn she held a more favorable opinion of him than her cousins. Consequently, she asked Melody if she *could* believe it of her family.

Despite the provocation, the girl responded with amusement, scrunching her nose as if she smelled something slightly foul and saying, "It is horrible, isn't it? I am a very terrible person because I would not be at all surprised if my brother did it. Matthew is a perfect beast. He cares not a whit for people, only the number of fish he can catch or birds he can shoot. The fact that he does both with alacrity underscores his general indifference to life. We are all God's creatures, are we not, your graces, trout and grouse as much as human beings? I am certain my brother could have knocked Grandfather over without thinking about it twice."

"Melody!" A woman shrieked in the hallway, her brown hair speckled liberally with gray and her chin narrowing almost to a point. "How can you speak of your brother like that? He is a fine, upstanding young man who loves his family and respects the sanctity of all life."

Trilling airily at her mother's distress, Melody said, "Oh, pooh, Mama. The duchess asked if I believed Matthew *could* harm Grandfather, not if he *did*. You know as well as I do that he is a fiend. He cares only for his own comfort and enjoyment and damn the rest. You yourself have said it dozens of times."

"I have, yes," Mrs. Gaitskill replied with a tight smile as she lowered herself into the fourth chair, "but to you, not to people outside our family and certainly not to members of the nobility. I hope you will forgive my daughter for her frankness and take everything she says to you with a grain of salt. She loves her brother, but like all siblings there are long-standing resentments between them that inevitably color her opinions. As their mother, I can assure you they are both too kind and decent to hurt anyone, let alone my father."

"Well, then, that resolves the matter, doesn't it? The word of a fond parent is all the duchess needs to remove Matthew and me from consideration as suspects," Melody said, her tone gently mocking. Then she laughed as she shook her head. "You know it is not that simple. You have read the descriptions of the duchess's thorough investigations in Mr. Twaddle-Thum's column. She requires proof of our innocence, not testimonials of our characters."

But her mother objected, asserting with quiet dignity that she never read the *Gazette*'s infamous gossip. "Nor any other reporter who resorts to rank speculation at the expense of good, honest facts."

"Hogwash!" Melody said, rolling her eyes to comical effect at the pious display. "Mama reads Twaddle religiously. We both do! And then we sit in the drawing room and have the most cheerful coze about its contents. She is just trying to make a good impression on you because of your rank. She cannot help herself. After so many years of serving as my grandfather's hostess and endearing herself to his guests, it is an automatic response."

Although Mrs. Gaitskill could not like this revelation, her expression remained placid as she looked at her daughter and said, "*You* are the fiend."

Her daughter laughed. "No, I am just trying to be helpful—precisely as *you* taught me. Lying to the duchess and her husband will accomplish nothing and only reduce the likelihood of their providing financial support to Fortescue's. We cannot make a good impression if we do not make an honest one."

The other woman agreed in theory but insisted that a judicious editing of one's comments was an act of civility, not dishonesty. "Regardless, you boldly announcing your brother murdered his grandfather is more harmful to the financial well-being of this institution than any white lie I could tell. Given Fortescue's unfortunate history of corruption—many years in the past but you know how these things can cast a long shadow," she added, darting a look that was at once awkward and apologetic at Bea, "we cannot allow any hint of scandal to be attached to it."

Although Bea could not speak to the specific depravity that had bedeviled an earlier incarnation of the asylum, she knew institutions of its kind were generally given to acts of immorality. The young and innocent were always the easiest to exploit, and finding genuinely charitable individuals to oversee their care was particularly challenging. It did not help that the positions were rarely well compensated.

Chiding her mother for making yet another false statement, Melody reiterated that she had not said her brother *had* done it. "Again, I said he *could* have done it. There is a significant difference in the two statements. But even that *could* is theoretical because in this case he actually could not have done it. Matthew left the house before Grandfather was killed. Several of the servants saw him drive away in the company of Mr. Hogan. There is no way he murdered our grandfather."

Mrs. Gaitskill was only slightly mollified by this explanation, for it exonerated her son of a heinous crime on what was at bottom a technicality—hardly the fervent endorsement of decency one desired for one's progeny. "I think Clifford has it right. You should be looking to the servants. The notion that any member of the family would harm my father is preposterous. We all held him in high esteem and valued his thoughtful input in our lives."

Her daughter chortled and said, "What a plumper, Mama! Grandfather was an officious old biddy and you know that as well as anyone. He always was, even when he was young, marrying you and your sisters off as soon as you turned of age."

Blushing at the candor in her daughter's voice, Mrs. Gaitskill nevertheless held her composure and defended her father's right to display concern for his family. "I fear my daughter has a flair for dramatics, which may lead you to misunderstand her feelings. She loved her grandfather despite what she says."

Readily, Melody agreed. "I loved him dearly but that does not mean I could not see him for what he was, which was a darling *and* a brute. He was quite without a conscience. But before you begin to wonder if *I* might have killed him, let me put your mind at ease. I was here, at the asylum, looking after Aggie, a sick little girl who is now on the mend. She had a terrible infection and her fever spiked as I sat with her. We were all very concerned. Mama even thought we might lose her in the night. You can confirm this with the head matron, Mrs. Chaffey. She looked in on me a few times to see how Aggie was faring."

"I will, yes, thank you," Bea said before announcing she had other information to confirm with the head matron as well. And since she was uncertain whether the girl knew about her grandfather's machinations, she leaned forward in her chair to watch her reaction as she explained. "According to a letter from Mrs. Chaffey that we found in your grandfather's room, she agreed to release you from your duties here in exchange for a generous donation."

Melody bounded to her feet. "The devil you say!"

Her mother gasped in dismay and ordered the girl to mind her tongue. "You are in the presence of a duke!"

The words went unheeded as Melody marched from the room, and Mrs. Gaitskill, further humiliated by her daughter's want of conduct, apologized for the horrendous behavior. "She is shocked to discover Mrs. Chaffey made such an agreement without telling her. They have a very cordial relationship, and she would consider this a betrayal of sorts."

Bea found it curious that Mrs. Gaitskill placed the blame for her daughter's anger squarely on the head matron's shoulders. "You do not think she is shocked to discover her grandfather made the arrangement behind her back?"

"Arranging things is what my father did: marriages for me and my sisters, positions for the servants, even a lease for the fishmonger so that he could move to a more convenient location," she said without any resentment. "It was a compulsion for him, and I could see no point in getting upset about it. Melody understood that. She is too clever to rail against something she cannot change. But she has given her all to this organization, including spending a sleepless night in a hard wooden chair to comfort a sick child, and the least Mrs. Chaffey can do is be honest with her."

When put in those terms, Melody's response seemed suitable, and yet Bea was still puzzled by Dugmore's treatment of his granddaughter. Why work to undermine her independence on one hand and bolster it on the other?

"Arranging things is what my father did," Mrs. Gaitskill said again in response. "He wanted Melody to marry and have children like my eldest, Dora, but he also recognized her limitations and wanted to make sure she was taken care of in the unlikely event he could not see her settled with a husband. I am sure that as soon as he extricated her from her obligations here, he intended to present her with a marital prospect more to her liking than Mr. Coombes. Melody is a trifle on the old side at twenty-one but hardly on the shelf. She could still make a match of it."

"Mr. Coombes?" Bea asked.

"A widower with whom my father sought to pair her," she explained, her lips pressed together in a disapproving frown. "It was not the most politic choice for her, as he is more than twice her age. He seems kind enough and possesses the means to provide lavishly for her but is hardly the dashing figure of which a young girl dreams. It was a misstep, putting Melody's back up in a way my father had not intended, and although she has always been devoted to her work at Fortescue's, she redoubled her commitment after he proposed the match. It was just that Mr. Coombes was so much older than she, and now Melody is quite firmly set against marriage in general, and I think my father understood how grievously he had erred. Paltry House was his way of making amends. Is the gesture a little on the sentimental side?" Mrs. Gaitskill shrugged her shoulders. "He was growing older."

Struck by the disparity in their ages, which was not reflected in any of the other matches Dugmore proposed, Bea asked how Mrs. Gaitskill felt about her father's high-handedness. "Melody is your daughter and if you have no objection to her spending time at the asylum, what right does he have to pair her with a man old enough to be her father?"

"You think I should be outraged by his presumption," Mrs. Gaitskill said with a shake of her head. "The truth is, I was grateful for his interest. Their own father had been generally indifferent to their existence before finally doing himself in with a dull pitchfork. The constable told a reporter for the county newspaper that he had been set upon by thieves in the field, but the truth was he was stumbling around drunk in the stables and fell. Thankfully, Melody takes after me in her practical outlook and sober-mindedness.

She knows that my father wanted only what was best for her and as far as he was concerned that meant marriage and children. He had many notions that now seem a bit antiquated. That was why he settled on Mr. Coombes in the first place. He thought all women need an experienced hand to guide them."

Before Bea could ask if those antiquated notions also included blackmail, Melody strode into the room trailed by a woman in a plain gray dress and sturdy shoes. "There is no cause for alarm, Emily has explained it all to me. She felt there was no point in raising the matter until she had the money in hand, and once she did, she planned to refer me to a sister organization near Spitalfields Market so that I could continue in my work."

"Well, that is a bit of a dirty trick," Mrs. Gaitskill said disapprovingly. "I had expected better from you, Emily."

Untroubled by the criticism, the matron shrugged her considerable shoulders and said, "When you conduct your business in an underhanded manner, you expose yourself to dirty tricks."

Melody clapped in appreciation, then rushed to make the introductions as Bea and the duke rose to their feet.

"This is an honor indeed," Mrs. Chaffey said, dipping into a curtsy, "for I have followed your career, your grace, and find your public spiritedness to be admirable. To give so much of your time to righting injustice when you could be attending fêtes and balls!"

It was, Bea thought, a disconcerting remark because the only reason she conducted her investigations was she found them highly gratifying and it seemed wrong to cast her own satisfaction as generosity.

Nevertheless, she murmured thank you and asked Mrs. Chaffey if she would mind answering a few questions.

"Mind?" she echoed with an air of confusion. "Who could

object to assisting the course of justice? I am happy to help you in any way I can. I will start off by affirming for you what Miss Gaitskill just said: I had indeed entered into a secret agreement with Mr. Dugmore to turn out his granddaughter without notice. And I was particularly ruthless during the negotiation over the price because the roof in the west wing has sprung a leak and I am desperate to fix it without asking the board of governors for more money. It seemed like the perfect solution, and I am sorry that Mr. Dugmore died before we had completed the transaction."

"I am too," Melody said, "for I would have loved to have seen his expression when he realized he had been bamboozled."

"Melody!" her mother cried. "Please, a little respect for the dead."

"You know I adored the old thing," Melody said fondly. "But this time he overstepped and deserved to be swindled."

"Not swindled," Mrs. Chaffey corrected, "outplayed. He should have put more conditions on his donation. I thought it might be an improving lesson for him."

Mrs. Gaitskill smiled wanly at this observation and said she very much doubted it. "My father was singularly immune to improvement. Like most men his age, he was very set in his ways. But that is neither here nor there. I would like to thank you, Emily, for your efforts on behalf of my daughter, and would request that if a situation like this one should arise again, you will consult with me before acting."

Alas, Mrs. Chaffey could not make such a pledge, for the roofs were so very fickle and could decide at any moment to admit torrents of rain to the upper story. "I know you understand because I have seen you move around the buckets in the hallways."

As her mother sought a reply, Melody asked Mrs. Chaffey

to confirm her presence on the night of the murder. "That is the other piece of information the duchess needs from you."

"You mean the evening you stayed here to nurse poor Agatha Johnson?" the head matron asked. "Yes, I can attest to that. Miss Gaitskill passed the whole night by her bedside. She would not allow me or one of the other matrons to relieve her even though we assured her the situation was not that dire. She was just so worried about her. That was why she took the unprecedented step of staying overnight."

"You say it was not dire and yet her little body was wracked with coughs and tremors," Melody said reprovingly, "How could I leave her?"

Mrs. Chaffey nodded her head in approbation and said to Mrs. Gaitskill, "You see—she is an absolute gem. I had to do something to ensure she could continue with her good works. There are so many children in need of love."

The girl's mother could not disagree with either part of the statement, for she knew not only that orphans wanted affection but also that her daughter was eager to supply it. She had made a similar observation scarcely ten minutes before, and Bea wondered if Mrs. Gaitskill was genuinely at peace with the possibility of her younger daughter dwindling into an old maid.

It seemed unlikely—that was, based on what she had said about her daughter's kind and gentle heart. If she truly wanted Melody to marry and have her own children, then how did she feel about her father providing the girl with a living in his will?

She would be against it.

But how against it, Bea wondered, and then marveled at the incoherent direction her thoughts had gone. If Mrs. Gaitskill did not want her daughter to inherit a plot of land, then killing her father was the exact opposite way to go about it. Her objective would be more favorably met if Dugmore lived long enough to accomplish his goal of thwarting her charity work and arranging her nuptials.

Unable to ascribe a motivation to Mrs. Gaitskill, Bea had enough experience with killers to realize that was not central to her project. The *why* was always the least significant part of the investigation. The far more important consideration was viability: Could this person have done it? If the answer was yes, then they were included among her suspects. If there was simply no way for them to have committed the murder, then their motive was irrelevant. They were not on the list.

Realizing she had not ascertained Mrs. Gaitskill's movements on the morning in question, Bea asked her to account for them now. "Or were you still abed?"

"Still abed at six-thirty?" Melody replied with a sly trickle. "Mama never sleeps past six, for there is always so much for her to do. Let's see, Grandfather died on a Thursday. That means Mama was in Mrs. Keene's office from six-thirty to eight-thirty deciding on the menus for the week and reviewing every item in the budget down to Grandfather's nightly cup of chocolate. I do not even have to be in the house to know that is where Mama was because it is where she is every Thursday. Mrs. Keene will confirm it, as will all the kitchen maids and most of the footmen. My mother can no more be considered a suspect than myself or my brother. I believe Clifford and Jesse can likewise provide solid alibis. As I told you, no one in the family could have done this horrid thing."

And yet one person's name was prominent in its absence: Ripley.

Kesgrave, noting it as well, asked if she thought the viscount was capable of murder, as she had failed to attribute an alibi to him.

Taken aback by the question, Melody appeared genuinely uncertain how to respond. "I want to say no because he is a flibbertigibbet, but that does not seem fair to him. He is a grown man, even if he acts like an unruly child, and as such he deserves the same consideration as Matthew or I. So, yes, I do think he is capable of murder."

But she lilted her voice upward at the end, so it came out more like a question than a declaration, and her mother, registering the same sense of injustice, insisted that of course the viscount could kill someone, especially if his victim was old and frail like his grandfather.

"Which is not to say that he could murder only someone who is weak and sickly," Mrs. Gaitskill quickly added in her nephew's defense. "He is lately arrived from the country, where men frequently lift large bales of hay and sheep, so I think he could murder someone who is not enfeebled."

"And he's been taking lessons with Gentleman Jackson," her daughter pointed out. "There is that too."

Mrs. Gaitskill, nodding firmly, held that this was true. "Ripley goes two or three times per week. I am sure with his training he is capable of killing all sorts of people if he puts his mind to it. But there are limits. He is not like Matthew, whose strength and skill are undeniable."

Her tone ringing with maternal pride, she stopped just shy of boasting of her son's ability to slaughter entire battalions of soldiers. Melody, seemingly aware of the danger, gave a subtle shake of her head, which caused her mother to flinch and tilt her eyes down. Both women fell silent.

Mrs. Chaffey, sensing an opportunity—or hoping to interrupt an awkward interval—suggested that now might be a good time for a tour of the facility. "I know you will be impressed with how happy and well taken care of our children are."

Although Bea felt a tremor of alarm at the thought of going deeper into the belly of the beast, she consented to the plan. "Just one moment, please. I want first to ask Mrs. Gait-

AN EXTRAVAGANT DUPLICITY

skill about shutting up her father's room so completely she did not allow the maid to finish cleaning it. I find that very curious."

"For shame, Celia," the head matron said chidingly. "Allowing your emotions to get in the way of the servants doing their job!"

Mrs. Gaitskill flushed lightly as she acknowledged the immoderateness of her reaction. "I realized right away that evicting Mary from the bedchamber was excessive and am embarrassed by my response. But I was just so furious at Matthew and Ripley for bickering over the room as if my father had merely returned to the country and was not lying under a sheet in the cellar. Of all the acts of disrespect! By rights the room should go to Matthew, but I hate the thought of rewarding his terrible behavior, for he should have known better. And Ripley—well, as Melody said, he's a flibbertigibbet. I do not expect him to behave with any decorum, and he will kick up such a fuss when I give the room to Matthew. And as the thought of listening to him whine about it makes my already frayed nerves vibrate, I decided it was easier to just keep the door shut. The season will be over soon enough and they can resume arguing about it next year."

Mrs. Chaffey hailed this solution as sensible, although she thought it would be prudent to permit the staff to perform their duties if for no other reason than the room should be aired out regularly, then suggested they start with the dormitories. She led them up a narrow staircase to the third floor. As the top step was slick with rain from a shower earlier in the day, Mrs. Chaffey cautioned them to walk carefully and lamented the deplorable state of the roof.

Every bedroom, it seemed, suffered from the same deficiency, and they were advised to step around, over and through eleven puddles. Despite the pools of water, the dormitories were clean and tidy, with neat rows of beds draped with woolen blankets in good condition. Not a single one was threadbare, and in the center of each bed, its head resting against the pillow, was a doll. Their forms varied—dog, cat, goat, sheep, pig, mouse, elephant—as well as their quality, and Ms. Chaffey explained that the children made the dolls themselves.

"It is the first thing we do when a new resident is brought to us," she said. "We ask the girl or boy what their favorite animal is and then they make a doll in its image. We call them talismans."

It seemed decent enough, Fortescue's treatment of its young residents, but Bea could not stop searching for evidence of cruelty.

The pristine beds, for example.

They looked so lovely, one after the other, their gray blankets tucked cleanly in the corners, and yet she saw something menacing in the perfection: a harsh and tyrannical precision that could be achieved only by ruthless repetition.

As the tour progressed, as they left the leaky third floor for the less soggy second and observed lessons from the hallway, Bea felt some of her cynicism fall away. The children appeared genuinely content, both at ease in their surroundings and lack of reluctance to speak up. One girl, about ten years old, interrupted her teacher to correct her addition—Miss Falk had failed to incorporate the one from the left column—and received a prompt thank you for her attention to detail. The children in the art room were garrulous but productive, and Bea, inspecting a dozen copies of *The Night Watch* made with varying levels of skill, was amused to note that one of the students had re-created the work down to the artist's signature. Comparing Rembrandt's mark to George's rendition of it, she could not tell the difference.

Clearly delighted by the fourteen-year-old's accomplishments, Melody invited them to gush in admiration over some of the less adept paintings by the younger pupils, fearful that their tender feelings might be hurt by the lack of attention.

Noting her thoughtfulness, Bea decided Mrs. Gaitskill's assessment of her daughter's skill with children was on the mark.

Chapter Twelve

By the time they returned to their carriage a half hour later, Bea was willing to concede that Fortescue's might indeed be the lone orphan asylum that treated its charges with kindness and did not seek to exploit their labor.

"Assuming their eagerness to show off their various projects to prominent visitors can be considered a reliable measure of happiness, and I rather suspect it can," she added as they crossed the wide lawn. "If they were abused or ruled by fear, I do not think they would have been so comfortable with us."

Kesgrave, hailing Jenkins, who jumped down from the driver's bench as they approached, agreed with her assessment. "Mrs. Chaffey oversees an orderly and benevolent establishment."

"And yet I cannot help wondering if it is perhaps *too* orderly," Bea murmured thoughtfully as she climbed into the carriage. "You noticed, I am sure, how immaculately the dormitories are turned out. Each bed was as perfect as the one before it. Can such a condition be achieved without a severe reprisal for failure? I am not saying she takes a whip to the children to get them to conform, but I cannot rule out some sort of psychological pressure. It seems as though—"

Her musing was cut off, however, by Kesgrave, who, the moment the carriage door was shut behind him, tugged her into his arms and pressed his lips softly against hers. Slowly, sweetly, he deepened the kiss, his hands moving searchingly across her body until his fingers rested against her stomach.

Ah, yes, *that,* Bea thought in amusement as she recalled the dazzling impropriety of her announcement. She still could not believe she had been so impudent as to inform the duke of his impending fatherhood in the front garden of a home for orphaned children.

All that dallying, all that worrying, all that dithering about the best way to tell him—and then to just blab it out!

Kesgrave did not seem to mind.

The stunning indecorum did not appear to bother him at all as he pulled her closer, his lips impossibly gentle as they moved over hers.

Bea felt her bones weaken, and her heart fluttered languidly as the ache of desire began to wend its way through her body. Leaning forward, she sought to deepen the kiss, to quench the wild craving that sparked and spiked, but he raised his head. Silently, he contemplated her in the changing light of the swaying carriage. Seconds passed, perhaps a minute, as he studied her with his gorgeous blue eyes, as cerulean as the summer sky, solemn and serious.

Finally, he spoke. "But truly, how do you feel?"

It was, Bea thought, an appropriate query and one that should have been easy to answer. Physically, she felt well. The bout of nausea that seemed to strike the moment she climbed out of bed in the morning was reliably quelled with a slice of plain toast, and the late-afternoon wave of fatigue that occasionally overcame her was a welcome invitation to retire to her office for rout cake enjoyment and to read for an hour.

And yet it was not simple, not really, for the minor alterations in her body were the least of her condition and it was the mental burden that presented the lion's share of her discomfort.

How did she feel?

The more useful question to ask would be: How did she *not* feel, for she was overwhelmed with quite an alarming mix of emotions.

To be sure, she was giddy.

Having been denied the ineffable comforts of maternal affection, she was joyfully bemused at the prospect of becoming a mother herself.

She could hardly wait to smother her own child in love.

But she was terrified too—and for the very same reason. Incapable of recalling the ineffable comfort of maternal affection, she did not know the first thing about caring for a child. Aunt Vera and Uncle Horace were her only examples, and neither one could be considered an encouraging template.

All she had learned from them was what not to do, for every decision they made to further her welfare had only deepened her misery.

And yet she was also relieved.

Oh, yes, she was hugely relieved to discover that she *could* get with child because the ability to procreate was not assured, not for any woman, and for much of her adult life she had considered the matter far less than most women.

Indeed, given how little attention she had paid to her own fecundity, she thought it would be a fitting reply for her fecundity to ignore her in return.

Her relief, however, was tempered by terror.

Women died in childbirth.

Women died in childbirth *all the time*.

It was such a commonplace occurrence that the church had a service to honor the women who managed to survive the ordeal: "For as much as it hath pleased Almighty God of his goodness to give you safe deliverance, and to preserve you in the great danger of childbirth."

As infrequently as Bea contemplated her ability to reproduce, she had thought about the hazards of the endeavor even less.

She was a spinster!

Spinsters did not have to worry about dying in childbirth.

In desperate poverty, yes, or in service to a tyrannical relative who made her fetch her embroidery sampler from a burning building.

If there was any consolation in passing from this life to the next alone and unloved, it was not having to die in screaming agony as an infant tore from her body.

She had felt herself so secure and removed from the possibility that she had been able to admire the aesthetic perfection of Joseph Hall's description when she had come across it in his *Epistles*: "Death borders upon our birth, and our cradle stands in the grave."

And now there she was, standing next to the cradle in the grave.

Bea did not want to die.

The exquisite happiness she had found with the duke was eons beyond anything she had imagined for herself, and the prospect of giving it up for a hint of an idea, for a figment of membrane and bone, hollowed her out.

And knowing she resented the sacrifice gutted her even further, for it seemed to be all of a piece with her upbringing. Deprived of maternal affection, she was incapable of feeling it now.

Already, she did not love her baby enough.

Perhaps she never would.

But Bea could not say all that, not in response to an anodyne question about her health, and what value would there be in giving voice to her fears? Saying the words out loud did nothing to alter reality. All it would do was cause Kesgrave to worry as well—and not just about her ability to survive the ravages of childbirth but also her ability to withstand its mental strain. Seeking to fortify her faculties before they collapsed entirely, he would take to listing all the women he knew who had successfully delivered babies.

Like Queen Charlotte, she thought, recalling their earlier conversation, who had safely delivered fifteen children.

He would cite her as well as the full complement of her progeny.

And in the order of their appearance in battle, per maritime tradition.

The prospect of just such a catalog was remarkably soothing to Bea's nerves, and she felt a frisson of amusement as she settled on a teasing answer to his question regarding her welfare.

"Truthfully, your grace, I am beside myself with anxiety at the recollection of all those perfectly made beds. I cannot imagine how it was achieved, for I have always been hopeless when it comes to tucking sheets," she said with an affected shudder. "I must warn you that if our child is anything like me, he will never be able to fold a blanket. I fear now more than ever you will regret having chosen me over Lady Victoria. Not only would she have left you untroubled by the deeper emotions but she would have issued cherubs with the dexterity to earn Mrs. Chaffey's approval."

Kesgrave disagreed with the basic premise of her observation, insisting that she fundamentally misunderstood what it meant to be a lady raised in splendor if she believed the coddled young woman in question knew a single thing about linens, let alone how to form a crisp edge.

"But do not try to distract me," he added with a severe frown. "I have noticed that you have been more tired of late and perceive now the cause. Are you sure you are well enough to go to Mrs. Palmer's this evening? I would be happy to send our regrets."

Bea chortled at the earnestness in his expression, which was solely for her benefit. "I know it well, your grace, for you have made little secret of your reluctance to attend the inaugural event of her political salon. As I have said several times since the invitation arrived, you are under no obligation to accompany me. You are free to go to the theater with Hartlepool or to your club with Nuneaton or a gambling hell with your cousin or even pass a quiet night at home with Marlow. I will be perfectly fine on my own. The worst that will happen is I will be given the cut direct by Lord Tierney for daring to suggest Parliament reinstate the income tax."

Kesgrave countered, however, with a long-suffering sigh and reminded her that he had vowed to stand by her for better or worse, and enduring the sanctimony of a roomful of politicians certainly counted as the latter.

Finding this statement unduly sanguine, Bea reminded him of the caricature of him currently on display in Mrs. Humphrey's window, which depicted him as a marionette puppet with her pulling his strings.

Surely, *that* was worse.

Or being chastised by Lady Jersey for allowing his wife to dash across Leather Lane with her ankles exposed.

As there was no shortage of examples, Bea was happy to spend the rest of the journey listing them, but the duke, in an effort perhaps to change the subject from his various humiliations, asked whom she deemed the most likely culprit. With great reluctance, she admitted it was Ripley, but only because he had no alibi. In every other respect, she felt absurd giving the peacocking dandy serious consideration.

Kesgrave empathized with her plight, then noted that the viscount's lack of alibi could not be overcome. "Either he is guilty or the servants must be considered. I suppose it is possible Jesse's valet lied about his being in bed? Or perhaps someone figured out how to manipulate time in the manner of Mrs. Mayhew to make it appear as though they could not have done it."

Bea, who had had this precise notion herself, smiled at the perfect alignment of their thoughts. She was also delighted that the topic of her fatigue had been well and truly dropped.

For now, at least, her pregnancy changed nothing.

She was reminded again of her interesting condition a few hours later when Mrs. Palmer eagerly welcomed her to her debut salon by asking if she was well rested, for the evening ahead would tax her greatly. "Indeed, I am sure after twenty minutes, you will be cursing my name and wishing you had never set foot in my home."

Bea, amused by the excessiveness of the picture she painted, reminded her hostess that she had acquitted herself well during their previous outing to a political salon, when they advocated for the reinstatement of the income tax. "And I still remember all the arguments as you described them to me."

"Oh, but we have given up on that cause!" Mrs. Palmer exclaimed without a trace of regret. "A good politician knows when it is time to abandon the field. We made our opinion known, and sometimes that is the best you can do. Tonight we are focusing on something much more important: legislation that will limit a father's ability to entail land away from his daughters. As I am certain you know, common law holds that an estate should pass to the eldest child regardless of sex, which is why an elaborate system of entails, strict settlements and uses was devised to keep the property in the male line. Now, we are not asserting that ancient estates should pass to an heiress's husband's family. Rather, our stance is that a woman should retain ownership of her inheritance regardless of her marital status."

Bea laughed.

It was a chuckle at first, little more than a light chortle, but as the audacity of Mrs. Palmer's proposition struck her, her humor deepened and grew until she was openly guffawing. Amused to the tips of her toes, she marveled at the utter absurdity of the other woman's presumption.

To be sure, she, Beatrice Hyde-Clare, had indulged in several acts of appalling insolence, such as elbowing her way into her neighbor's kitchens or literally barring several of the *ton*'s most illustrious members from leaving Lady Abercrombie's drawing room with her body. But she had never dared to propose that a woman should be considered an independent human being worthy of the same basic rights as a man.

She was, after all, a fully rational creature who comprehended the limitations of male generosity. It extended only so far as it did not disturb their comfort. And that applied to both political parties. The inferiority of women was among the few things upon which Tories and Whigs agreed.

As she struggled to contain her peals of laughter, heads turned and she wondered how her outburst would be rendered in Mr. Twaddle-Thum's arch account of the evening. As a proof of her contempt for the poor and dispossessed, no doubt. While London's downtrodden masses foraged for dinner, the duchess was spotted laughing uproariously at their expense while enjoying a sugared rout cake and port.

Kesgrave, who was in conversation with Nuneaton, looked at her curiously, and she shook her head as she pressed one hand against her belly to ease the sudden stitch in her side.

Mrs. Palmer, finding nothing untoward in this outburst, smiled blandly and waited patiently for the gales to subside. To that end, Bea took several deep breaths, some of which sounded alarmingly similar to the Austrian method, and slowly the wild humor of the moment faded to mild mirth.

"And what other goal have you set for us?" Bea asked with a teasing grin. "To stop the sun from setting? Perhaps teaching cows how to fly?"

Readily, her hostess acknowledged the immensity of her ambition but insisted politics was like a game of chess. "Asking for full parity is merely our opening gambit. You see, by starting with a proposal so outrageous even an accomplished lady Runner such as yourself cannot help but descend into a fit of laughter we are setting the stage for future moves. Next, when we ask for something equally transgressive but not as audacious, they will think we are being reasonable in comparison. That is how we will convince the House of Lords to make slight changes to the rules governing entails. Just give it a few years, your grace, and you shall see."

Bea, fully in control of her faculties despite the stray giggle that escaped her, commended Mrs. Palmer on her tactical brilliance. "I am delighted to serve as a foot soldier in your army. Now tell me how I may be of service. To whom should I speak and what should I say?"

But Mrs. Palmer shook her head, insisting she would never presume to put words in the duchess's mouth. "You are as clever as I, my dear, and far more courageous. If I had found myself suddenly under assault whilst reading quietly in my home, I am certain I would have aided my attacker by promptly swooning in fear. But you—you kept your wits about you and successfully fought him off. You are a Trojan, your grace," she said.

As she spoke, Mrs. Palmer's fingers clutched the delicate gold ornament that draped from a chain around her neck. Ivory and gold, with an intricately carved handle, it was a magnifying glass, slightly too small to be of any practical use and clearly intended for decoration. Many of the other guests in the room sported similar accoutrements, for it had become quite the thing to display a magnifying glass in some manner: a brooch, a bracelet, sleeve button, earrings. One woman had miniature magnifying glasses sewn along the trim of her gown like rosettes.

The style began in the immediate wake of Lady Abercrombie's murder mystery dinner party play, when Lord Bentham, ostensibly in awe of Bea's ingenuity in identifying the real-life culprit who had murdered their fellow guest, took to wearing one in tribute to her deductive skills.

In retrospect, of course, she recognized this decision for what it was: a calculating ploy to draw attention away from his own actions and toward hers. It was therefore particularly satisfying that the only reason she was able to repel his attack was she had been sporting the exact item he had made all the crack. Smothered by him, seconds away from suffocating, she had desperately grasped the magnifying glass hanging from her neck—a gift from Kesgrave that was at once sincere and sardonic—and drove it into his eye.

As soon as that information became known to the *ton*, interest in the craze increased to an intolerable degree, and now Bea saw magnifying glasses everywhere she turned. Even Mrs. Drummond-Burrell, the highest stickler among the Almack's patronesses, had adopted the fashion.

Deeply embarrassed by the tribute, she was more unsettled by it, for it made her feel vaguely like a lamb being fattened for slaughter. The more enthusiastically society praised her, the more viciously it would condemn her.

Bea knew it was not sustainable—their approbation.

Sooner or later she would make a misstep. Eventually, in the course of one of her investigations, she would accuse an innocent person or overstep her authority, and all the people who had raced to celebrate her would rush to denounce her. It was simply the way the beau monde worked, with its constant desire for new experiences. An investigative duchess was a delightful novelty until it was a dreadful pretension.

There was no point in fretting about her inevitable demise, however, for there was nothing she could do to avert it. Her fate was in Mr. Twaddle-Thum's cynical hands. Presumably, it would be he who would raise the first pitchfork in her general direction and skewer her with it the very moment tearing her down became more profitable than building her up.

What would the ton do with all their magnifying glasses then? Tuck them away in drawers with a faint hint of embarrassment?

To Mrs. Palmer, who had delayed the debut of her salon until in possession of her own specially ordered magnifying glass, Bea lodged an accusation of false humility, for the woman was famous for her refusal to shrink in the face of male contempt.

"Yes, but this was brutality," her hostess insisted. "There is a difference."

"But only in degree," Bea countered. "Brutality is merely male contempt in its most extreme form. But no matter! You are far too ingratiating in your manners to ever induce a man to murder you. I am sure none of your guests have the least idea you disdain some of them."

"*Some* of them?" Mrs. Palmer asked with a curious lift of her eyebrow. "It is more accurate to say 'most of them.' And I would include in that group my brother, Nuneaton, who does not care a fig about politics, which is the most objectionable stance of all to take. At least Mr. Darber believes in his heart women should have no legal standing. But that is neither here nor there. As much as I would adore spending the whole evening chatting with you, we have dearly held principles to undermine. You may start with Lord Hufnell, whose wife has deserted him. He looks quite forlorn standing next to the bookcase without anyone to talk to. Here, let me be the ideal hostess and introduce him to a conversational partner."

Striding across the floor, Mrs. Palmer identified his lordship as a leader among the Tories who was known for his fondness for speechifying and horses. "Alvanley once observed if Hufnell could give a speech while astride his stallion, it would be the pinnacle of his existence."

Although that description did not seem auspicious, Bea greeted Tufnell warmly. He was a gentleman of middle age, with tufts of dark-colored hair lightly grayed at the temples and sharp brown eyes.

Having little reason to anticipate the Duchess of Kesgrave's attention, he was slightly taken aback to have attained it. Nevertheless, he overcame his surprise quickly and owned himself thrilled by the opportunity to speak with her. "For there are a number of things I wish to talk to you about, your grace."

Alas, talking *to* her was an unduly optimistic understanding of what he wished to do, for in reality, he wanted to talk *at* her. Having read about her exploits in the *London Daily Gazette*—not at all his sort of thing, you understand, with its tendency to champion issues pertaining to poor people and orphans, but sometimes entertaining in its on-dits—he had several observations to make regarding her process.

Apparently, the manner with which she examined a murder scene was not commensurate with the way he would do it, and although he had never stumbled across a dead body in a darkened library, or, indeed, anywhere, he remained convinced he knew the best way to go about it.

The first thing: Do not touch the decapitated head of the victim yourself. Summon your valet or your butler.

"A footman will do if you have no other options," he added with a hint of reluctance, "but given their position in the household they are not accustomed to bearing the full weight of responsibility. Holding a door open is nothing like the immense duty of selecting a cravat."

It was, Bea thought, a particularly facile thing to say, for as far as she knew, all cravats were of the same basic size and color with slight variations in material (finest linen, cotton lawn or silk) and shape (rectangle or square).

But Hufnell had other bon mots, all equally unhelpful, and demonstrating the skills that had earned him a reputation as an accomplished debater, refused to yield the floor. No matter how forcefully she tried to inject a thought or observation into his lecture, he continued to speak as if she were not there.

Feeling invisible, she contemplated the option of simply walking away.

Hufnell would not even notice.

Ah, but he was a man who was accustomed to being listened to and would take offense at being abandoned midsentence. If he raised an objection, the topic of conversation at the party might shift from acts before Parliament to acts of the Duchess of Kesgrave, and she did not want to do anything that would undermine the success of the evening.

It would be a poor display of friendship to make Mrs. Palmer's inaugural salon all about Her Outrageousness.

Staying the course, Bea nodded blandly as Hufnell advised her to familiarize herself with the footprints of various small animals because sometimes what might seem like a murder was actually just a hunting excursion gone awry and discreetly surveyed the room for Kesgrave. He was two dozen paces away, by the fireplace, in conversation with a burly gentleman with auburn hair. By every indication, he was engrossed in the discussion, an expression of genuine interest on his face.

It was decidedly unfair—and yet entirely appropriate—that he would find himself more entertained than he had anticipated and herself significantly less so.

AN EXTRAVAGANT DUPLICITY

As it would be rude to stare daggers at the duke until he noticed her, Bea kept her eyes focused on Hufnell's face and tried her best to appear absorbed.

In this she failed utterly, for not a full minute later Nuneaton swooped in with an apology for not finding her sooner. "I promised my sister I would accompany you to the refreshment table but got distracted by Griffiths. He is so very gripping when discussing the fluctuations in the price of wheat, which went up a shilling this week but could come down by two shillings next week. I do not know how he sleeps at night, contemplating the instability in the bread market. But I am mindful of my duty now and must thank you, Hufnell, for doing my job for me. Now do let us go, your grace, before all the lemonade is gone. Katie has made it especially weak so that it may rival Almack's in its lack of flavor."

Given the viscount's perennial languor, Bea could only imagine how dull and glazed her expression must have been if he felt compelled to leap into action to rescue her.

Pulling her lips together in severe disappointment, she apologized to Hufnell for having to leave in the middle of their fascinating discussion. "For there are few things I relish more than getting helpful advice from someone whose experience is but a fraction of my own. I still have so much to learn. But Mrs. Palmer will be put out with Lord Nuneaton for failing to fulfill his obligation, and I cannot be allowed to come between a brother and a sister. I am sure you understand."

Hufnell swore that he did, as he had four siblings himself, two of whom were very quick to take offense. Then he complimented her grace on being such a stimulating conversationalist. "I see now that Mr. Twaddle-Thum has done you a disservice, for you are not at all outrageous, but insightful, unexpectedly well informed and cogent."

Although gratified to have overcome the vile gossip's twice weekly defamation of her character, Bea acknowledged it was a hollow achievement, for she had demonstrated none of those traits. Lord Hufnell was in fact describing himself.

Regardless, she murmured a grateful reply and accepted Nuneaton's escort. As they crossed the room to the refreshment table, she congratulated him on a timely interruption. Another few minutes, she swore, and she might have begun to snore.

"You were bored?" he asked, surprised.

Curious, she tipped her head toward him. "Is that not why you interrupted? To save me from the Tufnell trance?"

He commended her on her clever coinage—the Tufnell trance was as good as anything Twaddle had come up with—and assured her she had not looked bored. "If it was merely that, I would have left you to your fate because I myself am bored to flinders. No, my dear, you looked angry, as if you were about to clasp your hand into a fist and wallop his lordship on the nose. And even though you have nobody to blame but yourself because you encouraged my sister in this folly, I could not allow you to assault one of her guests."

As annoyed as she had been by Tufnell's critique of her investigations, she was nonetheless startled to learn the irritation had been readily apparent on her face. She thought she was better at hiding her emotions than that. "But a brawl at least would have made the evening entertaining for you."

Nuneaton acknowledged the comment with an abrupt nod and admitted it was a novel experience for him—acting against his own best interest.

He sounded so peeved by the development, Bea tried to offer hope by suggesting his concern for other people's welfare was most likely a temporary aberration. "It might have been something you ate. I am sure it will pass soon, perhaps as early as tomorrow morning."

Indignant, he said, "You dare to mock me when I just saved you from Tufnell?"

"According to your own report, you just saved Tufnell," she replied.

As with most gatherings, the crush of people was worse at the refreshment table, and Nuneaton turned sideways to slip deftly through the crowd. He procured two glasses of lemonade and handed one to her while cautioning her not to drink it. "I am merely playing out the scene in case Tufnell is still watching."

Reminded of her inability to nudge the conversation in the direction of inheritance law, she shook her head. "Your sister charged me with one responsibility and I failed her."

"I cannot believe it," Nuneaton said rousingly.

Appreciative of the vote of confidence, she assured him it was true. "I did not even broach the subject I was tasked with discussing."

"Well, yes, of course you failed her," Nuneaton said bluntly. "That is a given. I fail my sister three or four times a day. What I find impossible to believe is the claim that she gave you only one responsibility. That does not sound like Katie at all."

Bea laughed and admitted that it was one responsibility with several parts. "I am supposed to raise a particular topic with several members of the House of Lords, with Tufnell as my first target."

"Dear me," Nuneaton said with an affected shudder. "Is my sister seeking to overthrow the government again?"

"No, merely the system that oversees the distribution of property to the next generation," she replied mildly.

"Oh, just that," he said in a tone that matched hers.

"She thinks that if we propose something truly radical first, such as amending the law to allow wives to retain their property, then our next proposal—in this case, making minor changes to the rules governing entailments—will seem reasonable by comparison," she explained.

Nuneaton, who had taken a cautious sip of the lemonade, pressed his lips together at the sourness before calling his sister misguided. "She cannot genuinely believe that any of the men present in this room, let alone a majority of Parliament, would ever alter the convictions of a lifetime, especially one designed specifically to ensure their control. It does not matter how well-reasoned her arguments are or how devious her schemes are, no wealthy landowner is going to risk allowing a single square inch of his property to pass out of the family. It goes against hundreds of years of self-interest."

The viscount continued speaking, noting that hereditary law was so complex because it had been patched together by men determined to consolidate their power, but Bea was no longer listening. She was struck by his words: *no wealthy landowner*.

Over and over, it echoed in her head.

No wealthy landowner.

No wealthy landowner.

And yet there before her was Mr. Dugmore, a wealthy landowner with his grip firmly clenched around his family's necks to ensure they did precisely what he wanted.

This man had settled property on his granddaughter.

He ceded land—and well more than a square inch.

The bequeathment had been a curious one: a surprise to everyone and yet somehow reconcilable with what they knew about the man. It required some effort but every member of the family had found a way to make it sound reasonable. Clifford believed his grandfather was growing senile in his old age. Mrs. Gaitskill decided her father had become sentimental.

But what else about his behavior justified these conclusions?

In no other aspect of his dealings had he demonstrated cognitive impairment or mawkishness. Only days before his death he had threatened his grandson with debtors' prison and made plans to send an innocent girl back to the abusive stepfather from which she had escaped.

Now, considering the settlement in the context of centuries of primogeniture and decades of domination, she realized it was false.

The behest, yes, but also the document that bestowed it.

It was a fake will Melody quietly slipped into the mix to give herself the property.

That was why there was an older version in the pier table.

Bea had scarcely begun to wonder how the granddaughter accomplished the remarkable feat when she recalled Georgie and his preternatural skill at copying Rembrandt.

How quick Melody had been to draw her and Kesgrave's attention away from the orphaned boy's work. Noting their interest, she immediately showed them another painting.

Of all the motives for murder Bea had encountered in her career as an investigator, a counterfeit will was among the strongest, for having created the document, Melody then had to make sure it was executed.

And there was only one way to do that.

Her alibi presented an obstacle. She could not have been in St. James's Square murdering her grandfather if she was at Fortescue's nursing Aggie.

But it was only a minor impediment, for she could have recruited an associate—one of her former charges, for example, or even Mrs. Chaffey. Melody had already shown herself willing to corrupt an orphan who was in her care, and the head matron had revealed a cunning streak in her dealings with Dugmore.

It probably would not require much money to gain the cooperation of either.

Both prospects had merit, and although Bea wanted to dash across the room to get Kesgrave's opinion on her new theory, she restrained herself. Dashing anywhere at a staid political affair was indecorous, and it would be rude to abandon Nuneaton when he had been so kind as to save her from a public brawl.

She attended to him now as he noted that Tufnell was particularly virulent in his misogyny given his repeated humiliations at the hands of his wife. "I wonder why Katie even asked you to try to discuss the matter with him? She had to have known it was futile. Or perhaps she thought his lordship would be so impressed by your title as to allow you to make your case. Could she be that idealistic and naïve? Either way, she had gotten widely out of hand, and if Palmer is smart, he will tighten the bridle."

Bea, firmly pushing the theory of the fake will to the back of her mind until she could discuss it with Kesgrave, glanced at the viscount wryly. "You believe a woman should be restrained like a horse, but *Tufnell* is the misogynist?"

Disgruntled by the observation, Nuneaton twisted his lips and said, "If you are going to use my own words against me, then the next time you are in danger of engaging in public fisticuffs I will leave you to your fate."

"I will hold my tongue, then, for my aunt's sake," she said, imagining her relative's horror if Bea had indeed struck his lordship. "She is beside herself at the idea of her son brawling in the appropriate setting of Gentleman Jackson's salon."

"Speaking of our families, my uncle is in attendance and would welcome the opportunity to congratulate you on your marriage," Nuneaton replied. "He still cannot believe your parents were murdered or that you were not only able to figure out who did it but also coerce him into confessing in the middle of Lord Stirling's ball. Braxfield admires few people but holds you in high esteem."

In fact, Bea had done nothing to obtain a confession from her parents' killer. Simply confronting him with his own actions had been enough to break his mind, which had long been weakened by the horrendousness of his deed. It was because of that feebleness that he currently occupied a ward in a private asylum in Dorset rather than a cell in Newgate.

She did not care where he languished in madness as long as it was out of her sight.

"I would like to say hello to Braxfield and perhaps practice my speech on him before I make my next attempt," Bea said amicably. "I cannot leave here without trying to persuade at least one politician. Your sister will be so disappointed in me."

"Do not fret yourself over that," he said reassuringly. "Katie is disappointed in everyone despite their accomplishments. But, yes, let's do find my uncle so that you can refine your argument. He is accustomed to my sister's ways and will not be shocked when you advocate for a female prime minister."

"That is not the assignment," she said with a laugh.

"Not yet!" Nuneaton replied. "But give it some time."

Now Bea was the one who shuddered in feigned horror.

Chapter Thirteen

When Bea arrived with the duke at the Dugmore residence at nine-thirty the next morning, she found the house in an uproar. Ripley, his face bright pink with outrage, stood in the center of the drawing room, his finger pointed accusingly at his cousin as he charged her with the grossest betrayal. Melody huffed at him angrily and swore she had nothing to do with it. Her brother, who rested one arm against the mantelpiece like a proper Corinthian, sneeringly told the viscount to stop acting the fool, while Jesse waved his hands anxiously in the air in an attempt to attract their attention. Clifford sat silently on the settee with a stormy expression on his face, and Mrs. Gaitskill, entering the room from the door that connected to the parlor, ordered them all to be still, for the Duke and Duchess of Kesgrave's carriage was out front.

"They will ring the door at any moment, and we cannot have them step into a house that is as loud as ... an ... insane ... asylum," she said, slowly trailing off as she raised her eyes to see them perched on the threshold. At once, her features softened and a welcoming smile overtook her face. "Ah, there you are, your graces, we were just expecting you. Do come in and sit down. It is lovely today, is it not? Matthew was just saying he was to go fishing on the Heath, were you not, my love?"

"Yes, exactly, Mother," he agreed eagerly even though it was in fact a horrible day for fishing, for it rained torrents. "I was going to get my kit as soon as I finished my cup of coffee. May I offer you some, your graces?"

But Ripley would have no part of the tranquil scene his aunt was determined to present and marched over to the duchess. "I know you share my outrage, for you told me not to report any of our dealings to Mr. Twaddle-Thum and I respected your wishes. I did not say a word. But this missy over there"—he gestured at Melody—"told him everything! I cannot imagine a worse betrayal!"

"I did not!" Melody cried. "I would not know how to give him information even if I wanted to, which I do not!"

"A likely story!" the viscount derided. "But it does not explain how you and only you are mentioned in the article. There is not a single word about me!"

"It is not only me," she replied. "The orphans are included, as is Mama."

He threw up his hands in disgust. "Yes, all your grimy little orphans are mentioned as well. What do they have to do with *anything*?"

"If I had contacted Mr. Twaddle-Thum, then you may be sure I would not say a word about my charges, for I would never want them exposed to his wanton conjecture," Melody said.

Mrs. Gaitskill flinched as their voices rose higher and said, "Children, please, we have company."

"I am aware of our company, for I am the one who arranged it," Ripley growled. "*I* invited the duchess. She is *my* guest. And if anyone is going to worry about her opinion of us, then it will be *me*—even if Twaddle never says a word about it."

This argument failed to impress either Matthew, who told him not to be an ass, or Clifford, who asserted that the informant must be one of the servants. Mrs. Gaitskill shook her head and apologized for her family's unruliness. "The truth is, we are not bearing up very well under the strain of knowing one of us might be a killer."

"Not one of us," Clifford said irritably, gesturing toward the door with particular meaning. "One of *them*."

Ripley, begging for permission to disagree with his aunt, said he had been bearing up beautifully until Melody tattled to Twaddle and left his name out of it.

"I did not tattle to anyone, you imbecilic turnip!" she bit out.

"Children," Mrs. Gaitskill said again but without resolve. Seeming to have decided the damage had been done, she sank into the settee next to her nephew Clifford.

Jesse stepped forward with an awkward smile and threw his support behind Melody. "It is precisely as she says. She cares too much for the children in the orphanage to expose them to a reporter's speculation. The only one of us who would even think of doing such a thing is Ripley, and as you can see from his response, he is not responsible either. I wish we could be more helpful, but if you have come here to accuse one of us, then I am afraid you must leave disappointed."

Bea, casting a glance at Kesgrave, announced that she was unaware of the story in question but familiar enough with Mr. Twaddle-Thum's methods to know he did not need information to be supplied directly to him. "An eager network of servants, shopkeepers and cut-purses seems to keep him apprised of my movements. But I appreciate your discretion.

It is comforting to know that not every syllable I utter will be reported back to him."

"Well, in any case, this is nothing to trouble you, I am sure," Jesse said confidently. "It merely mentions that you visited Fortescue's yesterday and then wonders about your business there. It discusses my family's connection to the asylum, mentioning my aunt and cousin by name, but does not say anything about my grandfather, other than to note we recently suffered a loss."

Ripley growled deep in his throat but managed to keep his silence as Jesse handed Beatrice the newspaper containing the story in question. She glanced at it briefly before returning it.

"If you did not come to chastise us for the article, then why are you here?" Matthew said as he lowered his arm from the mantel.

"To ask more questions about Grandfather's murder obviously!" his lordship said snidely. "Her grace is not going to simply forget about it just because Twaddle is more interested in a parcel of orphaned brats."

"They are not brats!" Melody snapped.

Mrs. Gaitskill sent a quelling look to her daughter, who jutted her chin out stubbornly, and made a new effort to welcome the guests. "It is so lovely to see you again, your graces. Please be seated. Melody, do be a dear, and fetch a tray from the kitchens so that we do not keep our esteemed guests waiting a minute longer than necessary. They have already had such a discombobulating visit, and it has not been even five minutes."

Her daughter agreed at once, spinning on her heels to walk toward the entrance, but Bea forestalled her exit. "It is to Miss Gaitskill that we would like to put our questions."

The young lady's eyes flew open wide. "Me?"

"You see!" Ripley exclaimed triumphantly. "Her grace knows it was you who betrayed me."

"Good God, man," his cousin Matthew snapped, "do shut up."

The viscount opened his mouth to issue a stinging retort and promptly closed it again. Then he tossed himself sullenly into a chair.

Her fingers grasped tightly in front of her, Melody said, "I did not betray anyone. I have no idea how Mr. Twaddle-Thum found out about your visit and blaming me will bring you no closer to learning the truth."

"Thank you all for your fervent denials, but the duke and I are not here to discuss the column," Bea replied. "We would like to talk about your grandfather's will. If you prefer, we may discuss it privately, in another room."

Ripley, whose expression had remained belligerent, furrowed his brow in confusion as Mrs. Gaitskill said with baffled surprise, "My father's will?"

"No," Matthew said firmly. "Anything you have to say to my sister can be said in front of me. I will not allow you to browbeat her for information, especially as she knows nothing more than the rest of us. We are all confounded by what you describe as my grandfather's murder."

"Thank you for your offer," Melody said, "but I am content to remain here, surrounded by my family. I have no secrets."

Bea did not know to interpret this boast, for it was an especially bold statement to make when you had tasked one of your students with producing a fraudulent last will and testament to provide yourself with an independent living. Fleetingly, she doubted her own deduction.

Perhaps she had jumped to yet another outlandish conclusion.

But no, many of her wild suppositions had turned out to be correct.

And so it would be now, she thought.

"Very well," Bea said with an abrupt nod. "It is my belief that after we contact your grandfather's solicitor in Tamworth, we will discover that the will granting you Paltry House is in fact a counterfeit. The legitimate will was in the pier table with your grandfather's other sensitive papers."

While her mother blinked in shock and her brother scoffed at the effrontery of the charge, Melody chortled stiffly. "A counterfeit? What a funny idea."

"Yes," Ripley said thoughtfully. "It *is* a funny idea. I wonder why the duchess had it. I am certain she has an excellent explanation, for she is highly methodical in her reasoning. Do tell us, your grace, how you arrived at this conclusion. Is it because it strikes you as very strange that my grandfather would suddenly remove his objection to his granddaughter devoting her life to good works rather than making an advantageous marriage? Because it struck me as *very* strange. I said as much to Jesse at the time, did I not, Jesse? And you told me I was doing the old man a disservice. Even the most stubborn among us can have a change of heart—those were your exact words."

"And I believe it still," Jesse insisted. "Had he lived, I am convinced Grandfather would have come around to accepting Miss Cheever in our family. His first impulse was to scheme and threaten, but once he got to know her, he would have changed his mind. As I believe he did with Melody. He saw how valuable her work with orphans was and how much pleasure it gave her and decided he could not stand in the way of that."

"Do you even hear your own words?" Clifford asked jeeringly. "Seeing Melody's pleasure and deciding not to stand in the way? You are describing the two things our grandfather had contempt for the most: happiness and self-determination. Ripley is right. He would never have left her the property. It had struck me as odd as well, but I supposed he had become senile in his dotage. A forged will makes much more sense."

Mrs. Gaitskill looked at her nephews in horror, as if unable to believe what they were saying, but Matthew's expression was contemplative.

Something about the accusation resonated with him.

Melody chuckled again, more forcefully, but the sound lacked conviction. "I do not want to dignify the charge with a reply, but I fear I must say something or my cousins will continue to glare at me with suspicion. You must know, your grace, that even if such a diabolical scheme did occur to me, I would not know the first way to go about it. As I explained to you yesterday, I am an adequate artist at my best and could never make a copy of anything that would pass even the most routine inspection. You may ask any of my pupils, for they are often amused at my efforts to demonstrate a concept."

But mentioning her drawing classes was a mistake and Bea saw the moment she realized it. Her right eye twitched uncontrollably and the fingers clasping her hands together tightened.

Even so, she continued as if she had not made a grave tactical error. "I have nothing but respect for the law and would never dream of violating it. And my grandfather's trust. I could not bring myself to breach it for any reason. He was a kind man, and I held him in high esteem."

Matthew inhaled sharply and cried, "By God, you *did* do it! We all know our grandfather was a horrible man, and you would never say anything so blatantly false unless you were trying to hide something. I cannot believe your avarice—stealing from your own brother! Have you no decency?"

But his sister's outrage was just as fierce as she glared at him. "You inherited nine thousand acres and I secured for myself a measly three and *you* dare to call *me* avaricious? You are one man and can live in only one place at a time. You hated Paltry House. You called it damp and dreary and said it was too far from London to be convenient and too far from the country to be pleasant. Those were your exact words! But it was ideal for me, allowing me to continue my charity work at the orphan asylum while also providing a modicum of independence. I am certain it makes no difference to you."

"I cannot believe you could talk so offhandedly about your crime," he said, striding across the room to stand within an inch of her. "It is theft! It is forgery! You speak of good works, but instead you are a criminal."

"What is criminal is the way Grandfather used me as chattel to increase his wealth," she countered furiously. "He wanted to marry me off to a man almost three times my age so that he could enjoin the properties."

"So what?" her brother asked derisively. "He sought to do the same to me—and worse, for he threatened to have me consigned to debtors' prison if I did not comply—and yet you do not see *me* forging a will and stealing property from my sibling."

Melody cackled at the observation and said with searing contempt, "Because you don't *have* to, you bloody fool. It is all going to you regardless!"

Deeply unsettled by the scene, their mother fidgeted in her seat, alternately determined to rise to her feet to intercede in the quarrel and keeping her head down as if to pretend it was not happening. She shifted forward and backward, then sometimes up and down.

Finally, she stood and spoke firmly. "I will get that tea now. Yes, that is what I will do, for we all need to take a moment to clear our heads. Tempers are riled, and that is never healthy. Tea is soothing. So that is what I will do," she added, turning to Bea for permission to leave the room. "If you do not mind, your grace, I will fetch some tea and then we can resume this discussion calmly."

To this seemingly benign request, her son frowned and said petulantly, "I knew you would take her side. Melody can do no wrong, even when she has admitted to doing a great wrong."

"I am not taking anyone's side," Mrs. Gaitskill protested. "Tempers in this room are simmering and I simply suggest we all take a moment to allow them to cool down, so that we can have a sensible discussion."

"You see!" Matthew yelped in triumph. "That is her side, for if you were on my side, you would know there is nothing to discuss. There are no two ways about it. Melody is a thief and a forger. *And* a liar."

Further agitated by this argument, which perhaps contained a grain of truth, Mrs. Gaitskill repeated her desire for tea and, casting a cautious look at Bea to see if she would object, promised to return swiftly as she ran out of the room.

"There, see what you have done," Melody said angrily. "You've upset Mother."

"*I* have upset Mother?" Matthew replied dumbfounded. "That is rich."

Bea, who generally found squabbles to be an excellent source of information, decided this particular one had gone on long enough and asked its participants to sit down. Melody bristled and her brother scowled, but they both complied.

Ripley, who had watched the exchange with an astonished expression, said, "I do not understand how my cousin did it, for her handwriting is barely legible. Last week she left a note in my bedchamber and I had to ask four people what it said before Bevins explained that she had taken one of my cravats for an art project with the orphans. But the wills are identical. I saw them both and had no cause to doubt either."

"One of her students," Bea replied with a meaningful glance at Melody. "It was Georgie, was it not?"

Shamefully, the girl nodded.

"Then let us add corrupting a minor to her list of sins," Matthew said.

Tears welled in the corners of Melody's eyes at the charge, and her cousin Clifford, pursing his lips sympathetically, handed her a handkerchief. "Do not ruin it now by falling apart. I am mightily impressed by all that you've done and anyone who can get one over on Matthew is an out-and-outer in my book. Now do buck up, my dear."

Alas, this commendation only made her cry harder.

Ripley, shaking his head at the display, said, "I do not understand, your grace. How could Melody have killed Grandfather? She was at the asylum all night. She did not return home until summoned by her mother after the maid found him dead."

Bea, who had no intention of sharing her theories just yet, offered a vague reply about exploring various possibilities. She need not have bothered, however, for her response was drowned out by Melody, who sneered at her cousin and told him not to be more thickheaded than he could help. "Why in heaven's name would I murder a man who was going to be dead within the month anyway?"

Ripley laughed at the remark, as if she were the one who was being dense, then abruptly stopped as the grave implication of her words struck him. "Wait. What did you say?"

"Grandfather was dying," she said, glancing at each of her cousins in turn, all of whom wore either an amazed or blank expression. "Did none of you truly not notice how failing his health was?"

"He had gout," Jesse said with more than a hint of defensiveness. "I noticed that."

Melody smiled faintly as she shook her head. "Your critical faculties are as lacking as your observational skills if you actually believe that bouncer. He had tumors, not gout. Gout was the ruse he devised with his physician to hide the severity of his illness. He did not want us to know how dire it was," she said before directing her gaze at Bea. "You may confirm this with Dr. Pritchard. He will tell you the same thing, presumably in more detail."

Although, yes, Bea would verify the information with the physician—as soon as they returned to Kesgrave House, she would send Joseph or Edward—she proceeded now as if it was true. It would be foolish to lie about something that could so easily be refuted, and it did not seem implausible.

"If he took such pains to hide it, how did you find out?" Bea asked.

"I have nursed sick children at the asylum and have a sense of how an illness progresses," Melody explained. "Grandfather's condition never improved despite his diet, so I made it a point to be around when the doctor called and paid attention to what he said. Two weeks ago he told Grandfather to get his affairs in order."

"You eavesdropped!" her brother said accusingly. "Is there no transgression you will not dare?"

Untroubled by the new allegation, she calmly affirmed that she had indeed listened in doorways and hid in wardrobes. "How else do you discover information that is being deliberately withheld from you?"

It was, Bea thought, a rational conclusion, for there were only a few ways to overcome secrecy and none of them were socially acceptable. If spying did not satisfy, then one was left with breaking and entering or assuming an elaborate disguise to gain intelligence directly from the source. "And once you knew the truth, you began to plan."

Melody shook her head. "No, not immediately. It was only when he took out his will and waved it at Ripley, threatening to remove him from it, that the idea occurred to me. It was the first time I had seen the document. When was that?" she asked, turning to the viscount. "It was the day after you lost two hundred pounds at faro at the Red Lantern, so Friday of last week?"

"Saturday," he said with a bark of impatience, as if her failure to keep an accurate record of his dissipation was the true transgression.

"Yes, that is right, Saturday," she said smoothly. "Now that I know about the pier table compartment, I assume he usually kept the will in there, but on that day he left it on the desk in his study. And *that* is when I began to plan. I took it from the desk, brought it to the asylum and asked Georgie to make a copy with a minor alteration. He is a clever fellow, so he realized at once what I was up to and agreed. He knew if Grandfather had his way, I would never be allowed to return to Fortescue's. It took him three days, and the will was back on the desk by noon on Wednesday. As far as I could tell, Grandfather did not notice anything amiss and no harm was done."

Ripley gasped. "The day *before* he died! You expect us to believe it was a coincidence that someone just happened to kill Grandfather only hours after you had snuck your fraudulent will into his desk? Doing it a bit brown, my dear!"

Oh, but it was not, Bea thought, looking at Clifford, who was staring at Melody with a mix of dismay and respect. The unlatched panel that he had noticed while apologizing to his grandfather was the result of Dugmore returning his will to the secret compartment.

It was *that* coincidence she found difficult to reconcile. It seemed too implausible that the killer struck mere hours after Clifford stood over the vulnerable old man sleeping in his bed. As intertwined as the two events felt to her, Bea could not get around the fact that Dugmore was alive when Ripley entered the room at 6:08. If the body had been lying in the bed, then she could allow for the possibility that the viscount had simply not noticed his grandfather was dead. As that was not the situation *and* Clifford was seen reading the morning papers in the breakfast room, the only alternative was he had hired a confederate.

That struck her as equally implausible.

And yet he kept insisting that the culprit was a member of the staff, and recalling how frequently he'd made the assertion Bea wondered if he had been telling on himself. It would not surprise her that a man of Clifford's disposition—obsequious and sly and lacking in courage—would share the truth as if by compulsion. She could imagine the words flapping in his head like frantic birds trapped in a stable and his thinking, "Do not say it, do not say it," and the declaration spilling out of its own volition.

Or perhaps the reiteration had a more sinister purpose, such as setting the stage for the future implication of his accomplice. Already, the family had begun to repeat his theory.

Mrs. Gaitskill, for example, was convinced of it.

"I expect you to believe it was a coincidence because it *was* a coincidence," Melody said calmly in response to Ripley's query.

Clifford, his expression still appalled and admiring, asked why she returned the original. "Did you not risk that standing as the official will of record?"

"As my will was dated later, I knew it would supersede the older one," she explained, adding that it was fairly common for men of her grandfather's stature to alter their wills often.

"You'll note the one I replaced was from September, so he had recently changed it himself. My main goal, however, was to draw as little attention to the document as possible because you know how Grandfather was, kicking up a big fuss about every small thing. I was confident I could discreetly slip the new one in his desk drawer when the time came. And so I did."

Her cousins looked at her aghast, perhaps astonished by her methodical planning, perhaps appalled by her cool assessment, and stung into defensiveness, she added heatedly, "I had no choice! You all know it! Grandfather was an interfering old biddy who did not give a fig about what we thought or wanted. He knew best—end of discussion! And with the end growing nearer, he increased his efforts to marry us all off by using whatever underhanded means were at his disposal. All I did was follow his lead and implement my own sly scheme. Then I smiled sweetly at the old dear, said, 'Yes, darling,' whenever he brought up the subject of my marrying Mr. Coombes, and waited for him to die of natural causes. And that is all. I did nothing to hurt him. I never would! I think it is perfectly beastly that someone *did* kill him, but I do not understand why we must kick up the dust about it. It seems nonsensical to send a person to the gallows for killing what was naught but a walking cadaver."

"Melody!" Mrs. Gaitskill screeched from the doorway, her face ashen as she stared at her daughter in horror.

Kesgrave, noting her frailty, rose to his feet and relieved her of the tray before it slipped from her fingers. He placed it on the side table, then escorted her to the settee, where she melted like snow into the cushion.

Faintly, as if out of breath from running up a great many stairs, the older woman said, "I do not understand any of this. What are you saying, Melody?"

Instantly contrite, the girl rushed to her mother's side,

took possession of her hands and said gently, "He was going to die anyway, Mama."

As straightforward as this statement was, Mrs. Gaitskill shook her head uncomprehendingly. "For shame, my dear, we are *all* going to die."

"No, Mama, no. I mean, he literally was," she explained in a voice as soft as silk. "He was very sick. He had tumors, Mama. His right foot was encased in one, and I understand there were others in his body. According to Dr. Pritchard, he had only a few weeks left."

And still her mother shook her head, as if unable to believe any of it. "My father was dying and did not tell me. I cannot ..." She trailed off and stared at her hands clasped in her daughter's. Tears began to drop as she inhaled deeply and tried again to speak. "It is just that he relied on me so much —to run the household, to act as his hostess, to help him with his business dealings—and yet he did not trust me with this information. I cannot understand why he would not tell me something so vital. It is a great shock. And to discover this on the heels of learning about my daughter's perfidy. It is almost too much. I do not know what to do with myself. How can everything be so awful all at once?"

"Finally, Mother, you understand!" Matthew exclaimed. "Melody's actions *are* awful. We cannot let this stand. We must contact the executor at once and let him know we are contesting the will. Rothbart will be shocked to discover Grandfather nurtured a viper in his bosom. And we must send word to his solicitor in Tamworth as well to make certain that the will from September is legitimate. Knowing now of my sister's deviousness, I would not be surprised if the one we found in the secret compartment is also fake."

"I knew nothing of the secret compartment," she insisted. "If I did, I would have removed the original will to ensure nobody found it, and I would have burned the debts Grandfather held over your head because I have no more desire to see you trapped in a loveless marriage than myself."

The generosity of this sentiment had no softening effect on her brother, who merely rolled his eyes and said he could not trust a single word she uttered.

Mrs. Gaitskill whimpered at the exchange, as if their bickering were yet another unexpected disclosure she could not comprehend.

Ripley was equally confounded and looked at Beatrice with impatience etched into his features. "But who is the killer, then, your grace? It has to be Melody, does it not? She is our main suspect?"

Having asked the questions, he was quick to answer them himself. "She had the strongest motive, for who goes through all the trouble of creating a counterfeit will and then leaving its implementation up to fate? It does not follow any logical sense. She insists my grandfather was going to die regardless within a few weeks, but one cannot know that with any degree of certainty, can one?" he said thoughtfully, rubbing his chin with his thumb and forefinger, which grazed the edges of his high shirt points. "At best, doctors can make only educated guesses, and some are little better than butchers. Melody could not know if Pritchard's diagnosis was accurate, let alone his prognosis. He could have been wide of the mark or Grandfather might have undergone a miraculous recovery. It happens all the time."

Clifford, who had found much to like in this speech if his nods of agreement were any indication, murmured under his breath, "Well, not all the time."

"Melody could not risk either of these events happening, not if she wanted the will she had taken such pains to forge to stand," the viscount continued, his hands now clasped behind his back as he careened toward his conclusion. "She had to act, and given what we now know about her scruples—or, more pointedly, her lack of them—the duchess and I can arrive at no other conclusion than she is the killer. Cousin Melody murdered our grandfather."

Despite the seriousness of the charge, Melody regarded him with amusement and complimented him on his ability to make flawed deductions. "I was at the asylum at the time of the murder, as you well know. Mrs. Chaffey and several other matrons have attested to that. My alibi is undeniable. Can you say the same?" she asked, turning to look at the other men in the room. "Can any of you say the same?"

"I can, yes," Jesse said immediately. "Rawls has vouched for me, and he is above reproach."

"It has been established that I was in Hogan's carriage en route to the Heath at the time in question," Matthew reminded her. "So, yes, I *can* say the same."

"As can I," Clifford added, who had been ensconced in the breakfast room with various servants dashing in and out during the entire interval.

Even her mother chimed in, citing her standing appointment with the housekeeper to review the week's menus and accounts. "As you know, I was with Mrs. Keene from six-thirty to eight-thirty."

All eyes, then, turned to Ripley, who, far from having his own irrefutable alibi, was the only suspect who was actually in the room with the victim immediately preceding his death.

Indeed, by that measure, he was the only suspect.

All the relatives seemed to realize it at once, and they turned their eyes to stare at the viscount with varying degrees of disbelief and horror. He shrank from the attention, his shoulders rounding and marring the elegant lines of his tailcoat. He cowered like that for a moment, his eyelids blinking furiously, before he straightened his spine and called them halfwits.

"Think on it, you fools," he said with the untoward

aggression of a cornered hound. "If I were the murderer, then why would I summon the famously clever Duchess of Kesgrave to investigate?"

It was, he clearly thought, a winning argument, the coup de grâce delivered with élan, and he relaxed his posture as he looked at them with expectation, as if ready to receive their apologies. And yet it was he himself who had supplied the various reasons why he would have done that very thing when she and the duke returned to investigate two days ago.

His cousins listed them now.

"An excess of confidence," Matthew said. "You assumed the duchess would not find anything."

"You have made your desire for notoriety clear," Jesse offered.

Clifford nodded at these explanations and added, "As well as a hint of danger to burnish your reputation. You have been hell-bent on it since the moment you arrived in the city."

"Frankly, Ripley, you do not seem very bright to me," Melody said brutally before rushing to explain that she did not mean the criticism in a cruel way. "Rather in a sort of turnippy-provincial kind of way. It is not that you lack aptitude, merely sophistication. I can only assume it is easy to commit murder in the country and then mislead the local gentry."

The viscount turned purple.

Slowly, steadily, the flush rose in his cheeks until his entire face was the color of a beet and he looked on the verge of tears—whether caused by fury, frustration, embarrassment or fear, Bea could not tell.

"Shame on you all," Mrs. Gaitskill said, rising to lay a comforting hand on her nephew's shoulder. He flinched at the contact but did not step away. "You have no evidence of Ripley's guilt and I will tell you why you do not. Because he did not do it. He is as innocent as the rest of you."

Melody issued a mumbled apology for calling her cousin stupid, but the others remained silent, and Mrs. Gaitskill, shaking her head, owned herself disappointed. But, she allowed, they were grown men and free to behave as uncivilly as they chose.

Then she turned to Bea and invited her to leave, as it had been a morning of disturbing revelations. "Melody, Matthew, Georgie, my father, Dr. Pritchard," she said, listing the disappointments one after the other before repeating the doctor's name with inordinate ferocity. "How could he not trust me with the truth about my own father's welfare? He knows how much I fretted about him, how his aches and pains were never far from my mind. We spoke about it just last week! I specifically asked him what I could do to increase his comfort and he said I could induce him to take a little laudanum to ease his pain. That is all! Not a word about his mental suffering or how truly great his agony was. I cannot believe it!"

Matthew, seemingly indifferent to his mother's anguish, expressed his outrage at being included in the same group as his sister. "What have *I* done other than discover myself to be the victim of a swindle?"

"Your lack of charitable understanding—" Mrs. Gaitskill began only to be interrupted again by a cry of "You see! *Her* side!"

Shaking her head sadly, his mother apologized to Bea and the duke for withdrawing her hospitality. "But we must be left to figure out what is to be done. I know you agree that such a discussion is best conducted en famille. But you must know how very grateful we are for your time and consideration. Your assistance has been invaluable, your graces. As for my father's murder, you may return to continue your investigation at another time. Given where everything stands, I am more convinced than ever that Clifford's original theory is

AN EXTRAVAGANT DUPLICITY

correct and the culprit is either one of the servants or a stranger whose motive we cannot begin to fathom."

"My mother is right," Matthew said firmly. "We must be left in private to decide how to handle my sister's shocking betrayal. Bevins will show you to the door."

Bea, who had been shuffled to the side often during her tenure with the Hyde-Clares, including by Kesgrave at the Skeffingtons' party in the Lake District, was accustomed to such dismissive treatment. But the duke had never been ejected from a building in his entire life and he stiffened in insult. He opened his mouth to issue a stinging retort to Matthew, and as much as she would have enjoyed watching him cut the supercilious gentleman down to size, it would only antagonize him further.

The truth was, they could not return to the house to ask further questions if its owner bolted the door to them. They could huff and puff about the tyranny as much as they wanted, but even the Duke of Kesgrave was obliged to respect the boundaries of private property. The only reason she was able to shoulder her way into the Mayhews' home was the grasping mushrooms were delighted to have her attention. If the banker had been clever enough to imagine the far-reaching ramifications of granting her entrée, he would have removed her from the premises and continued to live in relative comfort with his wife.

Bea wondered if Matthew was thinking the same thing now.

Thanks to Mr. Twaddle-Thum's report, everyone in London knew the gravity of Mr. Mayhews' mistake and the path by which he was led to make it. The best way to frustrate the meddlesome duchess's efforts was to refuse to answer her questions. No one was obligated to respond.

But who was Matthew trying to protect: his sister or himself?

Given his fury over Melody's deception, Bea was inclined to believe it was the latter, but the Corinthian also had an unassailable alibi and could be guilty only if he worked with an associate.

Yes, your grace, everyone has an accomplice, she thought peevishly, annoyed at how frequently she considered the notion. She seemed to have just the one recourse for all the cousins save Ripley.

Only Ripley worked alone.

Well, yes, because he was the lone suspect without an alibi.

If she followed her own rule of thumb to favor the simplest explanation, then she should focus her attention on proving that the viscount was in fact the killer. And yet she could not conceive of his dirtying his hands with murder. It simply seemed too gruesome for him in the literal sense.

All that blood—ick.

It was far easier to envision his taking ruthless advantage of the grisly situation. He had been giddy from the very beginning, treating the whole thing as a great lark, and nothing, not even the prospect of a family member hanging for murder, had significantly dimmed his excitement.

His peacocking behavior was in keeping with her estimation of him.

Like Melody, Bea thought Ripley lacked intellectual rigor, and if he had the gross ill judgment to place himself in the middle of the investigation for the impish delight of watching the Duchess of Kesgrave chase her own tail, then he would have made a horrible muck of it.

It was this notion that kept niggling at her, for was that not precisely the state of affairs in which they found themselves: everyone with an alibi except him. If Ripley, with his limited intelligence, had murdered his grandfather in a bid for attention, then the plot would inevitably unravel in some spectacular fashion and he would be left holding the bag.

And that was the situation now.

Ripley should be her main suspect, not his various cousins and aunt, with their excellent alibis, and yet something held her back. It was his shirt points, yes, in one sense because they made it difficult to take him seriously.

But it was also the investigation itself.

Something about it had been off for her from the beginning. It had felt at once chaotic and futile, with Russell rambling, Aunt Vera whimpering, Flora commandeering, Holcroft brooding and she, Beatrice, observing nothing more sinister than an elderly man who had lost his balance as he climbed out of bed.

All of it—the chaos and the futility—had created a sort of exasperated indifference in her as she examined the crime scene cursorily at first, content to allow Flora to appease her ego in whatever extravagant fashion she required in the presence of her former beau, and Bea wondered if that strange apathy was an effect of her pregnancy.

Was she simply less interested in death now that she was nurturing life?

As she was not generally prone to mawkish sentiment, Bea thought the explanation was dubious but nevertheless allowed herself a moment to feel its truth.

Alas, it felt like nothing.

The cherub was too tiny and new to be anything but an abstraction.

No, it was also a distraction, she acknowledged, one of several she had had to contend with during the investigation. The discord between Flora and Holcroft had divided her attention as well. Either one alone would have undermined her focus, but the two combined allowed her to overlook the central clue at the heart of the mystery.

Indeed, she had *missed* the mystery.

It was that essential truth, that immutable fact, that undermined her now, for having made one egregious mistake, how could she trust herself not to make another? Her confidence had taken a heavy blow, and she could not dispel the sense that it was happening again. It was still so chaotic, with all the cousins and their motives, which at bottom was really just one motive—a desire to get out from under their grandfather's thumb—and their alibis and Ripley's antics and the ever-present threat of Twaddle's report.

It was a lot, she thought.

The investigation felt slippery, as though something was always sliding out of her grasp, and because she thought more clearly away from the noise, in a quiet place with Kesgrave, she forestalled the duke's cutting reply with a shake of the head. Then she thanked the family for their time and left them to argue in private.

Chapter Fourteen

Kesgrave responded to Bea's theory regarding Clifford's culpability with the same reservations he had shown to the proposition that Melody likewise employed a confederate. "You are doing so many contortions to make him fit when Ripley requires none."

As simplicity was one of her guiding principles, she could not reject the notion outright and instead explained that imagining the absurd cawker murdering anyone required her to twist her mind into an elaborate knot. Then she noted that the duke himself had made the strongest argument for Clifford's guilt when he pointed out that by taking only his own letters from the compartment revealed the identity of the thief. "Rather than solve his problem, he had in fact made it worse, the thought of which had to torture him as he was lying in bed in the aftermath of his great audacity."

Kesgrave, readily conceding that was true, asked her how precisely Clifford went about recruiting a confederate at two in the morning. "Did he wake up the servants who seemed most likely to consent to murdering their employer in exchange for money or decide among those who were already awake?"

"All right, all right," she grumbled as they entered the drawing room at Kesgrave House, which was cheerful and bright despite the dreariness of the day. "You may have that point."

Acknowledging her gracious concession with a dip of the head, he reiterated what Ripley's own family said: The viscount was just dimwitted enough to believe he could murder his grandfather and enjoy the attention generated by being suspected of murdering his grandfather. "It is the sort of plan a fame-seeking nick-ninny would devise. The body had been removed days before, so he assumed there was nothing to be found and summoned you on the understanding that you would poke around for an hour and leave. As far as he was concerned, that was all he needed to secure Mr. Twaddle-Thum's interest, and he had to do something dire after his ladybird wager failed to excite interest."

"Well, to be fair to him, that *is* what happened," Bea said with only a hint of bitterness as she sat down on the settee. "If you had been any less attentive, he might have gotten away with the perfect murder-cum-notoriety scheme—*if* that was his scheme."

"And he was unnerved to see us again an hour later," Kesgrave added. "He caught himself and smoothed it over, but he did squeal loudly and then resort to the Austrian technique to calm himself down. If he was guilty, then our return would have been an unpleasant surprise."

Reviewing his lordship's response from the perspective of his possible guilt, she had to agree with the duke's interpretation. She had attributed the viscount's restlessness to an inability to find the most flattering position to present himself and realized now it could have also been caused by nerves and anxiety. Noting the signs of a guilty conscience, she wondered if the odd discomfort she felt regarding the case was simply a dogged refusal to accept the obvious. Ripley could be both things at once: an absurd fop and a cold-blooded killer.

"He could not have known that he would be the only one without an alibi," Kesgrave continued. "He knew Matthew was fishing, but Jesse, Clifford, Melody, his aunt and a houseful of servants must have seemed like a sufficient number of suspects if the matter progressed that far."

As this point was as irrefutable as the others, Bea let out a low groan and, resting her head against the cushion, stared up at the vibrant fresco decorating the ceiling. "There is just something so deeply unsatisfying about Ripley being the culprit."

"It is his shirt points," Kesgrave said with wry humor. "You are prejudiced against Pinks of Fashion, and believe only Corinthians, rakehells, mushrooms and society matrons can be murderers."

"And politicians," she added, her own lips twitching at his suggestion. "I expect they can be quite lethal and I do not mean just by boring people to death with their oratory."

"I believe you consider that to be my exclusive province," he said as he took hold of her hand and sat next to her, appearing to get comfortable in the drawing room when she knew he had duties to see to elsewhere.

"Not death," she corrected ardently. "Never to death! Just flinders, which is a far less permanent condition. But seriously, Damian, the idea of Ripley as the villain feels inane and hollow, like opening a box and finding it empty. There is nothing there."

"But as you yourself just observed, you missed what *was* there," he said.

Determined not to brood about her failure, she extricated her fingers from his clasp and reminded him that Mr. Stephens had budgets for him to approve. "And did your grandmother not send a note requesting your presence as she gets set to fire her physician?"

"Set fire," the duke said.

Uncertain of the distinction, she regarded him curiously. "Excuse me?"

"My grandmother requested my presence for when she intends to set fire to her physician whom she believes is a warlock," Kesgrave explained. "She would like me there to bear witness to the tribunal and perhaps render judgment. I am not completely sure because her note was almost impossible to read. Her hand has been cramping more than usual lately, making it difficult for her to write, and that is the source of her complaint against Digby. She says he is making it worse with his potions."

Although reasonably certain he was teasing her, Bea would not put it past the dowager to impanel a jury against one of her doctors, for she was rarely satisfied with their treatment. Blandly, then, she said, "Yes, of course. And how does she propose to roast him: drawing room fireplace or kitchen stove?"

"The message did not go into that level of detail," he replied.

"It would not, no," she murmured before urging him to visit the dowager posthaste to discover her plan and then dissuade her from it. "But before you leave, do dash off a note to my aunt alerting her to your grandmother's intention to conduct witch trials so that she knows there are more shocking things than owning the patent for a steam engine."

His lips twitching, he shook his head and noted that with Mrs. Hyde-Clare's enthrallment to the aristocracy, she would take no issue with the decision. "Far be it for her to disapprove of burning infidels in the hearth if the Dowager Duchess of Kesgrave deems it necessary."

Bea laughed because it was both a joke and the unvarnished truth. "Unless, of course, the hearth belonged to the hated Lady Abercrombie. In that case, Aunt Vera would raise a bucket to extinguish the flames herself."

"While we are on the subject of physicians, I think we should discuss how your condition will affect your activities," he said.

She almost choked.

Startled by the sudden introduction of the topic she had feared for days, Bea swallowed in the wrong manner and her throat burned as she suppressed the cough that flailed to get out. Struggling to keep her expression placid, she marveled at how plainly he said it—as if her life were not about to undergo a fundamental alteration—and she supposed that spoke to the mundanity of it all. Of course he did not broach the subject with tepidity or tact. It was only a matter of common sense that a pregnant female would curtail her physical activities out of concern for her unborn child and cease all occupations that subjected her to lethal attacks in her own sitting room.

After all, she was sitting for two now.

It almost did not have to be said.

Almost.

She told herself to be grateful for how far she had come. What under any other circumstance would have been a short road—an alley, really—had extended for miles.

And she could not resent Kesgrave for his concern. Owing his very existence to the vagaries of childbirth, he understood better than most what was at stake. If his father's first wife had not died within hours of delivering a pair of sickly twins who themselves promptly expired, he would never have been born. That he would seek the opinion of an experienced physician was unsurprising, and having attained it, he would follow his prescripts to the letter.

Prepare to be put on a lowering diet, your grace, she thought churlishly, capable, it turned out, of feeling some resentment after all. No more rout cakes or meat pies. Only cooling fruits from now on.

Pineapple for every meal!

No, she would not suffer that atrocity again.

She was receptive to changes, of course, and would take all reasonable precautions. She had every intention of delivering the cherub safely. She was simply not convinced that a male physician, however highly credentialed or well respected, knew the best way for her to do that.

As these thoughts swarmed in her mind, Bea kept her expression neutral and strove for a convincing blandness as she responded with vague interest, "Oh?"

There was, she decided, no reason to adopt a defensive pose until she was firmly put in her place. Expecting that to happen momentarily, she was startled by a brusque knock on the door and the sight of Flora entering the room.

No, Bea amended, as she took in her cousin's posture, which was stiffer than usual, more upright, Flora *marched* in. With each step landing with force on the marble floor, she strode across the room until she stood before Kesgrave, whom she greeted with a formal courtesy, as if they had been introduced recently. Then she asked if he would be so kind as to excuse her cousin for several minutes, as she had something important she wished to discuss with her grace, the Duchess of Kesgrave.

And she said it just like that, employing the title along with the honorific, which was unusual to say the least, and the duke darted a confused look at Beatrice, who had no more understanding than he.

"Of course, yes," he said genially, announcing that he had business to attend to and had just been on his way to see to it. "Please stay as long as you wish. I will have James bring you some tea."

"I would appreciate that, thank you," Flora replied with rigid precision.

Although Bea had never seen her cousin in such a mood before, she naturally assumed it had something to do with her aunt and uncle. They were hardly a comfortable pair, frequently wrangling over domestic matters in which Uncle Horace had little interest, especially in the morning, when he tended to be abrupt and snide. If Aunt Vera had broached buying a new settee before her husband had finished his first cup of coffee or worried again about Russell's new brawling habit, then an ugly row might have ensued.

Ugly enough to send Flora scurrying to Kesgrave House to seek her cousin's assistance?

It was unlikely, for the girl had been exposed to their acrimony for almost two decades and knew that her mother's methods, although painful, got results. The new pedestal table in the drawing room had been the culmination of several years' work.

But it was not her parents, no, Bea realized suddenly. It was Holcroft.

Always Holcroft.

Either he had done something new to hurt Flora's feelings or the original offense continued to sting, and her cousin, indignant, frustrated and sad, desired an opportunity to vent her spleen to a sympathetic listener. The prospects for just such an exchange at 19 Portman Square were dim.

Before Bea could invite her to sit down or even welcome

her warmly, Flora said through tightly clenched teeth, "How *dare* you!"

Startled by the charge, Bea resisted the urge to look around the room as if to locate the true target of her cousin's fury. She knew it could not be herself, for she had had no communication with Flora in the past four and twenty hours, and yet it could not be anybody else.

"How dare you steal my murder from under my nose!" Flora said furiously as she withdrew a mangled *London Daily Gazette* from her reticule and waved it in the air. "How dare you wrest it from my hands! It was my investigation. Mine!"

Having asserted the claim with unwieldy ferocity, she seemed to pop like a bubble, losing her air all at once, and she dropped onto the settee as tears began to fall. "I am a useless ninny," she cried, "and everybody knows it. You! Holcroft! Even Mr. Twaddle-Thum! He never mentions me at all."

Astonished by her cousin's sweeping change in mood, from anger to misery in a fraction of a second, Bea stood awkwardly as Flora pulled her knees up to her chest. Then she wrapped her arms around them and gripped her hands tightly, giving no thought to the lovely brocade of the cushion.

Inconsequentially, Bea thought of Aunt Vera's horror if she witnessed her daughter's immense disrespect for the Duke of Kesgrave's finery. She would gasp and sputter as she calculated how much it would cost to reupholster the settee in an equally luxurious fabric.

No, she would faint at the audacity.

Hyde-Clares were not raised to tread easily in other people's houses.

Hovels, yes.

A small and ramshackle structure, perhaps with a roof that leaked during violent storms, they could trounce through as if they themselves owned the place.

But a sturdy home with pristine walls elicited a debilitating awe of perfection and an anxiety that even the most seemingly benign misstep could have irreversible consequences.

Hesitantly, Bea sat down next to Flora and lifted her hand as if to pat the girl comfortingly on the shoulder. Then, fearing the gesture might be an unwelcome presumption, she pulled her hand away and let it drop to her side.

"I should think being left out of Twaddle's accounts would be cause for celebration," she said instead. It was an attempt at humor to leaven the moment, but she also did not know how else to respond, her cousin's misery was so absolute. It certainly did not seem like the time to remind her of what Holcroft had said regarding the gossip's awareness of her. "You should be crying tears of happiness, my dear."

As benign as this statement was, it upset Flora further and the girl's shoulders began to shake as her sobs intensified. She laid her head against her knees, muffling her words, which made them barely distinguishable. "Of course I am doing it wrong. I do everything wrong. I am too stupid to do anything right, and you all know it."

Dampened by Flora's legs, the deeply felt self-pity nevertheless communicated itself clearly, and Bea struggled to understand its cause. Ordinarily, her cousin carried herself with a great deal of confidence, placating her mother, pandering to her father and persecuting her brother. Since unwittingly stumbling across a conspiracy in the Chancery Court and helping to apprehend its perpetrators, she had assumed an air of world-weary knowingness, which, though more than a little absurd, Bea found charming.

Nothing in her actions indicated a sense of inferiority.

Baffled, she said, "I do not know anything of the sort."

"But you do," Flora wailed, pressing her forehead even

harder against her knees. "You do! It is why you cut me out of the Dugmore investigation."

Yes, of course, the newspaper, Bea thought, comprehension dawning. Flora had known at once what it meant, her and Kesgrave's strange visit to an orphan asylum on the other side of the Thames. The fact that her cousin had readily perceived the significance argued in favor of a keen intellect, but Bea decided that was not the tack to take.

Rather, she addressed the charge forthrightly. "I did not cut you out of the Dugmore investigation because there *was* no Dugmore investigation. I swear! When we left the establishment, I was of the same opinion as you. It was Kesgrave who noticed something amiss and insisted we return. So if anything, it is the duke who cut you out. I can bring him back so you may rail at him if you wish, but I must warn you that his ego is very fragile in this regard. He fears you will supplant him as my investigative assistant, so please admonish him gently."

Flora, raising her head, shook it fiercely and accused Bea of mocking her. "You think I have nothing to add to the investigation. I am like a child, always in the way and having to be taken back to the schoolroom, where I can do no harm. You think I am insipid and facile, with my lifelong adoration of Incomparables like Miss Otley and my belief that only beautiful things have merit. And my horrible treatment of you! Always sending you to fetch my things as if you were naught but a servant and snickering behind your back when Mama called you dull for the way you silently trotted off to do her bidding. I deserve every ounce of your disgust!"

Aunt Vera's contempt was a revelation to Bea, who had spent her years as an unpaid companion with her head buried in one book or another. Reading had staved off the loneliness and despair of her situation, and she had not given her relatives the attention required to notice the extent of their scorn. But it made perfect sense to her, for Aunt Vera was just small-minded enough to deride a dependent for following her every order without a word of complaint.

Smiling faintly, she decided it was impossible to be appalled by this fresh example of her aunt's pettiness, for in truth it was not new. It was simply more of the same. "I trust you will not take offense if I observe that being called dull by your mother is a compliment. I can only hope you aspire to a similar height."

But this, too, was the wrong thing to say, for Flora cited it as yet more proof of Bea's disdain for her intellect. "You think I will laugh at your sallies and thus be diverted from the topic at hand. It is what Holcroft did for weeks, fobbing me off with stupid excuses, and I believed every one of them. I am exactly the ninny you both believe me to be. It is little wonder neither one of you trusts me to have a hand in anything, least of all my own future. I deserve every unhappiness."

Flora tightened her grip on her legs but kept her chin resolutely up, as if determined to confront her failures head on, and Bea returned her gaze steadily despite an intense desire to turn away.

Truly, she had no idea what to say.

That nobody deserved unhappiness—well, yes, obviously that.

It was a sweeping generalization, to be sure, and while there were no doubt exceptions, they did not include a young lady who had merely aped the behavior of the adults in her life. Flora had treated the poor relative in her midst precisely the way she had been taught to treat the poor relative in her midst, and it was unfair to resent her for failing to rebel against an injustice she did not know was unjust. The moment evidence appeared to suggest the need for a reevaluation, her cousin had duly reevaluated.

Bea genuinely thought that was the best any person could do.

She had said something to that effect in a previous conversation with Flora, when she discovered her cousin had embarked on the Chancery debacle in an attempt to make amends for perceived transgressions. If she thought her assurances would lessen her cousin's pain, she would happily reissue them now, but she knew Flora's outburst had nothing to do with the Dugmore investigation.

The problem was, she did not know how to address the real topic, for Flora had made her wishes known. For a week, she had seethed silently about her beau's treatment and never once mentioned it to any member of her family.

Clearly, she desired her privacy.

And yet there she was, in the drawing room in Berkeley Square, sobbing about Holcroft's ill treatment.

Surely, that constituted an invitation.

"It seems to me as though you have two options," Bea said with conversational certainty, as if the matter with Holcroft had been the subject all along—as indeed it had. "Forgive him or do not forgive him. That is it. Those are your two choices. Pick the one that makes you less miserable and then figure out how to live with it. Based on your irritability this past week, I rather think it is the former—or, rather, I hope for Russell's sake it is—but only you can decide. All I will add in regards to that is what is done is done. It is like what your mother said after you dropped an entire pot of tea onto the new rug: Do fetch a cloth, for there is no use in whimpering over spilled tea."

Flora, her expression lightening despite the tears that continued to stream down her cheeks, said, "It was Russell."

"Was it?" Bea asked curiously, unable to recall the specific details of the debacle other than she had dashed as fast as she could to the kitchens to get rags to sop up the mess. She had been only twelve years old at the time and still had understood to whom her aunt's comment had been directed.

Even with two footmen in the room, Bea had known.

"Yes," Flora said, the grip on her knees lessening as some of her composure returned. Slowly, she slipped her feet over the side of the settee and onto the floor. "He was bouncing all over the room, pretending to box with Michaels—he was the butler then, if you recall—and he swung out his fist and upset the tray, causing the whole thing to tumble onto the new rug. Poor Mama was beside herself. I think that might have been when she developed her aversion to bare-knuckle brawling."

Bea chuckled. "I do believe she was speaking to herself when she said there was no use in whimpering over spilled tea."

"Oh, yes, there can be no doubt," Flora agreed. "And it was chocolate, not tea. It was breakfast, if you remember, and Russell and I were allowed to have a small cup each. That was why Mama was in such a frenzy—because chocolate is so much harder to wash out than tea, especially weak tea the way the housekeeper used to brew it. She thought for sure the stain would be there forever, and we had had the rug for scarcely a month. And Papa was no help! He lowered the newspaper only long enough to note that light blue was an impractical color for a rug."

Although Bea had not mentioned the episode in an effort to divert Flora from her distress, it appeared to have had that effect. The stream of tears coursing down her cheeks slowed to a trickle, and she sought to brush them away with her fingers.

"Your memory of the incident is remarkable," Bea said, who was usually the one to recall events in vivid detail.

A hint of a smile trembled on her cousin's lips. "How could I forget? Russell was confined to his room for two full weeks and I got all the attention. Even Papa played draughts with me."

"Are you sure you did not trip him so that he would knock over the serving tray?" Bea asked.

Flora conceded that she might have slid her leg into her brother's path if she had possessed the cunning at six to come up with such a nefarious plot. "Alas, I would not engage in any daring schemes for another fourteen years," she said, her humor dipping as this thought led her back to Holcroft. She stared down at her fingers for several long moments before raising her eyes and continuing in a matter-of-fact tone. "He thought my life was in danger. Based on a puzzling series of events, he feared that someone might try to harm me to keep the Grimston affair a secret and he decided it was best if we had no further contact until the matter was resolved. But he did not do me the courtesy of informing me of that. Instead, he fobbed me off with lies and evasions and then expected me to be grateful for his sacrifice. I am *not* grateful!"

"No, I can see that you are not," Bea murmured and wondered what she could say to help the situation. Refuting the accusation lodged specifically at her seemed beside the point and yet she did not want Flora to leave Kesgrave House believing she held her in such low esteem.

"If he knows me so little, then maybe *I* do not know *him*," Flora added weepily, fury mixing with sadness to give her an air of true despondency.

Noting it, Bea reminded her that she had only two choices: forgive, do not forgive. "But I would caution you against looking at Holcroft's actions solely from your own perspective. As you yourself have observed several times, he is a staid gentleman known for his rigid morality—Holcroft the Holy, I believe, as Twaddle dubbed him. He is very careful and studied in his thinking. If he made a decision that strikes you as excessively ill conceived, perhaps you should consider why. Something drove him to it."

Flora pursed her lips thoughtfully. "You are saying he was too scared to think clearly."

"What I am saying is that if anyone's mental faculties are diminished, then they are Holcroft's," Bea said, stating her point clearly so that there could be no misunderstanding. "I am not seeking to excuse his treatment of you, for I agree it is unacceptable, but to propose an explanation other than he thinks you are a ninny. Holcroft is not given to rash behavior, and I think the fact that he did act rashly on this occasion might be an indication of his feelings for you."

Her cousin, allowing for the possibility, narrowed her eyes and said, "Perhaps, but he cannot confine me to my room like a small child every time the chocolate spills."

On the verge of asking how frequently Flora imagined her life would be in mortal peril, Bea gasped sharply as the image of the blemish on Dugmore's rug flitted through her head.

Light brown, yes, but still darker than the larger blotch to the left.

Examining the stain near the pier table, she had assumed Mary had made only so much progress before Mrs. Gaitskill shut up the room out of disgust for her son and Ripley's quarrel.

But now, with Flora's words ringing in her ears, she saw the darker stain differently.

What if it was not tea at all?

According to Melody's description of her mother's weekly appointment with the housekeeper, Dugmore drank a cup of chocolate every night. If his fingers were trembling so violently he could not properly secure the pier table's secret latch, then perhaps they were shaking too hard to grasp the mug.

Did it matter that an enfeebled old man's hands were so unsteady?

Frankly, Bea did not know.

And yet any divergence in his nightly routine struck her as significant.

Or at the very least worthy of further examination.

But she could not return to St. James's Square now, not with Flora across from her, her misery lightened but not dispelled. Resolutely, she returned her attention to her cousin and said, "That is a matter for you and Holcroft to discuss. I advise you to base your decision on how he responds to your concerns. If he will not acknowledge their legitimacy, then you will have your answer and can bring your association to an end calmly and maturely. It is better than your refusing to speak to him, which might serve only to affirm his judgment of you as childlike—if indeed that is the opinion he holds."

Even before Bea had finished outlining her proposal, her cousin nodded her head emphatically and she rose to her feet. "Yes, yes, that is exactly what I shall do. I have been in too much of a temper to think about it logically, but you are correct. I can use the remorse over his ill treatment as an opportunity to gain concessions. I am not obliged to accept his apology as it stands. We can negotiate. He has the most stylish curricle. Have you seen it, my dear? It is so very dashing, with its wooden gadroons and mustard yellow color, and I have asked several times to be allowed to drive it—only in the park, you understand, not on a thoroughfare such as Bond Street—and he always refused."

"And that is the tack you are going to take?" Bea asked, highly amused by the eagerness in her cousin's voice. "I will forgive you for treating me like a babe in arms if you will allow me to drive your carriage?"

"His *curricle,* Bea," Flora repeated with increased emphasis, as if expecting her cousin to display appropriate enthusiasm. "It is almost as splendid as a high phaeton. It goes particularly well with my new rose pink dress, which Holcroft admired when he finally deigned to visit. He said it brought out the green in my eyes, which is a lovely compliment, but I was too furious to appreciate it, let alone thank him for it. Perhaps I should change into my rose pink dress before seeing him. Yes, I shall do that. I will go home and change into my new dress and then send him a note asking him to call on me at his earliest convenience. And you must not worry, my dear, that my list will be all curricle drives and outings to the park. I will insist that future threats to my life be resolved by mutual agreement. Naturally, the same will go for threats against his life as well. It would never do if we talked endlessly about the risks to me and said nothing about the risks to him. And if he cannot be persuaded to treat me with the respect and dignity I require, then I will bid him adieu and wear my lovely rose pink dress to Almack's on Wednesday to find myself a more fair-minded beau."

Having established a course of action, Flora was impatient to implement it and she fairly ran to the drawing room door. She had just reached for the handle when she turned back to her cousin and apologized for not inquiring about the Dugmore case.

"Is that proceeding apace or do you need a consultation?" she asked in that familiar avuncular manner she had adopted since extricating herself and her beloved from a knife-wielding murderer. "As eager as I am to speak with Holcroft, I am never too busy to withhold my assistance. Shall we review your list of suspects?"

Suppressing a grin, Bea somberly assured her the investigation was well in hand. "Kesgrave and I have made tolerable progress," she added, imagining her cousin's approval if the culprit did in fact turn out to be the viscount.

Flora hailed this development as highly satisfactory and

swept out of the room, insisting that she did not require an escort to the door, for as her sister such courtesies were superfluous.

Delighted by her cousin's return to form, Bea granted this liberty and settled herself on the settee to contemplate the significance of the two spills.

Tea and chocolate, she thought, turning the notion around in her head. Tea and chocolate.

Nobody had mentioned the latter in any of their conversations, and although she wanted to point to that lack as conspicuous, she knew it was not.

Sometimes unimportant details were unimportant.

And sometimes the whole mystery rested on them.

Bea rose to her feet to summon the carriage just as Kesgrave returned. Noting her cousin's absence, he said, "I trust Flora left in a better state of mind than when she arrived."

"She has left her investigation in our capable hands," she replied wryly, "but remains available for a consultation should we run into difficulty."

He smiled and murmured "very good" before attempting to resume their conversation from earlier. "As I was saying regarding the physician, I have spoken with—"

But Bea did not want to hear it, not yet, for she had a thrilling new idea to explore and she wanted to pretend that not everything was about to change.

All those months of proving herself his equal only to be relegated to subsidiary the moment biology asserted itself.

It was inevitable and irresistible, and yet she sought to put it off just a little bit longer by interrupting his speech to announce she had made an advance in the case. "There were two spills: one tea, one chocolate," she said, threading her arm through his as she led him out of the room toward the entry hall. Her stomach rumbled, reminding her that she had forgotten to request a plate of cheese and fruit in the wake of Flora's frantic arrival.

Ignoring the pang of hunger, she explained her theory as they waited for Jenkins to bring the carriage around. Kesgrave found it compelling, and although he was at a loss to comprehend the relevance of spilled chocolate, he appeared content to speculate about its meaning as they drove to St. James's Square, as if complying with Bea's unspoken request to defer the doctor's recommendations until after they had identified Roger Dugmore's killer.

Chapter Fifteen

Ripley shut the door in their faces.

He did not do it harshly or meanly but rather with an air of distraction, as if he had just that moment been summoned to another room and had to resolve a pressing issue before he could even think of responding to the demands of the new callers.

Firmly, deliberately, his eyes turned assiduously away, he pressed the door closed.

Bea commented on the futility of the gesture, for the viscount had lauded her persistence on more than one occasion, and marveled at the way it managed to be both bold *and* craven. She glanced at the duke with amusement as she raised her hand to rap her knuckles against the wood and said, "I suppose this is another first for you."

Presumably, Bevins would respond in a moment to her knock—unless his lordship had resorted to physically restraining the poor butler. If that proved to be the case, then Kesgrave would have to pick the lock.

"Actually, it was a mainstay of my early adulthood," the duke replied, his own lips quirking in response, "as Marlow would not permit me to enter the house if I was noticeably drunk. Among his most strongly held beliefs is that a man should be able to hold his liquor without revealing the extent of his intoxication or abstain altogether. It was years before I was able to recite Hamlet's 'too too solid flesh' soliloquy while completely foxed."

It delighted her, all of it—a young Kesgrave working his inebriated tongue around "Fie on't! ah fie! 'tis an unweeded garden," an impertinent Marlow denying his own master entry—and Bea laughed as she tried to reconcile the image of his standing on the threshold of his home with his nose pressed against the door with the pompous bore who lectured with mind-numbing detail during their dinners at Lakeview Hall.

"I am not surprised to discover his standards are so exacting," she observed as she knocked again. "A lesser tyrant would have allowed you to fall back on the rhyme of 'double, double toil and trouble.' His horror upon learning you were to wed a drab spinster must have been so incoherent he himself could not recite a nursey rhyme."

"Of a certainty," Kesgrave replied, flashing a grin to soften the blow. "He could not have sputtered the first line of 'Ring a Ring o' Roses ' if he had tried. And his horror at your wild competence appears to be justified. The last thing he wanted was a mistress who would make him look weak by comparison, and your ability to repel Bentham without his assistance mortifies him to his toes. The next time you are attacked in your sitting room, do consider the servants and at least make some effort to summon help."

It was striking, Bea thought, the cool detachment with which he discussed a future assault upon her person, and she understood what it meant. He could only be so cavalier about her safety because he knew it was assured.

Smothering her resentment, she knocked even harder on

the door as she tsked with gentle humor. "There you go again, your grace, prioritizing the staff's tender feelings!"

As if he had been waiting for an indication of their increased frustration, Ripley opened the door and sighed heavily as he contemplated them with morose gloominess. "I do not mean to be rude, your grace, but this is really not fair. When my aunt said you could come back to continue your investigation, she did not mean an hour later."

But even as he offered this complaint, he stepped back to allow them to enter the house. "I suppose you had better come in and tell us what new horrible thing you have discovered about us now. We are still in the drawing room arguing over who killed Grandfather. It's perfectly beastly. It seems we are all just horrible people, eager to point our fingers at each other, although they are united against me, which I think is unfair. Melody changed Grandfather's will and yet somehow I am the villain!" he said, his tone a mix of outrage and sorrow. "It is extremely disagreeable to be accused of murder by your entire family. When I invited you here, I thought it would be merry fun, pretending to solve a mystery while courting Mr. Twaddle-Thum's attention. When you found the secret compartment with Matthew's bills, it was the grandest thing. I wanted your entire investigation to be humiliating interviews with my cousin. I never once considered what it would mean for him to be actually sent to Newgate. But now that they are all looking at me, I have been forced to contemplate what it means and I do not want any of my family to go to prison. Are you quite positive there is not a more interesting murder you would like to examine up the road? I heard Mrs. Montesquieu yelling at her husband last night for taking his mistress to the same opera performance as she and her sister. Maybe he has been slain in some horribly grisly manner that requires your attendance."

Appreciating the predicament in which the viscount

found himself, for it was completely of his own devising, Bea refused this offer. "We are here to speak to Mary."

"Good God!" Ripley said, goggling at her. "You mean to say Clifford was right all along? A servant *did* do it!"

"No," Bea said firmly, aware of how damaging a false accusation could be to a young woman without connections. "I do not mean to say that at all. I do not suspect Mary of anything. I merely want to confirm a theory regarding the stains on the rug."

The viscount's brow furrowed as he tried to make sense of this information in light of what he knew about the state of their investigation, which, he believed, was centered on Melody. Then he sighed and said, "You might as well join us in the drawing room so that you can put your questions to Mary in front of everyone. I do wish Mr. Twaddle-Thum had spent a little time writing about the corrosive effects of suspicion and how wretched it is to sit across from members of your own family and wonder if they are cold-blooded killers. It is deuced unfair of him to make murder sound so thrilling and fun."

Although she herself had laid an astonishing number of sins at the scurrilous gossip's feet, Bea was not entirely sure his lively columns were to blame for Ripley's grievously skewed perception of a murder investigation. The viscount's own enthusiasms and short-sightedness struck her as the more likely culprits.

Keeping these thoughts to herself, she asked him to send Mary up to his grandfather's bedchamber. "We shall talk to her there."

"The scene of the crime," Ripley said with a dramatic shiver, still incapable of grasping the seriousness of the situation despite his speech. "Are you sure you would not rather talk to her in the drawing room? As I said, we are all gathered there and herding everyone up to the second floor will take time."

"There is no need to herd anyone," Bea said. "We want to speak just to Mary."

Disgruntled at being excluded from events in his own home, his lordship nevertheless agreed to this plan and asked one of the footmen to summon Mary to his grandfather's room. Then he announced that he would be in the drawing room with his family speculating on the significance of the stain. "I trust you will attend to us after your interview has concluded."

Bea agreed as she and the duke mounted the stairs. Arriving at the second-floor landing, they turned to the right and entered the bedchamber, which was illuminated by weak sunshine peering through a break in the clouds.

"The stain is darker here," she said, pointing to a fat blotch surrounded by narrow drops. Then she gestured to a series of faint marks on the rug a foot to the left. "But over there it is almost entirely gone. I thought that was because Mary had cleaned this part of the spill. I thought the spill snaked along the rug until it hit the pier table, where it pooled near the edge based on the angle of the floor. But the one spill stopped, it did not snake, and the second spill began. That is the reason you can still see this blob plainly. It is chocolate, not tea."

"And you think he spilled the chocolate because his hands were trembling so violently he could not hold on to the mug," Kesgrave said, lowering to his haunches to get a better view of the stain. "He also could not close the table's compartment, which he accessed regularly, indicating his hands were shaking with more vigor than usual the night before his murder."

"A feeble old man is slightly more feeble," she murmured. "If the latter was caused by something—a substance in his food, for example, or drink—would anyone notice the difference?"

"Ah, so that would explain how Miss Gaitskill was able to be seemingly in two places at once," he said, following her line of thought. "The poison could have been administered at any time via any method. She would not have to be here at the precise moment he died."

"We know she is stealthy because she spied on Dugmore's visits with his physician without anyone being the wiser," she pointed out. "And she has demonstrated an aptitude for duplicity. Maybe she found a drug in the doctor's bag or secured it from the apothecary. She could have slipped it into his eggs at breakfast or tea and then toddled off to the asylum."

Kesgrave, conceding the general appeal of her theory, noted that the substance must have been very slow acting if its victim managed to get through the entire day without incident. "And it was not what killed him in the end."

Bea shook her head with frustration and said, "No, it is not, and positing two attacks—poison and bashing—does nothing but hopelessly complicate the matter. I can imagine Melody using a drug to make her already frail grandfather weaker to hasten his death or to simply debilitate him further so he would not have the clarity of mind to communicate with his lawyer. The more he tinkered with his will, the less likely the forgery would stand. But to have Melody's sneaky plan to undermine her grandfather's health intersect with another person's sneaky plan to kill him seems like too much of a coincidence."

"And yet that is precisely what happened at Lady Abercrombie's dinner party," he reminded her as Mary entered the room.

Breathless from running up the stairs, she apologized for

keeping them waiting and asked how she could be of assistance.

Bea presented her theory regarding the second splotch, which Mary confirmed and then lamented how much harder chocolate was to wash out of a rug's fibers than tea. "I was going to give it a good scrub as soon as I finished cleaning up the spill I made, but Mrs. Gaitskill ordered me from the room before I could start on the chocolate. I tried to argue that the stain would be harder to clean the longer it set, but Lord Ripley said not to worry about it because he would replace the rug anyway when he moved into the room. That caused another argument, which upset Mrs. Gaitskill further. She was already distraught."

Having endured several of the cousins' squabbles herself, Bea thought that response was only to be expected. "Mr. Dugmore regularly enjoyed chocolate at bedtime?"

Mary nodded vehemently. "Yes, your grace, it was delivered to his room every night at eleven as he was preparing for bed either by me or one of the other maids."

"Did you deliver it on the night before his death?" Bea asked.

"Yes, I did, your grace. I carried it into the room and placed it on the table next to his bed, right there," she said with a wave of her hand. "Then I bid him a good night and left."

"Did he frequently drop it?"

"His hands shook, so sometimes he would bobble the cup and I would find dried splatters on the table," Mary replied. "This was the first time he dropped the whole drink onto the floor, at least as far as I know. But the tremors in his hands had been getting worse in the last few weeks, and he was very tired by the end of the day. Just between you and me, I don't think Dr. Pritchard is very good because my previous employer had gout and his hands didn't shake like a leaf. And I do not think the chocolate was working."

"Working?" Bea repeated, stuck by the implication. "What was it supposed to do?"

"Help him sleep," the maid explained. "Mr. Dugmore had a terrible time sleeping through the night, always tossing and turning, because of his gout. And Dr. Pritchard said chocolate at bedtime would be more soothing than tea. He said having the same drink every night would help him prepare for bed. Routine is restful, the doctor said."

Although there was nothing remarkable about a gravely ill elderly gentleman having a difficult time sleeping, Bea was struck by the description because it differed so wildly from the one given by the viscount. Replying to an accusation from Jesse, he said, *He was alive and sleeping peacefully when I left.*

"Was it always like that?" she asked. "The tossing and turning? Or just on a particularly bad night?"

"Every night was a particularly bad night," Mary said. "The only time he slept soundly was when the doctor convinced him to take laudanum. Most of the time he would refuse because he did not want to form a habit. He said he would rather wake up every hour in his own mind than sleep through the night out of it."

Her remark corroborated Clifford's claim about being terrified that his grandfather would awaken at any moment and find him with his hand in the pier table—an assertion that ran counter to Ripley's own description.

But he was not alive or sleeping peacefully, Bea realized.

Dugmore was already dead by the time Ripley crept into his bedchamber at 6:08.

That made a lot more sense, she decided, as it also explained how his lordship felt comfortable enough to open the curtains to allow in daylight while Clifford could barely raise a candlelight for fear of disturbing his grandfather.

Bea tried to drum up a modicum of indignation at the lie, for Ripley had wasted her time and the duke's time and every member of his family's time, and yet the effort was futile. The simpleton had brought them there under a false pretense and flailed from one fiction to the next as various truths emerged. The boy was not a diabolical genius; he was precisely what he appeared to be: a naïve provincial with little sense or understanding. If he had just been honest from the beginning, then he would not be the prime suspect in his grandfather's murder and his family would not be united against him.

"It was the gout, you see," Mary continued with a forlorn shrug of her shoulders. "It gave him so much trouble. But he is sleeping peacefully at last."

Distracted by the new time frame for the murder—anywhere between eleven, when the chocolate was delivered, and six, when Ripley entered the room—Bea thanked the maid and allowed her to return to her duties.

As soon as she left, Kesgrave looked at Bea and asked what she had figured out. "I know it is something significant because you have that gleam in your eye: a little smug, a little impatient, a little annoyed."

Did she? Bea wondered.

Nevertheless, her answer conveyed her satisfaction when she said he would be a little smug too if he had realized Dugmore was already dead by the time the viscount entered the room at six in the morning.

Although clearly intrigued by the idea, the duke revealed no surprise, presumably because he knew the preening peacock was capable of any outrageousness. "I suppose we should go find out why Ripley lied."

It was easier said than done, however, for when they returned to the drawing room, they found its occupants engaged in a heated dispute, each person yelling louder than the next. Their voices were an indecipherable tangle, and Bea

AN EXTRAVAGANT DUPLICITY

was unable to identify a single line of argument. All she could distinguish were their expressions—the seething contempt on Matthew's face, the red-hot anger on Clifford's, the defensive fury on Ripley's. Mrs. Gaitskill was still sitting but she had pulled her body to the edge of the chair, which was flanked by the cousins. Her cheeks were bright red from the effort of yelling. Next to her stood Melody, whose hands were balled into fists that hovered in midair, as if at any moment she might strike a family member or supplicate to heaven. Jesse pressed his fingers to his ears, blocking out the noise while adding to it with what seemed like a perpetual scream.

Flinching, yes, at the primitivity of the scene, at the violence and the clamor and a sort of wrath that transcended generations, Bea could not fathom the speed at which the bonds of civility had broken down. She and the duke had been upstairs with the maid for less than fifteen minutes, and somehow in that brief span of time feral chaos had overtaken the company.

She stared agog.

Kesgrave whistled.

Like a governess quieting her charges, he produced a clear shrill sound through his puckered lips, and one by one the residents of 16 St. James's Square fell silent.

Characteristically, Ripley was the last voice to drop and Bea heard him insist that a secret twin was not implausible. Melody opened her mouth as if to refute the remark but did not say a word. Nobody did for several long seconds and although the room was quiet, their glares spoke volumes.

Mrs. Gaitskill broke the silence, suggesting that the cousins sit down so that the Duke and Duchess of Kesgrave could explain their business. "While they cannot be astonished to find the family in turmoil, given the discord we displayed little more than an hour ago when they left, we still owe them the appearance of decorum. You may all return to yelling at each other as soon as they leave," she added amiably.

Ripley, complying with the request, mumbled, "You were yelling too."

His aunt acknowledged the remark with a self-conscious smile and said she tended to do that when people accused her of bearing twin daughters in secret.

"I did not say you *bore* them in secret," the viscount replied, "but that you *raised* them that way."

"For God's sake," Matthew growled hotly. "Can you not hold your tongue for one bloody minute?"

Clifford snorted and said, "You are a fine one to talk. You have not ceased complaining about Melody's betrayal since the moment you learned of it."

Before the squabble could begin again in earnest, Bea raised her hand slightly and announced they had new information to impart. "The timing of the murder, originally thought to be between six-thirty, when Ripley left the bedchamber, and eight-thirty, when Mary found the body, is wrong."

"One does not need a snooping lady Runner to figure that out," Clifford said derisively. "Ripley killed him before he left the room."

"Careful, Clifford," Ripley warned. "Your disdain for Her Outrageousness will not endear you to Mr. Twaddle-Thum's readers."

Jesse exhaled a loud breath. "For goodness' sake, *hang* Mr. Twaddle-Thum. It is a matter of life and death now. We cannot continue like this, at dagger points with each other. We must know as a family who killed Grandfather."

Clifford insisted they did know. "It is Ripley. He is the only one among us who does not have an alibi. Unless someone wants to reconsider my servant theory."

The suggestion was roundly mocked, and Mrs. Gaitskill apologized yet again to the visitors.

Bea continued as if she had not been interrupted. "Mr. Dugmore was already dead when Lord Ripley entered the room."

The viscount gasped, as if stunned by the revelation, and while the rest of his family stared at him in either amazement or confusion, Melody laughed. "Leave it to Howie to lie to make himself appear more guilty, not less. Whatever were you thinking?"

"I was not thinking," Ripley said irritably, rising to his feet to stalk the drawing room. "The moment I saw him lying there, so small and sickly, I panicked. We had just had that hellish row the day before and the whole house had heard it. I knew what you would all think if I was the one who found him, especially at that hour because it was strange that I was there. Why would I be there except to cause Grandfather harm? It seemed so easy. I could just leave and nobody would be the wiser. I would return to my bed as though nothing had happened and wait for someone else to find him. But then Matthew saw me leaving! And it was already too late to do anything differently. I could not suddenly sound the alarm or say something like, 'Bye the bye, Grandfather is dead.' So I pretended everything was fine and returned to my room."

Mrs. Gaitskill shook her head, baffled. "But why would you invite the duchess here if you had something to hide?"

"I did not have *something* to hide," Ripley bit out furiously. "I had something to hide, which is different, as I am sure you understand. And it never occurred to me that Grandfather had actually been killed. The idea was preposterous."

Matthew, his eyes narrowed, asked why Bea was willing to accept the viscount's word about anything. "He is a liar and we all know it."

"He was dead, I swear it!" Ripley said, his voice rising in apprehension. "I could not believe it. At first I was so confused. That is why I threw open the curtains—so I could get a clear look at him. And I tried so hard to wake him up. I did. I swear! I shook his shoulder *very hard,* but it did not make a difference, as I knew it would not, because he was already cool to the touch. It was so shocking. I had no idea how long I sat there on the floor next to him before I realized I had to leave. So I closed the curtains as tightly as I could to make sure nobody would suspect a thing and crept out. And then Matthew ruined it all with his Corinthian ways! Fishing at six-thirty in the morning! Have you no decency at all?"

His aunt still did not comprehend. "But why create this ... this ... *circus*? Why make us turn on each other like the veriest savages? What did this accomplish?"

Distraught at the accusation, Ripley lost all color in his face and threw himself on the floor next to his aunt's chair. Taking her hand in his, he pleaded, "I did not mean for this to happen! I just could not bear your suspicions. You may deny it now, but you know it is true. As soon as Matthew told you what he had seen, you all looked at me with fear, as if I were capable of killing an enfeebled old man to save my inheritance."

"I do not deny it," Jesse said loftily.

"You see! I had to do something to prove I was innocent," Ripley insisted, squeezing his aunt's fingers so tightly she winced in pain. "I could not bear the thought that you would believe it for even one moment, Aunt Celia. Or any of my cousins, even Matthew. Especially Matthew. I know he thinks I am a provincial greenhorn with more hair than wit. You all believe I am just stupid enough to do it, even Melody, who sometimes laughs at my sallies and calls me a clever boy."

His cousin had the grace to blush. "You do have your

moments, Howie. I thought the escapade with the ladybirds was diverting. Asinine and juvenile, yes, but also diverting."

Although he flitted his eyes in her general direction, he kept his attention focused on his aunt. "I thought it was innocuous. Grandfather died of a fall! What harm could there be in allowing Her Outrageousness here to look around? And my plan worked!" he added, sweeping his gaze now around the room. "After the duchess left that first time, Matthew called me a great nodcock who did not understand anything, and Clifford chided me for not being able to take a little good-natured ribbing. The last thing I expected was for her to return an hour later and announce that Grandfather had actually been murdered. I have never had a greater shock in all my life."

Matthew laughed with disdainful glee. "You *are* a great nodcock! You would not be the only suspect in Grandfather's murder now if you had not been so eager to prove your innocence then. I have never seen anyone get their just deserts so swiftly or conspicuously. You will write us from Newgate, won't you, dear boy, and tell us what is all the rage among the prisoners? I expect they wear their rags *très effiloché,* but I trust you will correct me if I am wrong."

"*You* are the great nodcock if you do not comprehend what this means," Clifford snapped in a voice tight with anxiety, revealing that he understood the implication even if his older cousin did not. "Ripley is no longer the only suspect. If Grandfather was murdered in the seven-hour interval between when he got his chocolate at eleven and our cousin found him at six, then any one of us could have done it. All our alibis are useless."

Although spoken with an air of dire urgency, these words had little effect on Matthew, who raised his shoulders as if to shrug off the concern. He abruptly ceased this motion, however, as consternation swept across his features and he became aware of his vulnerability. By his own account, he had gone to bed at one-thirty on the morning of the murder.

That left him with no one to verify his movements.

Jesse, who had perceived the difficulty at once, eyed the drawing room door speculatively, as if gauging its distance, perhaps to figure out how quickly he could dash from the room.

As Bea wondered at his destination—Miss Cheever, she thought likely—Mrs. Gaitskill observed that not everyone's alibi was without use. "Melody was still at Fortescue's taking care of a sick child, and no amount of fantastical storytelling is going to refute that one inexorable truth. Ripley may invent all the secret twins he wants."

"Yes, Mama," her daughter said placatingly. "My well-being is secured, thanks to the horrible illness that ravaged poor Aggie's tiny body. How right you were to be so worried about her welfare. But I suggest you turn your attention to Matthew now, for it is his future that appears to be in jeopardy. His motive is as great as mine, if not greater, for he had no idea that Grandfather would die long before he could carry out the worst of his threat."

Clifford, murmuring appreciatively, complimented his cousin on being a spiteful kitten, for he had not thought she had it in her, while Mrs. Gaitskill stared at her son with a sort of bewildered confusion, as if surprised to discover he was still in the room. Ripley, arch and sardonic, welcomed Matthew to the club and received a hateful glare from him in return. Jesse, his eyes still pinned on the door, took two cautious steps forward, then looked around to see if anyone had noticed him inching toward the exit.

Watching him, Bea grew more convinced than ever that he did in fact still have an alibi and feared Miss Cheever might reveal the truth if she thought it would save him from

AN EXTRAVAGANT DUPLICITY

the gallows. He wanted to assure her that she must preserve her reputation at all costs and not worry about his welfare.

Worry about his welfare.

The words echoed in Bea's head once and then twice as the volume in the room grew louder: Melody chiding Clifford, Ripley goading Matthew, Mrs. Gaitskill touting the calming influence of tea as she rose to ring for a fresh pot despite the half a dozen cups from earlier that were ignored.

Bea could not fathom its cause, why the phrase would resonate so sharply, for there was nothing remarkable about it. People said it all the time.

Oh, but that was it, she thought suddenly, her eyes darting across the room to where Mrs. Gaitskill stood near the wall, her fingers grasping the bell cord so tightly her knuckles had turned white. Only a few minutes before Melody had said that very thing, assuring her mother that her concern for the sick child had been warranted: *How right you were to be so worried about her welfare.*

So trite and benign and yet rife with the most alarming implication, for there was only one reason Mrs. Gaitskill would lobby for her daughter to take the unusual step of remaining overnight at the orphan asylum: to make sure she could not fall under suspicion for her grandfather's murder.

Chapter Sixteen

I t was just a theory.

Having perceived the importance of Melody's comment in a sudden flash of insight, Bea knew she needed evidence to support it.

Without corroboration, it was nothing more than wild surmise.

Even so, she had managed to establish a reputation as an accomplished female investigator based on speculation that was far more outlandish.

Every hypothesis was absurd until the moment it was not.

With that in mind, she turned her attention to piecing together what she knew to create a viable narrative. Although she had done that very thing several times before, she was nevertheless daunted to realize she had never given Mrs. Gaitskill serious consideration because the matron had no discernable motive and suspecting her because she closed the door to the room felt flimsy. As a consequence, Bea had refrained from examining her with the same piercing skepticism with which she had scrutinized the assortment of cousins.

Contemplating the matter now, she still conceded a general lack of motive in the conventional sense. Mrs. Gaitskill neither sought anything from her father nor feared his reprisal. As far as she could discern, the pair had a cordial relationship, and she professed not to resent his interference in her children's lives.

What had she said?

I was grateful for his interest. Their own father had been generally indifferent to their futures before finally doing himself in with a dull pitchfork. The constable told a reporter for the county newspaper that he had been set upon by thieves in the field, but the truth was he was stumbling around drunk in the stables and fell.

'Twas not the way one generally talked about a beloved spouse, Bea thought now, and reconsidered the sentiment in light of the fact that she had never remarried. If Mrs. Gaitskill's own experience had been so unhappy that she would rather serve as hostess to her father than take another husband, then perhaps she did in fact object to Dugmore's determination to see her children settled in situations of his own devising. Having made a ruinous match for her, as well as for her sister Ruth, who resented being sold for a title, he could hardly be trusted to choose wisely for Melody and Matthew.

No, not Matthew, she realized, for the expression Mrs. Gaitskill had worn when her daughter pointed out his vulnerability had been one of befuddlement. In whatever scheme the older woman had hatched, she had not considered her son a factor.

And yet that struck Bea as strange, for the young man's predicament was the more pressing one. His grandfather had given him one week to yield to his demands or suffer the degradation of debtors' prison. By contrast, the plan he had formulated to direct Melody's fate, presumably to pressure her into accepting the suitor almost three decades older, had barely been settled. Dugmore had only just arrived at terms with Mrs. Chaffey, who had not informed Melody of her immediate dismissal. Money had yet to change hands.

If Melody knew nothing of the scheme, then what urgency could her mother have felt on her behalf? Furthermore, the two situations were hardly comparable. Losing one's position at a charity home for destitute orphans was not nearly as egregious as being leg-shackled for life to a woman you detested.

By any measure, it was Matthew who required his mother's assistance, not Melody. To be sure, the young woman had grown fond of her charges, and the thought of her being separated from her talented pupils might seem—

Talented pupils!

Bea stiffened as she recalled the many disappointments Mrs. Gaitskill had enumerated earlier in the day before evicting her and the duke from the house: Melody, Matthew, Georgie, her father, Dr. Pritchard.

Despite being absent from the room when her daughter confirmed the name of the artist, Mrs. Gaitskill had known precisely who had copied the will for her daughter.

Could she have reasoned it out on her own while she was fetching tea from the kitchens?

It was not impossible.

Mrs. Gaitskill knew her daughter's abilities and would realize the girl did not possess the skills to produce a convincing forgery. Comprehending that, she could have sifted through Melody's associates for potential accomplices and settled on the preternaturally gifted adolescent. With the limitation of the situation, it was not a particularly astounding feat of ratiocination, especially for a mother who was intimately acquainted with every aspect of her daughter's life.

As plausible as it was, Bea decided it was not likely, for

Mrs. Gaitskill had been gone so briefly and discovering that one's daughter had falsified official documentation to defraud her brother and betray her grandfather was a lot of information to synthesize. Rather than figure out how Melody managed to produce a forgery, she would probably spend the time fretting over her daughter's lack of moral compass and fearing her son's righteous anger.

Clifford cackled as Matthew snarled at Ripley and Melody asked Jesse where he thought he was going, and Bea, seeking to shut out the noise, closed her eyes so she could concentrate on constructing her narrative.

Suppose Mrs. Gaitskill knew all about her daughter's scheme to replace Mr. Dugmore's legitimate will with a forgery.

What would she do then?

She had only two choices: Thwart the plan or help the plan.

That was it, Bea thought.

Either alternative could be accomplished in myriad ways, but the options still came down to those meager two.

Thwart the plan or help the plan.

As Melody's false document had been unstintingly accepted as the genuine article, there could be no question as to which route her mother had taken. She had decided to aid her daughter. Whatever sinister scheme Melody had devised to secure a modest independence for herself, Mrs. Gaitskill had supported it.

Ah, but just how sinister was her scheme? Bea wondered.

Among the family, Melody was the only one who knew the extent of her grandfather's illness. She alone anticipated his imminent demise.

She alone, Bea thought again, her eyes flying open as she turned to look at Mrs. Gaitskill, her fingers still gripping the bell cord even as the housekeeper entered the room with a tray, her expression now vaguely devastated as she contemplated her only son, whose own features were arranged in a fierce scowl in response to his cousin's taunts.

It all made a horrible kind of sense—a mother blackening her soul to spare her child's—and Bea imagined she must have felt compelled to act swiftly and secretly before Melody had a chance to implement the second stage of her diabolical plan.

Only there was no stage two.

But Mrs. Gaitskill did not know that.

The stricken look on her face when she returned to the drawing room to hear her daughter describe Dugmore as a walking cadaver said it all.

The consuming futility of murdering a dying man struck Beatrice physically, and for a moment her stomach roiled. If only Mrs. Gaitskill had revealed an aspect of her plot to her daughter, then the useless tragedy could have been averted. She would not have been driven to patricide, and her daughter still would have inherited a minor property in short order.

And Melody—how would she feel when she discovered what her scheme had wrought?

Ripley saw it.

Despite his preening and peacocking and shirt points so high they threatened to poke out his eyes, he was not without any intelligence and recognized the look in Bea's eyes.

Not smug or impatient or annoyed.

Just horror and dawning comprehension.

Halting his words midsentence, he began to shake his head violently and pleaded with her to remain silent. Finally, it had ceased to be a lark. "Do not say it. Please, please, your grace, do not say it. *Please!*"

Aghast at the display, Matthew blinked at him in confusion and said, "Good God, man, have a little self-respect!"

Ripley laughed, a hollow and desolate sound, and he tugged at his cravat, as if it were suffocating him. "Do you not get it? Do none of you understand?" he asked, his eyes sweeping from one cousin to another. "She knows! The Duchess of Kesgrave knows which one of you killed our grandfather. It is over. It is all over and it is my fault. I did not mean for this to happen, I swear! I just wanted you to stop looking at me with suspicion. That is all."

Matthew pressed his lips with disgust at this seemingly nonsensical mea culpa while Clifford insisted he had only ever regarded him as a fool, never a killer. Melody marveled at the confidence with which the viscount excluded himself from consideration, and Jesse's shoulders seemed to round with relief.

Only Mrs. Gaitskill appeared cognizant of the housekeeper's presence, and she calmly instructed her to leave the tray on the table. "That will be all, Mrs. Keene. I will summon you when we are ready for teacakes," she said before turning to Bea with curiosity. "Now do tell us, your grace, what you have figured out. I am agog to learn the truth."

Bea, seeking the duke's gaze, was surprised to find that he was standing beside her, only a foot or two away. If she held out her hand, she could touch him.

"It is not the truth," Matthew said contemptuously, "but a theory."

Ripley turned suddenly toward his cousin, who was the only person in the room still arguing, and his eyes grew wide as the truth struck him. "Dear God, Matthew! Matthew did it!"

"I did not, you imbecile!" Matthew sneered.

But the viscount did not rise to the provocation, his manner gentle as he promised to find him the best lawyer in the country. "I will sell every waistcoat in my wardrobe to help raise the funds for your defense."

"Thank you, Ripley, but there is no need for such an immense sacrifice," Mrs. Gaitskill said firmly. "Matthew did nothing wrong. And I must say I am disappointed in you that you would think it."

He colored slightly at the rebuke and looked at Bea with confusion. "I am sure it is he, for he is the only one among us who is accustomed to killing creatures, such as birds, fish and foxes, and Grandfather had him all sewn up."

Melody, who had voiced a similar opinion about her brother when his alibi was assured, stared at him now with curiosity mixed with horror. Either seeking comfort herself or hoping to offer some to her mother, she wrapped her arm around Mrs. Gaitskill's shoulder and murmured consolingly that everything would be all right.

Mrs. Gaitskill shrugged herself free of her daughter's grip, walked over to the table and began to pour the tea. "I believe her grace might have a different understanding. I do hope you will share it so that we may all be put out of our misery. The uncertainty has made us all vile creatures."

Although Matthew looked as though he wanted to protest, he managed to restrain himself and sat on the settee with a hint of childish petulance. His cousins took seats as well with the exception of Ripley, who could not contain his agitation and fitfully refused the proffered cup of tea.

Kesgrave, taking advantage of the momentary distraction, brushed his fingers along the back of Bea's neck and asked if she was all right. "Your complexion has lost all color. I cannot like it."

"I am fine, your grace," she said with reassuring certainty before adding that she was perhaps a little unsettled by Ripley's entreaties. "This was naught but a romp for him. Like the ladybird race, it was a stunt designed to outrage the leaders of the *ton* and divert them with gossip. All he wanted was attention, and now a member of his family will stand trial for murder. It seems like an excessive reprisal for vanity and exuberance."

Kesgrave owned that he had also found the viscount's desperation highly distressing, for it had been like watching a small child realize his actions had consequences. "And yet I still believe it is better that a killer be brought to justice than not brought to justice."

In theory, Bea knew it was true. Violence engendered more violence and murder was a mortal sin and one could not be allowed to simply stride the world executing one's enemies as one saw fit. England was a nation that prized its laws, stretching back to the Magna Carta, and not even the king could act with total impunity.

Alas, in practice it was somewhat harder to reconcile.

Nevertheless, the die had been cast.

Ripley made his request to Russell, who duly relayed the appeal to Beatrice, and now here they were, in the drawing room in St. James's Square, about to condemn a middle-aged woman to the gallows.

Thank goodness his lordship had learned a valuable lesson about consequences, Bea thought caustically. His aunt might hang, but at least Viscount Ripley would be a better man for it.

As if aware of these thoughts, Mrs. Gaitskill looked at her inquiringly as she held up a cup of tea. "Do have a refreshment, your grace, as your throat must be parched from all your toils."

"Thank you but no," Bea said firmly.

When Kesgrave also refused, the matron leaned back in her chair, her fingers holding the saucer lightly and said, "Then I suppose we should begin."

Ripley, who continued to stalk the room like a caged animal, pressed his mouth so tightly the edges of his lips turned white. He offered no comment.

Her excessive calm, the way she appeared ready to engage in some light banter or listen to an entertaining anecdote about Prinny, further unnerved Bea, who stared at the teapot with wondrous horror.

But no.

Really, no.

Even if Mrs. Gaitskill had sought to end her own life with poisoned tea, she could not have arranged all the particulars in advance. The procedural challenges of such a feat were overwhelming. The theory was too fantastic to be of use.

Although perhaps it was not, Bea thought, as she contemplated the firm grip with which the murderess held her teacup.

According to her own account, Mrs. Gaitskill had spoken to Pritchard specifically about the laudanum the doctor had prescribed. She knew precisely where to find it and how to administer it. Aware of his nightly habit, all she had to do was add it to his chocolate.

It should have been easy and it would have been—if Dugmore had not dropped the cup.

Although Bea did not want to draw out the anguished moment by outlining her case against Mrs. Gaitskill in painstaking detail, she found she could not state the name of the killer without some preamble. "As you all know, I was summoned here to examine the suspicious death of the family patriarch, Mr. Roger Dugmore."

"Not suspicious," Matthew asserted peevishly. "An old man banging his head is how most old men die."

Although this was factually inaccurate, Bea abstained from offering a correction and instead reviewed the duke's observations that had brought them back to the house to investigate a murder. "Having conducted that investigation, I can now say with confidence that Mrs. Gaitskill killed her father in a bid to preempt her daughter from doing the same after discovering Melody's scheme to replace the legitimate will with a forgery. Ignorant of the advanced state of her father's illness, she did not realize that all Melody planned to do was wait a few weeks for him to die. She assumed her daughter would help the matter along. That is why she encouraged Melody to remain at Fortescue's to care for Agatha Johnson, so that she would be above suspicion when the will was read and she received the property, which was a surprise to everyone."

Melody, her face ashen, yelped as if in pain and allowed the teacup to slip out of her suddenly boneless fingers. It landed with a soft thud on the floor.

Matthew told his mother not to say anything. "Do not say a single word. It is all speculation and gossip. She knows nothing beyond what she has made up in her head. Her Outrageousness!" he jeered snidely. "The vaunted lady Runner is just an invention of a rumormonger who gets paid by the word. The more adjectives he heaps onto her head, the more money he makes. Hold your tongue, Mama, and you will avoid disaster."

Melody pressed her fist to her mouth as tears streamed down her cheeks.

Bea continued. "As Mrs. Gaitskill did not know the details of her daughter's plan, she assumed she had to act quickly. She arranged for Melody to stay overnight at the asylum and dosed his nightly cup of chocolate with laudanum. Then, when everyone was abed and enough time had passed, she slipped into his room to make sure the deed was done. Only he was not dead because he had dropped his chocolate. His weakness had been getting worse the closer he got to the end. He was not asleep. He was awake and alert and demanded to know why she was there, and Mrs. Gaitskill—scared, startled, worried about her daughter—slammed his head against the table. She assumed it would look like an accident. As Mr.

Gaitskill just observed, elderly people lose their balance and fall all the time. But the nightcap was bloodied in the struggle and she knew it would reveal the truth, so she took it with her. And that was her mistake."

Mrs. Gaitskill shook her head, causing her son to repeat his prohibition with increasing urgency. She ignored him. "It was in my fist. I did not realize it, you see, because I was so dazed by what had just happened. But I had grasped it when I took hold of his head and clutched it during the entire encounter and simply forgot to let it go. It was not supposed to be like that, so bloody and violent and Father wrenching his shoulder to shrug me off. Dr. Pritchard swore to me laudanum would put him to sleep gently and peacefully."

Melody keened as if in physical pain, her dark eyes huge against her pale face, and said with stricken confusion, "Dr. Pritchard *instructed* you on how to kill Grandfather?"

"Do not answer!" Matthew said frantically. "Do not speak. She has only Ripley's word that he was already dead. Ripley's word means nothing."

His mother, seemingly unaware that he had even spoken, replied only to his sister. "No, dear, nothing like that! I expressed concern for my father's pain and asked if anything could help ease it and he said he had left laudanum for him but Father was too stubborn to take it. And then I made a point of clarifying how much he should take and what terrible things would happen if I misjudged the dosage. The wretched man said nothing about his true condition!"

Flinching at the censure in her mother's tone, Melody opened her mouth as if to defend the doctor's discretion but no words emerged.

"I did not want to cause him pain," Mrs. Gaitskill said fervently. "It was the last thing I wanted to do. You must believe me! You cannot imagine what it was like, lying in my bed, wondering at every moment if it had happened yet, if it was over. I did not *want* to visit his room. I tried not to go. Even as I was creeping through the hallway, I told myself I would not enter. I would just press my ear against the door and listen. But I could not resist. I had to know if it was over. It was unbearable not knowing. So I went in and when I raised the candle to look at him in bed, he was glaring at me. I acted without thinking, knocking his head back so that it banged against the headboard. The knock stunned him. But I knew my father. He would regain his wits in a second and then there would be hell to pay. There was nothing else to be done, for I was already sunk. So I put down the candle, grabbed his head in both my hands and bashed it against the table two times or maybe three because I thought it would look more natural if he fell forward rather than backward. Then I pushed him onto the floor and ran from the room. It was not until I had returned to my own bedchamber that I realized I had the nightcap in my grasp. I burned it."

Melody was beyond words, her face splotchy now from the sobs that had overwhelmed her. But Matthew remained coherent if horrified. Moisture gathered in the corners of his eyes as he asked on a strangled cry, "For God's sake, Mama, why?"

"I had no choice," she said with deepening anxiety, seemingly upset with his inability to perceive the direness of her predicament. "You know what your grandfather was like. He would have had me in irons for attacking him."

But this explanation meant nothing because it did not answer the question he had asked. "Why not intercede with *Melody*? If you knew about the fake will, why not destroy it and tell *her* to stop defrauding her family?"

Mrs. Gaitskill stared at him aghast. "What would *that* have solved? My father would have never ceased his meddling. He was determined to marry Melody to Mr. Coombes and asked for my help even though I told him I did not approve.

And if the plan for Mr. Coombes could not be brought to bear, he would have picked out another suitor, maybe one who is older and has fists like tree trunks. He would never have allowed her to choose her own husband or to continue to work with orphaned children. He was determined to ruin her life as he ruined mine, as he ruined my sister Ruth's, and I thought the forged will was a good solution. And then there is you, my love," she said to Matthew, her voice softening as she smiled at him fondly.

He recoiled as if struck, appalled to find himself entangled in her murderous scheme in any way, however tenuous.

"I knew nothing about his plan to send you to debtors' prison if you did not consent to marry Miss Sneed," she continued with a faint hint of disapproval for his failure to confide in her. "I knew he was hoping for a match but did not realize he had taken steps to ensure it. The second I learned of it, I felt twice as sure in my decision. Your grandfather did not care about your happiness, whether you and Miss Sneed were suited. He did not care about my happiness or whether my husband was a decent man. All he wanted was money, land and power. And I am sorry, truly sorry, for the way it happened. I regret to the bottom of my soul that nothing went according to plan. That infernal cup of chocolate! If he had just drunk it as he did every night, then none of this would have happened. What confounded luck! And then to have the Duchess of Kesgrave come sauntering in to examine the room for evidence! That was more terrible luck."

But it was not the work of fortune, bad or otherwise, but Viscount Ripley, and at this reminder of the part he had played in his aunt's downfall, he ceased his wild pacing and collapsed into an armchair as if his legs could no longer support him.

"If only I had not shut up the bedchamber, then there would have been nothing for her to examine," Mrs. Gaitskill murmured on a remorseful sigh. "But I was so troubled by what had transpired in that room that I could not bear the sight of it and when Matthew and Ripley started bickering over it, I welcomed the excuse to shut the door and never look at it again."

A tear hovered on the tip of Matthew's lashes, then dropped gently onto his cheek. "It is always her. You always chose her."

At that charge, his mother lost some of her composure and she crossed the rug in three brisk strides to comfort her son. Wrapping her arm around his shoulder she said, "I chose you both. Old tyrants like your grandfather live for decades and I knew he would settle your future as surely as he settled mine. I did it for both of you. I want you both to be free. I could not have known he would be dead within the month regardless. Only Melody had the sense to figure it out. I told you she is clever. Now she is free, and I cannot wait to see what she does with her freedom. I do hope, Matthew, you will overcome your churlishness and allow her to keep Paltry House."

He laughed bitterly at her words as he shrugged free of her embrace. "Yes, Mama, it is my churlishness that is the problem here."

With seemingly nothing else to say, his mother stared at him blankly.

It was endemic, the vacuity, and the occupants of the room looked at each other with the same baffled emptiness, all their words gone, all their anger vanquished. Even Ripley, whose frivolity had brought them to this place of desolation, blinked with a sort of dumbfounded muteness.

He was all out of pleas.

Indeed, he was all out of everything.

Bea found the silence unnerving.

Ordinarily, the revelation of a killer was a chaotic affair, with people yelling or shouting or gasping or seeking to snuff out her life in some violent fashion such as suffocation or gunshot or internment in a subterranean room.

Somehow, the stillness was worse, for it made her feel stranded there, in the Dugmore drawing room, like a ship becalmed at sea. In the absence of a ruckus, Bea felt her part keenly: She had condemned a woman to the gallows.

Again and again, she kept doing it, consigning people to their death.

'Twould be easier to bear if they were all Benthams, all calculating and cruel, but scattered among the assortment of miscreants and scoundrels were a few pitiful human beings acting in desperation.

All tragedies were meaningless, but there was something particularly useless about this one, and Bea wondered if the futility itself was the distillation of motherhood: the willingness to do anything for your child, even make a sacrifice that was ultimately without point or purpose, and still feel justified.

If that was the case, then she very much feared she lacked all proper feeling, for the only thing she felt as she stood in the middle of the drawing room was sadness at the stunning waste.

Matthew, turning away from his mother's vacant stare, looked around the room as if to find the chair farthest away from her and then lowered slowly onto the settee.

He knew, Bea thought.

Of all of them, he was only one who comprehended the depth of the stupidity.

She felt his misery keenly, and it pulled her deeper into her own despair.

It was strange, the way she kept exposing herself to the desolation of other people's lives. It never got better, and yet she still felt a pang knowing this time would be the last.

What a macabre thing to regret.

If she had any sense, she would be grateful to the cherub for sparing her future revelations.

Alas, she had no sense, none at all, not when so much of her identity was entangled in her ingenuity, and sorrow for herself mingled with grief for the family.

Oh, very well done, your grace, she thought scathingly, to stand amid the wreckage of the Dugmores and feel sorry for yourself.

She had to leave, and shaking herself violently to throw off the malaise, she did now what she always did: Raised her eyes and sought out the duke.

And there he was, waiting, his gaze steady and constant.

Staring into the gorgeous blue of his eyes, she told herself that it was a fair exchange. The happiness she had found with Kesgrave was worth any number of murdered corpses.

Wryly amused by the observation, she felt some of her melancholy lift as the duke cleared the way for their exit. He had a quiet word with Matthew, then a brief one with Ripley, before leading her toward the hallway. He sought out the butler, who was apprised of the situation and agreed to send for the magistrate.

A few minutes later, they were outside, striding down the steps to the pavement, where a strong breeze greeted them.

There, she thought, not becalmed at all.

Jenkins hailed them with a tip of his hat, opening the door to the carriage, and as Bea climbed inside she tried to think of something irreverent to say to break the silence, to lighten the solemnity. The air in the carriage was so heavy and glum.

Kesgrave had to feel it too, the devastation, and suddenly it struck her as patently unfair, the way she kept dragging him into these wretched situations.

No doubt he was heartily sick of it by now.

The cherub had offered him a way out, and she had no right to be surly that he had grasped it.

Even so, it was easier said than done, and to improve her low spirits, she reminded herself of the exchange and called up an image: the elegant duke standing on one side of the scale and a pile of rotting carcasses on the other.

Flora, who was adept at drawing, could handily produce the illustration, and Bea decided to commission her cousin as soon as they returned to Kesgrave House.

Not to hang in Mrs. Humphrey's window or publish in the dailies, of course, but to place in a spot where she would see it every day and remember that her strange ability to identify murderers had brought her there.

It was enough.

Kesgrave sat on the bench across from her and took possession of her hand. Squeezing it softly, he noted that the color had returned to her cheeks.

"The physician said that women in your condition tire easily, and I see that is the case," he observed, as if their conversation on the topic had not been interrupted first by a furious Flora and then by the denouement of a murder.

It was only to be expected, given his singular focus, and although she was not surprised by his obduracy, she was nevertheless unprepared for it.

Even so, she resolved to absorb the blow without shrinking, and she tightened her shoulders as she said, "And is this the doctor your grandmother calls an ignorant quack or the one she hopes to cook on an open spit?"

The duke's lips twitched as he replied, "Neither, although I assure you Taub and Digby are estimable men of medicine. In this case, however, it is the one whom Tilly calls supremely competent. Shaw delivered her three children safely. He cautions that you will be very tired at first but that will get better in a few months. He recommends as much sleep as possible."

"Ah, yes, I see," she said, striving for nonchalance. "I suppose he advises against pregnant ladies reading late into the night, as he harbors an ardent disapproval of literate females."

"In fact, he revealed no such prejudice," he assured.

Of course he did not.

She had only been teasing.

On a more serious note, although nothing in her tone indicated the gravity she felt, she said, "But he does possess firm opinions about pregnant ladies following rigid courses of training."

Now Kesgrave nodded. "Naturally, yes."

Closing her eyes, she pictured the scale.

Those stunning blue eyes.

That mound of decaying flesh.

"He said I should move your first lesson back an hour to allow you to sleep later in the morning," he added. "He also suggested we shorten them from an hour to forty-five minutes each to make time in your schedule for naps, but I think we can take a wait-and-see approach."

Utterly astounded, Bea snapped her eyes open.

Kesgrave, continuing as if the earth had not miraculously shifted on its axis, explained that Lady Abercrombie swore she had more energy when she was carrying her children than when she was holding them. "She attributes it to all the pâté she ate and insists that pregnant women should have it with eggs as least once—"

But the exact nature of the countess's prescription was lost as Bea hurled herself across the carriage, knocking Kesgrave over as she smothered his face in kisses, and as they slid onto the floor, the duke mumbled something about discussing the gestating habits of the English gentlewoman more regularly before succumbing to her ardor.

※

*Bea and the duke return this fall
for another adventure.
Until then ...*

Meet Verity Lark
*Mr. Twaddle-Thum
*Duke of Kesgrave's illegitimate half-sister
*Exception to every rule

On sale June 2

Also by Lynn Messina

Beatrice Hyde-Clare Mysteries Series

A Brazen Curiosity

A Scandalous Deception

An Infamous Betrayal

A Nefarious Engagement

A Treacherous Performance

A Sinister Establishment

A Boldly Daring Scheme

A Ghastly Spectacle

A Malevolent Connection

An Ominous Explosion

A Lark's Tale (BHC Expanded Universe)

An Extravagant Duplicity

Love Takes Root Series

Miss Fellingham's Rebellion (Prequel)

The Harlow Hoyden

The Other Harlow Girl

The Fellingham Minx

The Bolingbroke Chit

The Impertinent Miss Templeton

Stand Alones

Prejudice and Pride

The Girls' Guide to Dating Zombies

Savvy Girl

Winner Takes All

Little Vampire Women

Never on a Sundae

Troublemaker

Fashionista Spanish Edition)

Violet Venom's Rules for Life

Henry and the Incredibly Incorrigible, Inconveniently Smart Human

Bea Tees

The Bea Tee
Beatrice's favorite three warships not only in the wrong order but also from the wrong time period. (Take that, maritime tradition *and* historical accuracy!)

The Kesgrave Shirt
A tee bearing the Duke of Kesgrave's favorite warships in the order in which they appeared in the Battle of the Nile

Available in mugs too!
See all the options in Lynn's Store.

About the Author

Mistress Lynn Messina is the author of 14 novels of questionable morality, including the *Beatrice Hyde-Clare Mysteries* series and the *Love Takes Root* series of lurid romances.

Aside from writing scandalous fiction to corrupt well-behaved young ladies, Mistress Messina hosts a Socials page where a certain dubious gentleman by the name of Mr. Twaddle-Thum regularly shares scurrilous and certainly false gossip.

Mr. Twaddle-Thum is likewise the author of a worthless little news sheet known as *The Beakeeper.* It prides itself on being filled with nothing but utter tripe and nonsense. It can, however, serve as a remedy for a spot of Sunday afternoon ennui.

Mistress Messina resides in the uppity colonial city of New York with her sons.

Made in the USA
Coppell, TX
15 April 2023